DR. ERotic

A ST. LUKE'S DOCUSERIES NOVEL

max monroe

Dr. ER
A St. Luke's Docuseries Novel
Published by Max Monroe LLC © 2017, Max Monroe

ISBN-13: 978-1548266752
ISBN-10: 1548266752

Editing by Silently Correcting Your Grammar
Formatting by Champagne Formats
Cover Design by Perfect Pear Creative

dedication

To Shakira.
Our "Hips Don't Lie" either.
Well, unless they've gotten bigger. Then our hips *are* fucking
liars. Those extra inches have nothing to do with the fact that we
finished off an entire large pizza, garlic breadsticks, boneless wings,
mozzarella sticks, French fries, and a chocolate chip pizza cookie in
one night.

And to everyone who ever wonders if we're writing about them.
We are.
Just kidding…?

prologue

━━━━━━━━━━━━━━━━━━━━━⊰❈⊱━━━━━━━━━━━━━━━━━━━━━

Scott

THE COOL, WET ENDS OF MY HAIR TICKLED AT MY NECK AS I PULLED ON A fresh scrub shirt and tucked it into my pants.

I was working a double shift, and the last several hours had been some of the messiest I'd seen in a while. Blood, fluid, vomit—you name it, I'd been covered in it, and a shower in the locker room was the only thing that made me feel remotely human again.

Slamming my locker shut, I reclipped my ID badge onto the front pocket of my shirt, dropped my phone into my pocket, and made my way out the door.

Several coworkers smiled and nodded as I passed them in the hall, but both food and coffee were necessary for not only my health, but the health of those around me.

When it came to hunger and caffeine withdrawals, I didn't get grumpy; I got punch-drunk. Fucking slaphappy. And sometimes, a little unnecessarily rude.

One of my very few flaws.

The cafeteria in sight, I picked up my pace and yanked open the door, dodging an exiting nurse as I stepped inside.

Normally, I would have perused, inspected, considered a plan of attack for winning her over with my charm and wit at such a close encounter with a cute female, but my priorities occasionally flip-flopped—though, it was rare—and this was one of those times.

Coffee and food then *sex.*

Speaking of coffee, a familiar body lurked in front of it. One that I found amusing despite any lack of caffeine or sustenance—the one and only *Dr. Obscene.*

He, along with me and one other head of department, had been chosen, approached, and optioned for a new reality medical show, *The Doctor Is In,* set to run for thirty-six weeks, with one weekly, hour-long episode airing every Tuesday night. While all of the episodes had been filmed at the same time, Will's were the first to air, and fucking hell, he was having a time of it.

Nudity, borderline inappropriate bedside comments, and from what I'd heard through the rumor mill, an insurgence of new patients with desperate determination to have their chance at the good doctor. He was struggling, but to an outsider like me, the entertainment value was endless.

"Will Cummings!" I shouted, calling his attention across the seventy-five feet of space between us.

His head jerked up at the sound of my voice, and a genuine smile curved the line of his mouth up at the corners. I understood—I'd be happy to see me too.

I headed straight for him—he was right in front of the coffee, after all, and I stuck out my hand to greet him.

"Scott," he said easily, taking my hand to return my shake.

A mental film reel of his most recent episode made my smile shift slightly. The poor schmuck had been far too liberal with his behavior in front of the cameras, and aside from how much I enjoyed watching all of the ways his normally golden intentions shone a little less brightly, I felt bad for him. Will Cummings was a truly good guy.

But no show these days was after a truthful portrayal of three men in their medical prime, saving lives and taking names and being stand-up citizens in the process.

Today's world was about drama and flair and making the stars of "reality" television as entertaining as possible—much of the time to the detriment of their overall character and existence.

That's why I'd taken my philandering ways off-camera and off-site from the hospital—and for a brief period of time, curtailed them entirely—while we were being filmed. While Will got caught with his pants down time and again, when my episodes aired, I knew they wouldn't catch me at all.

I smiled slyly at the thought.

"Stop looking at me like that," Will said with a groan, and I couldn't hide my amusement. He was too fucking easy to rile sometimes.

"Touchy, touchy. Someone's in a bad mood."

"Just you wait," Will grumbled, stirring his coffee violently enough that it almost sloshed out of the cup and onto the counter. "You will be too."

I laughed. Oh, Will. He really was too naïve. "You're assuming everyone is as good at looking like an asshole as you are." I reached out to shake his shoulder teasingly. "You really are the best."

"Oh no, Scott," he disagreed, a new layer of acid in his voice. "I assure you, as much as the rest of us try, we'll never top you in the asshole department. Just ask Mandy. And Sarah. And Monica."

Well, fuck. *That stung.* I smiled through the discomfort, but hearing each of those names felt like salt in an open wound. I'd mis-judged those situations; stuck around too long thinking they felt as casually about me as I did about them. They didn't deserve the way I'd taken off, but I wasn't a relationship guy. Not at all.

"I guess you really are in a bad mood," I muttered, knowing I'd mostly brought this on myself. He was obviously sensitive about the public scrutiny from the show, and I couldn't blame anyone but my-self for the *Mandy, Sarah, and Monica* ammunition I'd provided.

"Sorry, Scott. Just…with the show and everything…and I haven't had my coffee." He shrugged, his whole body a six-foot-something line of apology. "I guess you're right. I am the biggest asshole." I almost laughed. God, Will was a nice guy to a fault.

Still, I didn't waste the opportunity his apology provided because, like he'd said earlier, I really *was* the bigger asshole. "Well, at least you recognize it now."

I gave him a pat to the back and headed out while I was on top.

It was time to save lives, coffee consumed or not.

Twelve weeks later...

It's official. I really am the luckiest son of a bitch in New York City. Amazing sex with three different women, three different nights this week with no hard feelings and the hottest show on reality television—I felt fucking unstoppable. On top of the world, like nothing could bring me down.

Dr. Erotic.

That's what they've decided to call me. Just thinking about it makes me smile.

While Will had to bury his head in the sand, I've stretched mine toward the light. The glory, the fame, the good times.

The stint of celibacy I'd done during filming had been more than worth it, and now I was ready to use it to secure a life of the opposite.

I, Scott Shepard, was officially Dr. Erotic—and I'd take his power and recognition right to the streets of New York City and into the pants of willing women.

Are you ready for me?

CHAPTER *one*

Harlow

Seven weeks later...

"SO, WHAT DO YOU LIKE TO DO IN YOUR FREE TIME, HARLOW?" BARRON asked after he took a hearty sip of his wine. He'd ordered us a third bottle of red—*a Merlot, maybe?*—to share with our meal, and he made a point to let me know every detail of its rare and vintage quality.

"Amazing," my date said as he swirled his glass around and grinned. "I'm impressed by the legs on this one. Did you notice how the subtle tones of oak and chocolate liven your palate?"

Barron Alexander Conrad III—*my date's full, and let's be real, very pretentious name*—had been rambling on and on about the wine's legs since the server left the bottle at the table. I literally knew nothing about wine. Tannic. Oaky. Full-bodied. Every word he spoke bled together into a single word in my mind: ostentatious.

When it came to wine, all I cared about was how many glasses it would take for me to get buzzed.

I fought the urge to roll my eyes and just nodded in fake agreement as I tilted the glass to my lips and finished off my first glass from this bottle.

First dates, man. I fucking hate them.

Hell, I loathed anything that could end up in a relationship in general. I wasn't a commitment-phobe or anything like that. I just knew that long-term commitments weren't my thing. I'd been burned once, and I'd learned my lesson. I'd spend the rest of my life keeping my hands away from the proverbial hot stove, thank you very much.

I forced a smile. At least, I hoped I was smiling. *Do smiles taste like vinegar? If so, I'm definitely smiling.* "Well…I stay pretty busy with work. And when I'm not working, I guess I enjoy going to dinner with my friends, reading, seeing movies, going to concerts…" Blah. Blah. Blah.

God, I sounded just as boring as Barron.

Why do I even agree to these things?

Because I needed sex.

I know. Believe me, I know.

But I really did need sex.

Short of swiping right on everything within a two-mile radius on Tinder, dates like these were the only option for a hookup, particularly the kind that ended in penetration, without donning clear heels and a belt as a skirt and hitting the street corner. Though, if this didn't work out, that option was sounding more and more like it had merit.

It's been too long, and I've reached the point where my daily masturbation sessions just aren't cutting it.
I need a penis, guys.

"How long have you been with *Gossip*?"

I sighed internally. At both the sound of Barron's too nasal voice and the ridiculous job I still called my own. "I guess it's been about four years now." *Too fucking long.*

Gossip was an online and print magazine, and I'd been on their payroll as a columnist for several years. The goal of the magazine revolved around digging, swindling, or bribing the firsthand scoop and juicy gossip from the rich and famous of the world, particularly the ones residing in New York City.

It was trashy and trope-y and just about everything you would expect from something titled *Gossip*.

Celebrities, as a rule, were all the same; they loved when we noticed them but hated us when we hung their dirty laundry out to dry.

Although, it should be noted, I wasn't completely on the dark side like some of my fellow columnists in the industry. I only gave my readers *mostly* factual celeb news with very little embellishment. I followed the yellow-brick road to reality, even if I stepped off onto the grass every once in a while. Other conniving vipers ran around in the forest looking for the juiciest poison apple to plant in a celebrity's hands.

With that said, I derived unmitigated pleasure from writing about some celebrity heartthrob who'd fucked his nanny while his wife was on a movie set thousands of miles away—his nanny having spilled the beans *with* proof—and I didn't think that would ever change.

Of course, the same went for the cheating wives and the asshole celebs who treated their assistants and staff like shit.

To make a long story short, my job at *Gossip* had started out as a short-term plan after I'd graduated college and left an awful mess of a relationship, but somehow, it had turned into a career. Hell, at twenty-nine years old, when I looked back on my life, I wasn't even sure why I was still working there.

Seriously? Why am I still there?

I stabbed my fork into the asparagus on my plate and wondered how I'd reached this place, making a career out of something I didn't enjoy, and going on first dates with men like Barron just because I was that desperate for a penis. Good Lord, when I really thought about it, my life's train had derailed off the motherfucking tracks.

As if on cue, Barron grinned from across the table and held his fork out toward me. "You need to try this," he urged me, motioning the fork for emphasis, and I shook my head. "Just try it, Harlow. Their lobster is to die for," he said and nodded toward the fork that was now two inches from my face as if I were somehow *still* questioning what he wanted me to do despite the step-by-step tutorial.

"Uh…" I grimaced once the fishy seafood smell hit my nostrils. "I'm not a big fan of fish."

"But it's lobster."

"Yeah…fish…lobster…pretty much anything that swims in bodies of water… I'm not a fan."

"C'mon," he continued, and I had the urge to smack the fork away from my face. "No one can resist Daniel's lobster."

"Actually, I can."

He stared at me and I stared at him; *Mortal Kombat's* theme song played in my head.

For the love of God, move your fork away from my face.

Eventually, after what felt like an hour, he took the bite of lobster himself, moaning his delight out loud. "God, it's good."

If dinner was a preview for later, it was safe to assume I should just get the fuck out of here before the bill came. Fake some kind of emergency. Text one of my friends to save me from the inevitable disaster that would most likely occur before the evening was through.

Good plan, Harlow! Text Amanda.

Amanda was one of my oldest and closest friends from college, and this wouldn't be the first time she'd helped me get out of a similar situation.

While Barron stayed mesmerized by his wine and lobster, I discreetly slid my cell phone out of my purse and texted my best friend with the hopes that she'd have the perfect fake emergency. And then, I'd beg her to help me execute it.

Me: Help. Me. I need an emergency.

Amanda: Nope. Not this time, Frances.

Me: What??? I'm dying here! (And stop calling me Frances. You know I hate that.)

Frances Harlow Paige. My full name—almost as bad as Barron Alexander Conrad III—that I didn't go by anymore and no one ever called me. Trust me, Harlow, as unconventional as it was, suited me much better.

But occasionally, my best friend liked to be a bit of a bitch and taunt me with the fact that I'd been named after my grandmother.

Fucking Frances. God, that name was the complete opposite of me.

Amanda: Considering it's your actual first name *and* I think it's adorable, I'm ignoring your request. And maybe you should give this one a shot, Harlow. He could be an amazing guy. He could be THE guy.

Me: Now is not the time to begin a career in motivational speaking! This guy keeps talking about his wine's legs and shoving lobster in my face. I need help in the form of a fake emergency. Anything will do. Come pull the fire alarm. Call in an anonymous bomb threat.

I hit send and then thought better of it. Bomb threats and fake fire alarms sounded a little too dicey. I just wanted Amanda to help me out of the situation, not get arrested and questioned by the FBI. *Though, maybe I should do it myself. It'd probably end in a cavity search…*

No. NO. Thinking like that was a new all-time low for me.

Me: Wait…don't do those! They could end badly… Oh! Call me and tell me someone has three hours to live, and I need to get there as soon as possible to say my last goodbyes. PLEASE. I'M BEGGING YOU.

Amanda: Nope. You start your dates, you finish them, missy.

Fucking hell.

Unless I could execute a fake emergency on my own, and obviously, with no thanks to Amanda, I was stuck. Which explained why I ended up staying through dinner. *And* the boring conversation. *And* the mundane cab ride to Barron's place…

Fingers and toes crossed the sex is actually worth this hassle…

Barron's bedroom was exactly what I'd expected. Everything had its place, perfectly angled to showcase its worth and opulence, and all of his paintings, sculptures, and furniture made it obvious he wasn't shopping at Target. It was a lux, sophisticated apartment with a view of Central Park to boot. Too bad it felt completely devoid of personality.

Further surveying the surroundings, I spotted two armoires that I absolutely adored. *Hmmm… I wonder if there's any fucking chance he got those from IKEA?*

I started to ask him, but when I glanced down at his face—which was currently between my thighs—I decided that now probably wasn't the time to talk about his furniture.

Okay, yeah. I admit it.
I am currently in Barron's bedroom, and he is, in fact, giving me oral right this very second.
Can I be honest with you guys?
It's awful.
But thanks to my focus on interior design, you probably already guessed that.

"Does that feel good, Harlow?" he groaned against my skin, and I bit my tongue to avoid saying something along the lines of *Please, stop. I think you're actually making my vagina sad.*

"Mmm-hmmm." I did my best to feign enjoyment. A little sigh. A well-timed gasp.

"God, you taste so good."

Oh, fuck. Ouch. What's he got a spear on the end of that thing?

Ugh. I couldn't do this much longer. I'd always been a lover of the oral, but holy moly, my vagina could only take so much of whatever he was doing with his tongue. I feared she might end up with some kind of emotional trauma if I let this go on any longer. *Do they have therapy sessions and antidepressants for pussies?*

Maybe if we just skip the foreplay and go to the sex, it'll get better?

Some women might have given up, but sex was the reason I'd sat through that dinner and engaged in the most boring small talk ever to exist in the history of humans. Goddammit, I was getting some glimmer of enjoyment out of this if I had to take his penis hostage and do all the fucking myself.

"Fuck me, Barron," I whispered, redirecting the sad sex train and forcing it somewhere more illicit. He looked up at me with a gleam in his eyes.

Yes. Keep going, Harlow. This just might work…

"Please, fuck me, Barron," I said again, and instantly, he took action.

The man was on a mission as he quickly removed his pants and briefs, revealing a nicely shaped and sized penis. *Thank God.* And after the world's quickest condom placement, he moved between my thighs and started to slide inside of me.

Okay. This is better…

One thrust. Two thrusts. Three more thrusts and I was actually starting to enjoy the feel. Hell, I was even starting to think the entire mundane night had been worth it. The mouth didn't match the penis, that was for damn sure. His conversational and oral skills were subpar compared to what he could do during sex.

"Turn over," he urged between panting breaths. "Let me see your perfect ass, baby."

Ugh. Baby. God, I fucking hated when guys called me baby. *Still, it's okay. This is at least going in the right direction. Don't lose focus, Harlow.*

Barron didn't give me a chance to make the move myself, instead, he gripped my hips and flipped me onto my belly. Only, he wasn't superior in the skillset, fumbling the maneuver with a bobble, a shove, and collapsing onto me with the force of his weight. His chest hit my back, and my body catapulted forward, my forehead smacking into the headboard of his giant king-sized bed with a loud and piercing thud. Instantly, my vision blurred, and a jagged line of pain shot behind my eye.

"Oh, holy mother lover!" I cried and held a hand to my forehead. Hot embers focused at the point of impact, making it hard to breathe through the intensity. "Jesus, Mary, and Joseph at Applebee's! What the hell!"

"Oh my God," he said behind me. Shock clung to his voice. "I'm so sorry, Harlow. Oh my God, are you okay?"

I pulled my hand away from my forehead to mutter some nonsense about him maiming me being okay—and realized I probably wasn't okay. Bright red blood covered my fingers and palm, and now that I'd moved my hand, a little puddle of it was soaking into the fine silk of his pillowcase as we spoke. Whatever had happened to my forehead during the throes of Barron's passion for my ass, it appeared it'd done some damage.

I turned toward him.

"Oh, fuck," he muttered when he caught sight of my injury. "That's a really big gash, Harlow."

Uh…ya think?

"Mind grabbing me a towel so I can, you know, not bleed all over your bed?" *Any more than I already have anyway…*

"Shit. Sorry," he muttered and hopped off the bed, his now deflated penis flapping in the wind as he jogged toward the bathroom.

I sighed out loud. This was literally the worst fucking night ever. It honestly deserved one of those internet articles about terrible first-date experiences.

Not even a minute later, Barron had a towel pressed to my forehead, his worried gaze assessing my face. *I guess it's nice that he's concerned.*

"Thanks," I said, and he grimaced.

"God, I'm sorry."

"It's fine."

I mean, it really wasn't fine, but what was I going to say in this situation? *Yeah, you should be sorry. You give awful oral, and while fucking me, you managed to toss me into your headboard that just so happens to be made out of glass crystals.*

Which, why the fuck was that his headboard? I was lucky I didn't lose an eye.

I stood up and walked into the bathroom to assess the damage for myself, and Barron didn't follow me. I looked back just in time to watch him touch the bloody pillow with his hand, move his fingers closer to his face in horror, and faint dead away into the middle of his plush bed.

Jesus Christ.

I shook my head in disgust but stopped nearly immediately. Dizziness took root in the base of my skull and radiated outward, threatening to drop me like the fucker in the other room if I wasn't careful. After a glance in the mirror, a noticeable and still-bleeding gash on my forehead swelling, I knew I needed stitches.

All I'd wanted was penis. And yet, for my trouble, I was getting a solo trip to the emergency room. *No chance in hell I'm waking up Minnie Mouse in there to go with me.*

Jesus. *It might be time to consider the convent.*

CHAPTER *two*

"Yo! Scott!" Justin, one of the day nurses, greeted me and I slapped him a high five.

It was the changing of the guards, the switch of the shift, and things in New York City were about to get motherfucking interesting.

Trust me, as a doctor of ten years, and the head of the Emergency Department at St. Luke's Hospital for the last three and a half, I'd seen just about any injury you could conjure in your depraved mind—and then some.

From stabbings, shootings, and muggings to broken kneecaps from a trip on the crowded sidewalks to sex toys trapped deep within the female genitalia—medicine in an emergent capacity knew no boundaries.

Fortunately for my patients, I didn't know many either. While *work* was the most important part of work—always—I didn't think that meant I couldn't have fun at the same time.

Most attending physicians would use their station as head of the department to get *out* of night shifts, but not me. The nights were when you met the most interesting characters, experienced the weirdest of cases, and I'd always been a night owl anyway. I did this shift as often as I could.

"Another day, another dollar," I shouted back as Justin pushed open the door to the locker room.

He paused with a smirk. "Do they shove them in your G-string, *Dr. Erotic?*"

I laughed. Not only was I comfortable with the nickname my ever-growing reality show fame had brought me, I lived for it. Nine weeks of being on the air, and I felt like I was on top of the world. Some might call me outgoing—others might call me an attention whore. Either way, I didn't mind living in the limelight.

"I guess it depends on how good of a job I do," I teased before signing off with a wave and picking up my pace. I wasn't necessarily late, but I had shit to do before my shift started.

Around the corner and into the thick of it, I dodged a bed in motion and high-fived the patient, an often-drunk man named Barney who showed up here when he got into more trouble than the actual big purple dinosaur. Believe me, this Barney didn't spend his days sitting around a campfire singing nursery rhymes. The man made a career out of drunken shenanigans that resulted in injuries I had to fix.

"Suck dick, Dr. Shepard," he called over his shoulder.

"Only if you pay me, Barn," I struck back.

We really liked each other.

No, really, we do. He just has a unique way of showing it. As for me...
Is your job this entertaining? I didn't think so.

As soon as I rounded the corner, I made a beeline straight for the desk, teasingly shoving Sherry, a cute little nurse from Tennessee, out of the way on the computer, and logged in to my sign-in. As of now, 10:58 p.m., I was officially on the clock.

Now that the formalities of the facility were out of the way, it was time for *my* formalities. My routine, my comfort zone, my way to get ready for all of the gruesome things these overnight hours could throw at me.

The warm-up. With questionable vocals and dance moves better than most toddlers, I took to the open airwaves, using my diaphragm to project fully into the space.

"Oh, baby, when you talk like that," I sang, calling the attention of several nurses around me. I turned up the volume on the computer behind the nurse's station, and a slow Latin beat thumped an instantly familiar rhythm.

"My hips don't lie," I crooned along with Shakira after missing a few lines while I was busy climbing atop the desk chair.

Most of my coworkers smiled. They were used to my routine—I'd been doing it for years, changing out the song every week or so—a musical warm-up for the things to come on the night shift in St. Luke's Emergency Department. Though, I had to admit, Shakira found her way into the rotation the most. There was something about her that kept me mildly obsessed. *Probably all of the tongue control that comes with rolling Rs.*

There weren't many patients in here yet, the real mayhem of a weekend overnight in New York City was just starting up. But the ones who looked on with mild distrust and disbelief at my antics until the rest of the staff fell victim to participating one by one, the beat of Shakira too powerful to resist. I watched as some of their faces melted to amusement, while others skipped surface-level delight and jumped straight to recognition.

Yep, I'm that guy. Dr. Erotic, here in the flesh. There was a GIF of me out there hip rolling as I did one of these very warm-ups, something they'd featured heavily on the show, if I wasn't mistaken.

A few cell phones appeared, but I was used to that, me popping up on YouTube and Facebook and Insta-fuck and whatever else there was to post elaborately staged pictures of fake reality these days.

*I'm not anti-social media like it might sound. I'm just a liver,
a doer, a partier of sorts. I'd much rather be out and about
than posting pictures of myself with my dinner plate. If Shakira
appeared in front of me right now, I wouldn't waste my time
taking her picture, if you catch my drift.
Although, when one of the episodes aired featuring her song,
"Whenever, Wherever," she tweeted me, and I'd be lying if I didn't
admit it thrilled me. I just wish "tweeted" meant something more
physical—dirtier. Seriously, I'm down with whatever freaky shit
she's into.*

"Dr. Shepard!" Debbie, the head nurse in charge of admission yelled, completely interrupting the climax of my performance. In her midforties with a generic blond bob, serious hazel eyes, and little to no makeup, Deb was the walking, talking dictionary definition of "business." She meant it, she enforced it, and she got shit done.

In real terms, she was a pain in my ass.

"Geez, Deb," I grumbled as I climbed down from my perch halfway on top of the desk. "Why do you always have to undermine my performances?"

She smirked and shook her head. "Because they're terrible. And you're needed on stage B, aka Bay Two, for an actual patient, that has to do with your actual job."

"I'm offended, Deb. You should know better than anyone that the warm-up is a crucial part of my process. Working conditions are integral to success. Would you consider patient care without your gloves?"

"Scott—"

"I think not!" I cried, fake outrage making my voice carry. Several sets of eyes followed us closely.

"Stop making a scene," Debbie chastised. "Aren't you tired of making a fool of yourself?"

"I'll never tire of it, Deb," I vowed solemnly. She sighed. "Not ever."

"Fine. Then make a scene in Bay Two. But do it while you're sewing up a head lac, would you?"

"I live to serve you, my sweet emergency goddess."

"Jesus Christ," she grumbled, shoving the patient chart into my chest. "They don't pay me enough for this shit."

Fortunately, Sherry found me far more amusing than Deb did, if the glowing smile on her face as she looked on was any indication. I winked at her as a reward.

"Scott!" Deb yelled from across the room.

Whoops. Patient in Bay Two. Apparently, I wasn't moving fast enough.

"I sure hope you're close to bleeding out," I told the faceless patient behind the curtain as I approached Bay Two. "You've interrupted my performance, gotten me scolded by Deb—"

The chink of the curtain hooks rang out into the space as I yanked it back, and I immediately stopped speaking.

Well, I'll be damned. She's cute. Shoulder-length, half-curl-rumpled hair, sexy smoky eyes with glowing green irises, and a body that could kill. She also had a fucking mess on her forehead, a blood-soaked rag and both of her hands pushing into it, but that was just a surface detail.

"You know what?" I asked her rhetorically. "Strike all of that. Don't you even worry about interrupting me."

She rolled her eyes and sank back onto the bed. "I wasn't worried about you at all. The gushing, bleeding wound in my forehead? That concerns me."

I smiled at her candor and sarcasm and then nudged at her hands with my forearm. "I'm concerned too. Truly. So move your hands."

She narrowed her eyes, and I laughed. "I'm concerned. I promise." I made an X over my heart with one hand and grabbed some gloves from the tray beside the bed with the other. "This is my job."

"According to your argument with Deb, performing is your job—"

"No, no," I interrupted as I popped the second glove into place.

"You can't actually use my argument with Deb as evidence. That's just routine. It's mundane, actually."

"Listen, Doctor…?"

"Shepard. Scott Shepard. You can call me Scott."

"Listen, Dr. Shepard…"

I laughed at her obvious disinterest.

"Can you just treat my injury?"

"Of course. If you just move your hands."

"It's fucking bleeding! I'm holding pressure. Everyone says to hold pressure."

"That's true. Until you get to the hospital. Where the doctor—" I pointed to myself "—that's me—needs to actually look at the cut to assess and treat it."

"But what if what it needs is pressure?"

"I'll apply some."

"Promise?" she asked, big, mischievous eyes turning doey right before my own. *Wow. That's talent.* Usually, my conversational opponents didn't have as much expression control as I did. I was impressed.

"Promise."

"Ow," she muttered as she pulled her hand with the blood-soaked cloth away. "Fucking ball sac."

I shook my head, amusement making my cheeks feel heavy. "And here I thought I was looking at a forehead."

"Shut up," she mumbled. Again, I found myself smiling at her.

Grabbing some cleaning solution and a swab, I cleaned up the area until the actual laceration was visible. Four, maybe five, stitches, tops.

"Oh, this isn't bad at all."

"Says the person not bleeding." She held up the rag in her hand as evidence, the corner of her mouth curling up in protest. "Look at this."

I shrugged. "Head wounds bleed a lot."

"Because they're a big deal," she hedged. Thanks to the head injury, she was careful with any expressive use of her eyebrows, but I could tell the restraint took effort. I'd never seen it done, but uninhibited, I was convinced her eyebrows would be able to contort themselves into an illustration of the middle finger.

"Only sometimes," I argued easily.

The patient's medical file that Deb had so gently shoved into my chest felt like it would slow the conversation down, so I did the Cliff Notes version of surveying any important, life threatening information and tossed it to the side and grabbed a syringe and suture kit. With a quick and gloved hand, I pricked the area with a fast-acting dose of numbing agent and gave it a few seconds to take effect.

"I'm really starting to dislike you."

"Only starting?" I asked with a mocking smirk. "I haven't liked you yet."

"I was being polite."

I laughed, poking at the area a couple of times to test her level of feeling. She didn't even flinch, so I grabbed my needle and thread and got to work. "Really? This is you polite?"

"Is this you professional?"

I shook my head with a frown. "Professional is such a dirty word. Stuffy and boring. Who the hell wants to be professional?"

"Most physicians."

I pretended to yawn. "Bor-ing."

Her eyes lit suddenly, the way they always did when people realized who I was. For the first time, maybe ever, something panged in my chest that wasn't excitement.

"Ohh. You're—"

"Scott Shepard," I finished for her, looping through the skin once, and then again.

Her eyes narrowed, but she smirked at the same time. The skin I was working on shifted slightly, but she showed no signs of discomfort. "Right. Dr. Scott Shepard."

"That's me," I agreed with a smile. "And you are?"

She rolled her eyes. "The lady with the head wound."

"You know it says your name in your chart, right? All I have to do is look at it." I'd given it a glance to assure myself that she had no allergies or serious medical history just before giving her the dose of numbing agent, but now, a more thorough perusal seemed pertinent.

"Yeah, but what fun is that, Dr. Shepard?"

"Fine," I agreed. "What should I call you, then?"

"How about *Bleeding Woman Thanks to Horrible Sex with a Guy with a Fancy Name*?"

I laughed a little before clearing my throat and wincing. "Well, it's a little long. But I guess I can work with it. I would love to know how someone gets a head lac from horrible sex. It sounds like a really nice story."

"Sorry. It's an awful story that I'll never relive. Not even for your amusement."

"Geez. Fine. It's like you want me to sew this up and leave you alone or something."

She smiled, and it consumed her entire face. So much so, I thought the corners of her mouth might loop all the way around to form a circle. "That would be nice."

I laughed again, completely smitten.

Jesus. I hadn't had this much fun talking to a woman in a long time. Hell, I hadn't even spoken this much to a woman in a long time. Usually, we exchanged several heys and then went straight to making out. Not entirely flawed when your goals were what mine were—a night of fun and fucking—but not exactly mentally stimulating either.

"Well, you're in luck," I told her as I tied the last stitch and clipped off the excess. "You're all set."

I, however, wasn't feeling that lucky at all. I didn't want to be done working on her yet. Too bad I hadn't thought to stretch it out a little bit. Her conversation was too engaging to leave brainpower for scheming.

"Great!" she chirped, sitting up in a hurry and swinging her legs around and off the side of the bed.

"Whoa, whoa, whoa," I urged with a hand to her shoulder. "Take it easy, Sex Victim. I've got to sign off on your chart, and you have to get discharged."

"But if you sign off on my chart, you'll see my name," she said. It could have sounded weird, but with the way she said it, it just sounded flirtatious. Enchanted by her cool, witty demeanor and the sweet swell of her breasts, I was more than willing to go with it.

"I won't look at your name," I promised easily.

Because I wouldn't.

At least, not until she was already gone. And, depending on how off my moral compass was at the time, I might even look at her phone number too.

Chances are good I'll be dialing those digits in the near future.

Truth was, that fucker very rarely, if ever, pointed true north.

CHAPTER *three*

Harlow

THERE WERE TWO THINGS I WAS CERTAIN OF BEFORE I OPENED MY EYES. ONE, I should have put my phone on silent, and two, my face felt like someone had tried to give me a facelift without anesthesia—or so I'd imagine.

I had no idea what time it was, but from the way the sun's rays were trying to set my bedroom on fire, I knew it was at least after nine. Which, considering the events that took place last night, was still too fucking early to rise and shine.

When a garbage truck outside my SoHo apartment started serenading me with its trash-crunching powers, I groaned audibly and opened my eyes for the first time.

The world didn't look any more beautiful or optimistic despite daylight's glorious rays. If anything, the harsh sunlight made me want to go back to sleep. I was maybe thirty seconds away from accomplishing the heavenly task when my phone started chirping again. *Oh my God, who is calling me right now?*

I hadn't even started my day, but already, I wasn't a fan.

I rolled to my side and snatched my phone off the nightstand before violently tapping the green phone icon to accept the call. "Stop it," I muttered into the receiver. "Stop. The. Calling."

"That bad?" Amanda's slightly amused voice filled my ear, and I sighed in annoyance. My best friend was a morning person. And while, normally, I didn't mind mornings, spending a couple hours in the emergency room to get my face stitched up after my date tossed me into his headboard sans a sexy ending didn't equal a happy start to my day.

I should've found a way to disconnect all contact to the outside world and hibernate for the next seventy-two hours.

"Oh, hello, traitor," I greeted. "Just FYI. You basically fed me to the horrible first-date wolves last night."

"Excuse me?" She barked out a laugh. "How was your awful date my fault?"

"Because you wouldn't help me escape it!"

"Oh, c'mon, Low. You were being ridiculous. You fucking asked me to call in a bomb threat to the restaurant." I rolled my eyes. *I took that one back, goddammit!*

"I just needed a fake emergency," I retorted. "And since you refused to help out your best friend, I ended up in the emergency room last night, thank you very much."

"What?" she asked on a shout. "*The emergency room?* Oh my God! Are you okay?"

"Just a minor head injury that required some stitches. No big deal."

"No big deal?" she exclaimed. "How is that no big deal, Low? What in the hell happened?"

"Well…let's just say that if you ever enter a man's bedroom and his headboard is made out of glass crystals like he's Don fucking Corleone, do not engage in sexy times on his bed. You might end up bleeding all over his pristine white sheets after he accidentally tosses you toward it."

"Holy shit, Low! You got injured while having sex last night?"

"It'd be nice if your side of this conversation would stop ending in questions. And we really don't need to rehash it. I'm fine. My head is fine. Everyone is just fine, *no thanks to you.*"

The phone went dead silent for a few moments until Amanda's stuttering giggles filled the void. They started out quiet, but eventually, her laughter dam broke, forcing breathless—and far too loud— laughs over the airwaves.

I cringed in response. My head wasn't ready for the noise. "Stop laughing, asshole! It's not that funny."

"OhmyGod. Yes, it is," she disagreed, nearly snorting. "I can't believe you ended up with a sex injury."

"You're a terrible best friend."

"Hey, now," she retorted, only mildly offended. "I made sure you were actually okay first before I found enjoyment out of the logistical side of your injury. Cripes, I can't believe Barron the Bore fucked you straight into the emergency room last night."

"Wait…Barron the Bore? That sounds like an established nickname."

"Uh…"

"Did you know he was boring before you set me up on this thing?"

Amanda had set some kind of goal of finding me a man who would encourage me to settle down. Obviously, it was a lost cause. I would never settle down, and the only reason I'd agreed to the date in the first place was because my craving for penis had gotten out of hand.

"Uh…" she muttered again.

"Amanda Marie," I urged in my best mom voice impression. "Tell me the truth right now."

Silence.

That double-crossing bitch. She'd known Barron was as thrilling as a bowl of oatmeal before she'd set me up on that goddamn date from hell.

"I'm hanging up on you now," I muttered in warning before

doing just that. I tapped the red phone icon to end the call and tossed my phone onto the sheets beside me.

The damn thing pinged a moment later with a text message notification.

Amanda: I love you.

Me: No, you don't.

Amanda: Yes, I do. People click with all sorts of unexpected personality traits, Low. I really thought there was a chance you would hit it off.

I sighed heavily. Then something occurred to me.

Me: You're still laughing, aren't you?

Amanda: Yep.

Me: I need a new best friend.

Amanda: You just need to give your best friend the exact, detailed version of your sexcapades last night. Also, I feel like I should warn you, if you're looking for a new best friend, you don't give a very good first impression.

Me: Hey!

Amanda: #sorrynotsorry

She really was a bitch. Luckily for her, I kind of liked that in a friend.

Amanda: Details?

I sighed again. All this fucking exhaling was wearing me out.

Me: It wasn't anything too exciting. After Barron attempted the worst oral in the history of oral, we moved on to the sex. And while we were doing the sex, which surprisingly, wasn't terrible sex, he tried to flip me over and ended up pushing me toward his headboard. Which, that fucker was made out of glass crystals. Word to the wise, glass crystals and foreheads are no bueno.

Amanda: Why in the fuck is his headboard made out of glass crystals?

Me: Exactly my point.

Amanda: What a weirdo. I'll admit it's hilarious, but I'm glad you're okay. Take some pain medicine, caffeinate, and call me later once you've finished working.

Amanda: P.S. I need your help with packing! Like seriously, how does someone pack for a long trip to Europe in only one suitcase. It's impossible. Help. Me.

I'd almost forgotten that my best friend would be leaving for her big trip to Europe soon. Her PR company had recently signed this up-and-coming—*and extremely hot*—Spanish musician named Mateo, and the lucky bitch would be gallivanting all across Europe for the next month promoting him.

If that didn't remind me I needed a career change, I didn't know what would.

Although, PR was definitely out for me. Actually, anything related to celebrities was out. I'd had more than my fill through my *Gossip* column.

Me: Ugh. Stop flaunting your Europe trip in my face.

Amanda: Love you ;) And you better call me later or be prepared for a full-on catfight.

Me: Calm your tits. I'll call you later.

By some miracle, I found the strength and willpower to move from bed, but it didn't take more than the beginning of the climb to realize I wasn't going to be a big fan of movement today. "Ow, fuck," I muttered to myself and held a hand over my newly stitched forehead as I slowly stood up beside my bed.

Sex injuries are no joke.

It was safe to say last night sucked serious goat taint.

There is no penis out there that's worth this kind of hassle.

The mere idea of attempting another first date or even one-night stand had me shaking my head. *Never again, Harlow. Never fucking again.*

Sure, a girl needed the D sometimes, but holy hell, I'd maybe give changing up my masturbation routines a try first before attempting another situation that resulted in last night's version of hell. Even if the hottest guy with the most perfect penis were sitting in my living room right now, with his sexy man parts hard and on display, I'd tell him to get the fuck out. *Take your bad-news penis somewhere else, fictional dude of my daydreams!*

Plus, I needed coffee, ibuprofen, and a long *Gossip*-column writing session. There was literally no better motivator than the fear of losing your job over a missed deadline.

But even though I'd been one of *Gossip's* lead columnists for over three years now, I still had no idea how I'd managed to achieve that promotion. It wasn't like writing gossip columns about the rich and famous was my life's passion. When I wasn't actively searching for my next column inspiration, I certainly wasn't sitting around obsessing over Rhianna's new hairstyle or if Bradley Cooper and Jennifer Lawrence would be a good match. Though, from a gossip columnist's perspective, I do, in fact, think those two would be fucking adorable together.

The negative spin most people hear about gossip columns was true: *Don't believe everything you read.*

Even I dabbled in overexaggeration and occasional embellishments for the health and longevity of a story, but my morals had limits. I'd never once in my career written or published something slanderous that was truly detrimental to someone's life.

But did I bring my readers the sexy scoop on their favorite celebrities?

Of course.

And that was why, after my unfortunate trip to the emergency room last night, and my first introduction to the undeniably sexy physician, Dr. Scott Shepard—*because holy hell, he is sexy as fuck*—I knew exactly what my readers would love to hear.

Hello, Dr. Erotic. Harlow Paige readers are about to get the scoop.

If I'd learned anything last night, besides never have sex with a guy named Barron, it was that Dr. Scott Shepard was exactly as advertised—seductive and charming with a smile that flirted even better than he did. Sandy brown hair, deep chocolate eyes, and a tall, sculpted body that screamed touch me, the man was walking sex, even when he wasn't having it. He even had a bit of a beard, and generally, I wasn't a fan, but somehow, Scott could even pull that off *and* make it sexy, something about his overbearing confidence was built to convince me—and other women—that everything about him was Goldilocks level *just right*. And I couldn't deny I'd quite enjoyed our banter session—probably more than the sex that landed me there.

But that was as far as it went for me.

Sure, he was handsome and charismatic, and it was easy to get lost in his chocolate brown eyes. But I didn't make a point of playing with fire, and Dr. Shepard was a smoke show waiting to burn your motherfucking hands. That man most likely had a different woman every night of the week. Which was part of the reason why I'd all but demanded he didn't look at my name while he tended to my sex injury wound. The last thing I needed was to be on a first-name basis with a man like that. When you played with fire, you most likely got motherfucking burned.

Plus, if I was being really honest, while I was sitting on his ER bed, I'd already made a mental note to bring my readers the Dr. Erotic dish, and I couldn't remember how medical files were set up. Was it just my first and last name? Or my whole name?

I had a feeling it was probably the former, but I didn't want to take any chances on the latter. Sure, he'd promised not to look at my name, but what if he *did* look at my name? Would he see Frances Paige? Or Frances *Harlow Paige?*

I definitely did *not* want Dr. Shepard to be privy to the fact that I was using myself as an inside source for a column that just so happened to be about him. That was just bad business. A gossip columnist never revealed her sources unless it was for good reason—read: never.

Three ibuprofen, half a cup of coffee, and fifteen minutes later, I was cozy in my favorite writing spot and my fingers were ready to make this column my bitch.

Paging Dr. Erotic fans! I've got some dirt to dish!

Dr. ERotic: Certified, Class A flirt and Commitaphobe.

Between Grey's Anatomy *and* Scrubs *and even Joey Tribbiani playing Dr. Drake Ramoray, sometimes, I wish that the hot doctors I see on TV and in movies were, in fact, real-life doctors. Wouldn't it be nice if Dr. Avery was your family practitioner or Dr. Carlisle Cullen was your dermatologist?*

What if I told you that there's a real-life version of your hot doc fantasies residing in an emergency room in your city? What if I told you his name is Dr. Scott Shepard, better known as Dr. ERotic from the reality series, **The Doctor Is In?**

Slow your roll, ladies. Before you start plotting your next medical emergency, read the following warnings carefully...

Dr. Scott Shepard is not the next Dr. McDreamy, or even McSteamy.

Sure, he's sexy AF. And his signature smirk has the power to bring all the ladies to his ER.
But I have the Gossip that might have your, "Oh yes!" turning into a "Hell no."

An inside source revealed that Dr. Shepard does, in fact, live up to his Dr. ERotic title. Not only is he easy on the eyes, but he's a certified, Class A flirt.

Word on the street says the reality star and emergency room physician is a total commitaphobe and his little black book is filled with nurses, fellow doctors, supermodels, actresses, and even the up-and-coming pop star, Laney Lane.

Yikes! At this rate, he's going to need to start purchasing his little black books in bulk...

It appears that monogamy and commitment are a big no-no for Dr. Shepard.
Don't go looking for forever in Dr. Erotic's direction.
But for my favorite adventurous ladies who'd love to get an insider's view of Dr. Shepard's bedroom, an orgasm, and nothing more, an insider tells us he frequents NYC hotspots such as Club Indigo and Melt, and has occasionally been spotted taking the subway to work.
Get out there, ladies. A city full of fun is waiting.

Kisses,
Harlow Paige

CHAPTER *four*

"OOH, SCOTT," ONE OF MY COMPANIONS FOR THE EVENING, BRENNA, giggled directly into my ear. I hadn't done anything, said anything, touched her anywhere that mattered, but she was primed regardless. Ever since that first episode aired, my personal relationship workload had gone down significantly.

Hell, it was almost like the damn show was foreplay. And maybe it made me an asshole, but I wasn't complaining.

It'd been almost a week since the mysterious, shit-talking woman of my dreams had come into the ER and left without even giving me her name. I knew next to nothing about her and I wasn't sure a woman of my dreams actually existed, but she'd starred in a couple of the erotic variety since that night. *Close enough.*

The instant I'd walked away from her ER bed, grinning and ready to take a closer look at her medical file, a gunshot victim had rolled through the doors on a gurney and in need of five hours' worth of surgery time. Thirty minutes after scrubbing into the OR, and with my hands inside the man's opened chest, I'd given a quick verbal order for Deb to discharge *Bleeding Woman* from Bay Two. She'd done as told, efficient as ever, doing all of the paperwork to release her before setting it aside for my signature for legal purposes.

By the time I'd remembered to track down my sexy mystery woman's name, it was half past four in the morning, and the result wasn't what I was expecting at all.

A woman as witty, antagonistic, and drop-dead hot as she was should not be named Frances.

Jesus. *Frances.* No wonder she hadn't wanted to give me her name.

But even with a name that should be left in the corner and five hours of surgery time to get over her, I was still interested—a reality even I found surprising.

Unfortunately, four numbers into copying down her phone number—a practice that was actually highly illegal—Deb stole the file back and threatened to castrate me in my sleep if I looked Frances's information up again.

Something about a Hippocratic Oath and patient confidentiality, and then another little bit about what a manwhore I was.

She wasn't far off on any of it, especially the bit about it being morally, ethically, and legally wrong. So, as a way to cope, I'd called up three of my not-even-remotely close friends, Hilda, Brenna, and Esmeralda, and strolled over to Club Indigo for a night out of drinking, dancing, and sex.

Of course, that was only my surface reasoning, as good as it was. I was really here, at this club, on this night, because Pamela Lockhead was too.

Mysterious, right?

Assistant to the assistant of the mayor or something equally ridiculous, Pamela Lockhead was also young, impressionable, easily swayed by good flirting and appropriately placed dirty talk, and liked this club on Thursday nights—or so I'd heard.

As far as I could tell, she was the most direct route to the mayor.

I'd been working this connection for months, trying to get a meeting with him. I know it seems a little cliché to be making this huge outcry about public health policy—and a little ridiculous to be chatting up a few women as a means to do it—but changes to the current policy and protocol the last administration put in place as a Band-Aid were absolutely vital, and I was willing to work with what I had. And I, Scott Shepard, had the ability to flirt like no other. Initially, I'd tried to go through the proper channels. I'd met with several heads of emergency departments from other hospitals here in the city, and eventually, even approached a lobbyist group known for targeting health care reform. Just being in contact with that many politicos made me itchy. And in the end, it hadn't moved fast enough for my interest anyway. The only option was to return to what I knew—malleable women like Pamela Lockhead.

I knew it sounded terrible, but I'd seen the effects of political shortcuts to public health up close and personal on, unfortunately, several occasions now. Terrorism and other public attacks were the unwelcome way of our current world, and that kind of medical emergency added an angle to our procedure that we weren't properly prepared for. Short on funding, training, and an appropriate list of priorities, the policy had been built on paper, for looks rather than for implementation. Quite frankly, it tied my and other professionals' hands in ways that occasionally prevented us from actually administering care when the public was in need. And to me, that was unacceptable.

I wasn't thinking of running for office or anything—*don't worry*. They'd fucking crucify me in a court of public opinion. But as the guy in charge of saving lives at St. Luke's Hospital, I wouldn't mind a little fucking help from the law doing it. At the very least, finding a way to avoid having it work against me.

And, as I sat here tonight with Bippity, Boppity, and Bimbo Barbie, I'd never felt my sacrifice was greater. Hopefully, Pamela was witty enough to give me a little verbal sparring as conversational foreplay at the very least.

I wasn't actually planning on sleeping with Pam to get to the mayor, just spending a little time making her feel good—*emotionally*—by tending to her ego and flirting the line with inappropriate in an effort to secure an ally on the inside. My morals and boundaries are mostly questionable, but I usually start out with the best of intentions.

Flirting in the name of public health isn't a crime, is it?

While Brenna blew in my ear like a gnat, I watched Pam weave through the crowd on her way to the dance floor, separating from the women she'd come with and making coy glances at any and all eligible men around her.

She was primed, in search of male company, and ready to give in to the first guy who showed her interest. Now was the time to make my move.

Up and off of the sofa, I winked at my company and gestured to the dance floor. One of them made a move to follow me, but I shook my head.

No, no, sweetheart. You stay here. Scotty's got some work to do.

Pam had short, dark, cropped hair and a dress a size too tight to be sophisticated, and I lasered in on my target and prowled. I had to give myself a short mental pep talk to dial up the charm. Normally, this was the epitome of my scene. Flashing lights, writhing, dancing bodies, too tight clothes, and women who were more than willing to loosen their inhibitions.

But tonight didn't feel the same, and I wasn't sure if it was the game, the long chase, or the fact that no one seemed as interesting as *Bleeding Woman* anymore. Which, to be honest, probably had a lot to do with the challenge she presented.

Nonetheless, I shook off any and all uncertainty and tapped Pamela on the shoulder. As much of a flirt as I was, I had a rule of thumb about physical contact.

Never touch a woman with any form of intimacy until she consents—and no one can consent through the back of their head.

But as soon as she turned around and surveyed me, it was a different story. I was up to her standards, possibly even exceeded them, and she made her interest more than a little visible by plumping up her lips and thrusting her chest forward to garner attention.

"Hi," I greeted, leaning in to the shell of her ear to tackle a multisensory approach. She shivered as the air from my hot mouth made contact with her clammy, post-dance-exertion skin.

"Hi," she purred back, kicking her hips slowly back and forth to the building beat of the club remix of "Believer" by Imagine Dragons.

I held out a hand in an offer to shake, but she rejected polite pretense, grabbing it and placing it on her swaying hip. I smiled. *This might be even easier than I thought.*

"I'm Scott."

She smiled and pushed her body into mine, forcing me to move to the same sexy beat. "Pamela."

"Hi, Pamela."

"Hi, Scott."

Internally, I laughed. It was really fucking sad how ridiculous these conversations actually were.

"You look familiar," she said. A twinge of discomfort flared in my stomach before I tamped it down. I wasn't sure if being known as Dr. Erotic of reality show stardom would be a good thing or a bad thing as far as getting a meeting with the mayor was concerned.

"Oh, yeah?" I asked, unwilling to offer up any unnecessary information. "Been to the hospital lately?"

"That's it!" she chirped, snapping her fingers right in my face. *Here we go.* "You're that doctor that Harlow Paige wrote the article about."

Okay. There were at least two things in that statement that weren't at all what I was expecting.

Article? I was thinking TV show.

And who the hell was Harlow Paige?

"Huh?" I asked eloquently. Really, I was doing a stellar job executing my plan so far.

"Harlow Paige at *Gossip*. She just wrote an article about you. Dr. Erotic, right?"

"Yeah," I admitted, not recognizing one word about the article, but I was completely familiar with the nickname.

"Did she say nice things?" I asked teasingly, trying to bring the conversation back around to something that would get me somewhere. Pam shook her head with a smile.

"Not really. Apparently, you're a great flirt but terrible with commitment."

Fuck. This was going somewhere, all right, but not at all where I wanted. *Though, this article sounds pretty fucking accurate.*

I racked my brain for the answer, for what I could say to change her mind about whatever she was convinced I was like, so I'd have enough time to win her over, to make her an ally, to—

"So, you want to get out of here?"

Wait…what?

I laughed to myself and nodded before I could think twice about it. "Yeah, Pam. Yeah, I do."

God bless women wanting things that are bad for them.

What? I told you I always start out with the best of intentions.

But I was a single guy, and Pam was an attractive, willing woman who seemed pretty well informed on the score. Whoever this Harlow Paige was had given Pam the speech for me.

Who said a little work couldn't lead to a lot of play?

CHAPTER *five*

Harlow

NEVER THOUGHT I'D WITNESS A WOMAN FEEDING FRITOS TO A SMALL HAMSTER hiding inside of her purse in public, but I guess I'd severely underestimated the glorious people watching opportunities on the subway.

Because that happened. Actually, it was *still* happening.

As the subway slowed to a stop, I glanced up at the sign on the platform, and quickly realized I still had six more stops to go. And for the first time in my life, I wasn't disappointed by this fact. I had Hamster Lady, and she apparently had enough Fritos inside of her pocket to put her little rodent buddy into a food coma.

The train's doors shut, and its wheels squealed as it picked up speed, down the dark tunnels of the city toward the next stop. All the while, the rodent lover sitting across from me pulled another Frito out of a clear, plastic sandwich baggie and held it toward the opening of her purse.

Her miniature, furry—*and possibly infected with rabies*—pal looked up at her as she looked down at him, and they shared a little moment before he grabbed the Frito with two hands and started chowing down on the salty goodness until it was completely gone.

I swear to God he smiled once he was finished, and even though I'd never been a fan of anything that resembled rats, I was fucking mesmerized by the tiny disease incubator.

Before I could witness him munch on Frito number three, my phone buzzed inside my pocket and grabbed my attention.

Amanda: Look, I know I'm a little late to the party here, but please forgive me. I've been busy since the second I stepped off the plane. Managing an international PR tour ain't exactly easy. It's a fucking pain in my ass. Anyway, I just read your column about Dr. Erotic. Fucking tell me that he's the one who stitched your sex wound!

Sex wound? I grimaced. She made it sound like I'd obtained an injury to my vagina, not my forehead.

Amanda had only been gone for a few days, and already, I missed the hell out of her. But, with that being said, I never revealed my inside sources. Even when they were me.

Me: My lips are sealed. I will never give up my sources.

Amanda: You're such a fucking tease. And I know it was you! OMG! I can't believe he was your doctor in the ER! I love his episodes so, so, so much. So sexy and fun. God, you should've boned him. Please, Please, Please…,Make my year and tell me you boned him.

Me: Seriously? You honestly think me having sex with Dr. Erotic was even an option after my earlier bone from the evening had been the reason I was in the ER in the first place? What kind of floozy do you think I am??

Amanda: Hmmm... what's the rule on double boning in one night?

Me: Same guy = Awesome. Different guys = A little too loosey-goosey for me.

Amanda: Yeah, but there has to be an exception for this case, though. The first bone wasn't a full bone. Pretty sure that makes it a null and void bone. Which means, you could've boned Dr. Erotic with a clean slate for the night.

Me: Your last text bone count = 4. That's a lot of bones, dude. It appears to me that someone is jonesing for the penis. Probably of the Spanish variety...

Amanda: Shut up. I do not want to bone my client.

Me: Liar.

She was full of baloney on this one. Pretty much every woman in the world saw Mateo Cruz and *immediately* thought, *muy caliente*. With a voice like honey and a face like sin, everyone wanted to get inside the pants of the next big thing in the music industry. Including my best friend, even though she refused to admit it.

Amanda: And don't think I didn't notice you basically admitted that Dr. Erotic took care of you in ER. Did you at least get his number so you can bone him after you've fully recovered? Which, pretty sure you should be good to go by now...

Me: Leave me alone. Go bone your Spanish client.

Amanda: I don't bone my clients!

Me: Then go find someone to bone so you stop talking to me about boning. Anyway, I actually do have to go. I have an appointment in like ten minutes.

Amanda: An appointment to bone Dr. Erotic?

Me: Stop saying bone.

Amanda: I bet Dr. Erotic has nice bones…

Me: That doesn't even make sense.

Amanda: I meant BONERS. I bet he has nice boners. I know they say the eyes are the window to your soul, but I'm pretty sure Dr. Erotic's eyes are the windows to his penis. A man with those gorgeous fucking brown eyes, and who looks the way he does, has to have an ah-mazing penis.

She had a bit of a point. Scott Shepard's eyes were like ooey-gooey chocolate morsels that contained the power to make *any woman* melt. But I didn't need to add fuel to the already burning fire of penis metaphors. I had to change the subject.

Me: What about Mateo? Shouldn't you be servicing his penis right now under the pretense of "PR"?

Amanda: Shut up.

Me: You're totally going to go for a ride on the Spanish stallion. I know it.

Amanda: I miss you. But you're an asshole. He's my client. Business and BONE-ING do not mix.

Business and Bone-ing... Real fucking clever...

Me: Just couldn't help yourself, huh?

Amanda: Nope. :)

Instead of simply putting my phone back in my pocket, I turned it off and *then* put it in my pocket. Otherwise, I would've received no less than ten more text messages about bones and boners and Dr. Erotic.

Plus, I didn't want to be in the middle of my doctor's appointment while my phone lit up with "bone" texts.

Forty minutes later, I was sitting patiently on my doctor's exam table while he gently assessed the stitches on my forehead with gloved hands.

"These healed very nicely," he said with a little nod of approval.

At the young age of seventy, Dr. Barry Williams had been my doctor for my whole life. From diaper rashes to upper respiratory infections to that time I'd managed to catch the flu when I was twenty-one, this guy had been privy to it all.

"How did you manage this one, by the way?"

"Uh..." I searched for a sugarcoated version of my sex injury. Dr. Williams was also a good family friend and golf buddies with my dad. The last thing he needed to hear was that my date had basically fucked me into his glass headboard. "Just a clumsy moment, I guess."

He quirked an amused brow. "Was alcohol involved during this clumsy moment?"

I wish there had been more... "Of course not, Dr. Williams," I lied. "You know I'm a good girl who stays on the straight and narrow."

A barking laugh left his lips. "Yeah, and I'm one nomination away from being the next Democratic candidate for President."

"*You are?*" I feigned gullibility, and he smirked.

"I'm guessing you don't want to tell me what really happened because you're afraid I'll tell your dad?"

"I know you'll tell my dad," I retorted, and his smirk turned into a full smile.

"You're just going to feel some tugging as I pull these out, okay? It might feel a little strange, but it shouldn't hurt," he instructed as he started the removal process.

I nodded and shut my eyes in preparation. Even if it wasn't supposed to be painful, it still wasn't fun having a doctor remove fucking stitches from your head.

"Whoever did these did a fantastic job. You're probably not even going to have a scar once it's fully healed," he updated as he tugged gently on the sutures, and I grimaced from the odd sensation.

"It was Dr. Shepard at St. Luke's." I opened my eyes as I spoke. He focused as he finished up.

"Wait…" He quirked that brow again. "The ER doc that's on that reality show?"

"Yep. That's him."

"My wife loves that guy," he muttered. "She never misses an episode. Every Tuesday night she's in front of the TV waiting for that stupid *Dr. Erotic*."

I giggled. "He's quite the character. A lot of women love him."

"Uh-oh…You think I should be concerned?" he teased, and I shook my head.

"Nah," I responded with a smile. "You've got that older distinguished gentleman thing going for ya. Plus, you're a hot doctor too, so I think your marriage is safe."

"Thank God," he joked and set his instruments on the metal tray beside the exam table. "There. All set, Harlow. It healed nicely and shows no signs of infection, but just keep an eye on it over the next few weeks and give me a call if you have any issues," he instructed and headed toward the counter to scribble something down on my medical file.

"Okay. Sounds good." Tingly needles shot up my legs as I jumped down from the exam table and came to a jarring stop on the ground. *Ow.* Twenty-nine years young and already ailing. I was going to be fucked when I got older.

"Oh, and tell your dad I'm going to kick his ass next month at the charity event."

"Will do." I grinned and grabbed my purse from the floor. Before stepping out of the room, I snagged my phone out of the front pocket and turned it back on. Amanda could send as many "boner texts" as she wanted now that good old Barry wouldn't be within eye shot. "See ya around, Dr. Williams," I called over my shoulder as I headed out of the exam room and toward the exit.

Fifth Avenue buzzed with traffic and the smell of grease as I jogged toward the subway entrance en route to my office at *Gossip*. I panicked briefly as my phone started ringing inside of my purse, thinking it might be my boss calling to ream me for missing some sort of scoop, but I smiled once I saw the caller ID.

"Give me the good stuff, Claude." His soft chuckles fed some sort of hole deep in my soul.

Claude was my dealer. Well, not of the drug variety, but when it came to juicy pictures for my *Gossip* column, he was the guy with the goods. Paparazzi weren't normally a source of good karma and soul replenishment, but Claude was different—likeable. I couldn't even explain exactly what it was about him, but that intangible something was there all the same.

"Would a certain *monsieur* on *The Doctor Is In* be of interest to you?" he asked through his thick French accent.

Jesus. *Scott Shepard strikes again.* I felt like this guy was following me everywhere, even though the one and only time I'd seen him was over two weeks ago inside of his ER.

Hmm. I guess it could also be Dr. Obscene, but last I heard, he was settled down in a pretty serious relationship.

"Are we talking Dr. ER?" I asked to double-check.

"*Oui.*"

Immediately I perked up, my eyebrows lifting toward my

hairline. "Color me intrigued."

"Ah, *Mademoiselle* Harlow," he responded, and I could hear the smile in his voice. "I have a few shots you're going to love."

"Fantastic. What's the story?"

"Dr. ER at Club Indigo last night enjoying drinks with not one but *four* lovely women."

That charming son of a bitch. I grinned. "Do you know who the women are?"

"I believe one is an up-and-coming actress from Spain, two are famous Russian models. The other woman he spent the majority of his evening with, I'm not so sure who she is, but she is quite stunning."

"Did they leave together?"

"*Oui.*"

"Sounds like Dr. Erotic is living up to his name, then."

Claude chuckled. "It appears that way."

Good God, I was beginning to love Scott Shepard. Well, at least the columnist in me was. If he kept this up, I'd have enough material for months. Maybe even enough to fill a novel with my columns specifically dedicated to him. *Dr. ERotic: A* Gossip *insight.*

I'd have to think about the byline, but I had at least fifty Scott Shepard-inspired columns to figure it out.

"How many photos are worth my time, Claude?"

"Five."

"How much?"

"Five hundred."

"A piece?" I questioned skeptically. "Oh, c'mon, Claude. You know me better than that."

He laughed. "Can't fault a working man for trying, *mademoiselle.*"

"Yeah, and you can't fault a working girl for calling you out on your bullshit," I retorted. "I'll give you one thousand for all five."

"Twelve hundred," he countered.

"Eleven hundred and that's my final offer," I stated firmly. "And you should know that I still have three messages from Raoul. He appears to have also been at Club Indigo last night…"

He groaned. "I detest that guy. He's rude."

"He's paparazzi," I interjected. "You know, just like you."

He laughed. "You drive a hard bargain, *mademoiselle*."

"I've learned over the years, Claude," I explained, and he knew exactly what I was talking about. When I first started working for *Gossip*, I'd once paid Claude two thousand for a single photo. Obviously, this money never came directly from my pocket, only my employer's business account, but still, I'd paid it, and my boss had all but strangled me.

"Okay," he said on a sigh. "We have a deal. Cut the check, and I'll send the photos over."

"Full files, please," I added. "No less than 1080hp in quality."

"You got it, *mademoiselle*."

"*Merci*, Claude."

"*De rein. Au revoir*, Harlow."

"*Au revoir*." I hung up the call and hopped onto the subway.

While I waited for my stop, I fired off a quick email to *Gossip*'s accounting department, letting them know they needed to send one of New York's paparazzi sharks eleven hundred dollars for five photos. It sounded like a lot of money, but in the grand scheme of things in the entertainment and media industry, it was mere peanuts. Some celebrity photos could go for millions. Snag a shot of a celebrity's baby or catch an athlete in a compromising position with someone who wasn't his wife or girlfriend? Gold mine.

An hour later, I was sitting inside my office and had just finished up the mundane task of replying to hundreds of waiting emails when a new one from Claude landed prettily in my inbox. One click was all it took to open Pandora's box of compromising images—a very handsome physician with his arms wrapped around not one, but two beautiful women. They were tucked away in the VIP corner of Club Indigo and appeared to be very cozy. Not to mention the other pictures of Dr. Shepard dancing with a mystery woman, and then, later that night, leaving the club hand in hand with her.

Yep. Claude had given me the exact shots I needed.

And now, I had two options. I could either make up my own assumptions or try to find out the scoop from the source…

Definitely talk to the source. I didn't know why, but I really wanted to enjoy a phone conversation with Dr. Erotic himself.

After a few quick calls to my various connections in the city, I had Scott Shepherd's direct cell number in my hands.

And three rings later, his voice in my ear.

"Dr. Shepard."

"Hello, Scott," I greeted. "How are you doing on this beautiful Monday morning?"

"Uh…who is this?"

"My name is Harlow Paige, and I write—"

He cut me off. "That *Gossip* column," he said and I smiled. He'd been paying attention, it seemed. "I know who you are, Miss Paige, but what I'd like to know is why are you calling me?"

"I have a few unanswered questions."

"According to what I've heard, you write about me like you know it all."

I grinned into the empty space of my office and tried not to let his fast-talking ways get me off track.

"Well, now I have more."

"And you think I have the answers?"

He had the fucking answers, all right. Whether or not he gave them to me was another thing entirely.

"I'm certain you do."

"All right." He chuckled, completely at ease. He obviously wasn't too upset about the call either. "Even though this conversation will no doubt end up in another one of your columns, I'm intrigued. How can I enlighten you?"

"It appears that you had a very busy and interesting evening last night," I stated and silence filled the line. *There's no way he forgot about the four women, right?* "At Club Indigo…" I hinted, and he finally cured himself of amnesia.

"Oh. Oh, yeah. I was at Club Indigo last night enjoying drinks with a few friends."

Jesus. How often did this man find himself surrounded by models? Was it, like, an every night thing? Or like an every Tuesday, Thursday, Sunday thing? How did it work with this guy?

"A few friends?" I questioned, but I couldn't hide the sarcasm from my voice. "I'm sure you mean *a few women*."

"Well, I know this might come as a surprise, but I do have friends that just so happen to be women," he retorted, and I couldn't stop myself from smirking at his response.

He was good. Too fucking good.

"And the mystery woman you left with? Who is she?"

"Mystery woman?" he avoided.

"Yeah," I answered. "The brunette in the killer heels that you left Club Indigo with last night."

"Hmm…" he started and then paused for a brief second. "I left with a brunette in killer heels? You know, that sounds like something I'd enjoy, but for some reason, I don't remember it."

I shook my head and tossed my pen on top of the photos I'd printed out for closer inspection.

"You know what's crazy, Dr. Shepard?"

"What?" he asked, amusement lengthening the sound of his A.

"That I'm sitting here, looking at a photo of you holding hands with the brunette as the two of you leave Club Indigo."

"Really?" he questioned, but his voice lacked any kind of concern. "That is crazy."

"Oh, c'mon, just tell me the truth," I coerced, turning my voice slightly seductive in the hopes that playing his game would pad my score. He chuckled softly.

"She's just a very nice woman I met that night."

"And the two of you left together?"

"We did."

"And did your other *friends* meet up with you guys later?"

"Nope." The pop of his p was almost smug, the bastard. He wasn't giving me anything juicy, and he knew it.

"What's her name?" I asked. This time his laughter was rougher, uninhibited.

"I'm not telling you that, Miss Paige. And not because I have anything to hide, but because it's not fair to my female companion with the killer pumps."

"Female companion?" I questioned, doing a little something a judge might call leading the witness. My boss would just call it good investigating. "So, the two of you are an item?"

"No. We're not an item. Just friends."

"Just friends that leave clubs together at midnight?"

"Yep," he answered, and I could hear the cocky smile in his voice. "That sounds like us."

I couldn't exactly fault him for not giving me the woman's name. I mean, I was obviously calling him for an inside scoop, and it wasn't fair if he gave me a name of someone who didn't want her name in the media. I definitely respected that.

But still, he wasn't exactly giving me a lot to work with.

"Anything else, Miss Paige?"

"Nope. That's all, Doc. Thanks for your time," I said, and before he got another word in, I ended the call.

As I stared at the empty Word document on my laptop, I knew I needed a little something more to make Scott's big night out a *Gossip*-worthy story. Which meant, now that we'd put out the money for the photos, I'd have no choice but to embellish—*only a little, of course.*

With my fingers to the keys, I typed out the headline.

Four Women in One Night.
Is Dr. ERotic the next sex superhero?

CHAPTER *six*

PERSONAL IPAD IN HAND, I SCROLLED THROUGH THE NEWEST COLUMN BY Harlow Paige, another brilliantly written trash piece about yours truly, and shook my head.

Honestly, I wasn't even doing it on purpose. It was like an involuntary muscle tic triggered by reading paragraph after paragraph of pure and utter bullshit.

Four Women in One Night.
Is Dr. ERotic the next sex superhero?

As nice as the title sounded, the meat of the column was a whole lot less flattering, and a whole lot more bordering on derogatory.

I'd fucking fed her information, for shit's sake. And still, it seemed as though she'd done nothing more than write whatever the fuck she wanted. I was the puppet master, and women's emotions were nothing more than the objects at the end of my strings—apparently.

What she'd failed to mention was that even if I had been with the four of them at once, it would have been an informed decision by four consenting adult women who knew how not to take life so seriously.

Not only does he have a harem of women keeping him warm and cozy at night, but an inside source revealed that Dr. Erotic is always looking. Even the female patients who stroll through his ER doors might be graced with his famous flirtatious banter and charming ways right before he finds a way to ensnare them in his web of sex.

Inside source? What fucking inside source? And, yes, I might have flirted with my patients on occasion, but I never fucking slept with them. I enjoyed chatting up the opposite sex, but when it came to my job, I knew the boundaries.

And asking my patients out on dates with the intention of sleeping with them? That was a definite hard limit for me. Hell, throughout my entire career, I hadn't ever been tempted to do something like that.

Well, besides sexy Frances who came in with that head lac a few weeks back…

Okay. Well, obviously, there were exceptions to every rule, but no one is perfect.

And despite my better judgment, I kept reading the trashy article until the end. Harlow Paige managed to cap this one with a fucking bang.

What do you think, ladies? Should we spread our legs and put out the Bat Signal in the name of Dr. Erotic? Is he really the next sex superhero of New York City?

The jury is still out for me, but all I can say is that he might treat banged-up bodies, but from the looks of it, he bangs more bodies than them all.

Kisses,
Harlow Paige

I actually had to admire gall like that.

Tossing my iPad into my locker a little less gently than intended—after all, it wasn't the iPad's fault—I shut the door and tucked my scrub top into the waistband of my scrub pants.

With another night shift on the horizon, I didn't have time to sit and cry into my Cheerios about a stupid column from a less than reputable news outlet. *Gossip* wasn't where readers went for facts anyway.

I decided not to give any credence to the voice in my head that suggested maybe the reason this smarted so much was because of how close to the truth it actually was.

I double-checked the clip on my ID badge and headed for the door of the locker room with purpose. I wasn't going to think about Harlow Paige and her column anymore, and I wasn't going to be on the lookout for Frances. She should have had her stitches out a couple of days ago, but I guessed she'd gone to a different doctor.

Most patients follow up with their primary care physician, my medically trained mind reminded me.

Whatever. Her loss, right? It wasn't like we were going to be soul mates. At best, I would have given her a few orgasms, sans head injury, and we would have moved on.

The strains of our warm-up song started to play as I wandered down the hall, so I picked up my pace with a smirk. Sherry had obviously been paying attention when I told her all about our song of the week.

Maybe I'd have to give some attention to stoking that fire a little. She seemed pretty eager to have some X-rated fun—and smart enough to recognize that fun was all it was.

I'd made some poor choices in the past with Mandy and Sarah. They were two ER nurses I'd gotten to know on a biblical level, and unfortunately, had hurt a little bit in the process.

I'd been so eager I hadn't paid close attention to the looks on their faces, the cues in their actions, and the obvious attachment each dalliance built. They were looking for a relationship, and no matter who was doing the looking, I was always the wrong direction. I spent over a hundred hours a week at the hospital working, and I had too much fun doing what I did when I wasn't. I didn't have a yearning for kids, and I had no desire to live outside of the city with a picket fence, white or otherwise. Settling down wasn't for me.

Believe me, heartbreak was *never* my intention. Emotions and feelings were something I strived to keep *out* of the equation when it came to women and sex. Obviously, with Mandy and Sarah, I felt pretty fucking badly about the way things had ended.

Rounding the final corner onto the Emergency Department floor, I watched as my mom climbed to her feet in the chair behind the nurses' station and cranked the dial on the volume for our song of the week—*Pour Some Sugar on Me*. There was irony in the extremely horrendous timing of song choice and the way it lined up with my mother's unexpected visit.

Christ. Nicole Shepard was a lunatic. Gray-salted dark brown hair and rubber clogs on her feet, she was getting older with every day that passed—not that she was giving in to it willingly. The chair she was standing on jerked, and my heart flipped over in my chest.

Thankfully, Beverly, a pretty new nurse from Albuquerque with tanned skin and glowing turquoise eyes jumped forward to stabilize the wheels.

My mom's hips rolled as she lip-synched the words, and the jam-packed ER floor took immediate notice. It was only mildly embarrassing—after this many years as her son, I was pretty fucking used to it. Not to mention, it completely reaffirmed our genetic connection. My mild-mannered, serial monogamous father was another story entirely. If it weren't for our similar looks, I'd have thought my mom stepped out on him.

I strode quickly toward her, her eyes following me as I did. "Pour your sugar on me, Scott. I can't get enough!" she shouted. I cringed and laughed at the same time.

"Gross, Mom. No thanks."

She smiled, unfazed. "Sugar meeee. Ye-ah."

I reached forward and turned down the volume on the computer, and the groan of our disappointed audience was audible.

"Yeah, yeah," I grumbled to the room at large before extending a hand up to my mom. "Can you get down now, please? We're packed, and I don't really have time to sew up your future head laceration."

She took my hand as instructed, carefully climbing down and straight into my arms for a hug. "And that's how you'd treat your own mother," she clucked teasingly in my ear.

I pulled back and dropped a kiss on her cheek. "I guess, if I really had to, I'd find time to sew you up," I conceded with faux indifference.

"Aww." She patted my cheek. "Now that's the Dr. Erotic I know and love."

I rolled my eyes at my mom's ridiculous use of my nickname.

"Break any hearts lately?"

I smirked. "I never break hearts." At least never intentionally, that was for damn sure.

She scoffed and pulled away to walk around the counter and lean into it. "So only four or five, then?"

"I'm kind of busy, Mom," I avoided, picking up the chart from the counter and rounding it.

She pursed her lips. "Mmm-hmm. That's the usual too."

"Mom—"

"It's fine, Scotty."

"What brings you to town anyway?"

"Your father's god-awful schoolmarm of a wife invited me to their anniversary party."

I laughed. "That doesn't mean you have to go."

"Of course it does! I can't let her win."

"*Mom.*"

"She listens to Christian music, for Pete's sake."

"Linda is a nice lady."

She scoffed. "Nice. Exactly. I don't trust it."

"Well, trust it or not, they've been married for fifteen years now. It says so on the invitation."

She gave me a mocking smile and patted my cheek a little too roughly to be loving. I grabbed her hand to stop the assault and trapped it between both of mine.

"Look, if you're well behaved, I'll let you go with me."

"I'll go on my own."

"Mom," I chastised.

"Fine. I'll be good. Whatever the hell that means. But you have to give me some kind of a reward."

That sounded a bit like blackmail…

I quirked an amused brow. "A bribe, you mean?"

"Don't mock the bribe, Scott." She winked. "I did it all the time with you."

"Fine. What do you want?"

"The party is Saturday, and I have no plans for tomorrow night," she said quickly. *Too* quickly.

My eyes narrowed, and the hair on the back of my neck stood up. My mom was notorious for trickery. Honestly, I blamed myself for not seeing this one coming.

"So, by no plans, you mean you've made plans for both of us without my knowledge, and now, in exchange for also escorting you to a party where you will, in all likelihood, *not* behave, I get to take you somewhere else I'll hate."

"You doctors are smart." She grinned like the Cheshire cat. "All that schooling. It must be good for something."

I sighed and smiled at the same time.

"So where are we going tomorrow night, dearest Mother?"

"*Kinky Boots.*"

"*Kinky Boots*…the Broadway show?"

"I'll meet you at your place at six forty-five," she said by way of answer, scooping her purse up from the desk and walking straight out the automatic doors.

I looked around, and set after set of eyes jumped away.

Good Lord, my mom knew how to make an entrance *and* an exit. That woman was hell on wheels, and I'd rejoice the day she found a man who kept up with her feisty ways.

With no choice but to give in to the fact that I'd be seeing fucking *Kinky Boots* tomorrow night, my mind wandered to an irritatingly recurrent thought, and I decided there was something I had to do before I got consumed by the exciting—*and oftentimes bloody and gross*—world of emergency medicine.

"I'll be back in just a minute," I told the ER charge nurse for the night. Beverly nodded. She was a lot more lenient than Deb, the slave driver.

Against my better judgment, I stepped around the corner, scrolled through my recent calls, and clicked one to dial. It rang back in my ear as I waited.

"Heeello?"

"Harlow?"

Yeah. So, apparently, the article was bothering me a little more than I wanted to believe. But this was good. I could talk to her really quick, get all of my gripes off of my chest, and then get on with my night and my job.

"That's me. Who's this?"

"It's Scott."

"Scott who?"

Scott who? Was she serious?

"Scott Shepard. You've called me before. Don't you have my number saved in your phone?"

"Ohh. That Scott. Sorry, I know a couple, and I didn't bother to look at the caller ID when you called."

I ran a frustrated hand through my hair. "Who in the hell doesn't look to see who it is when someone calls?"

"Sometimes, I don't. Is that all you needed?"

"Is that all I needed?" I nearly roared. What an irritating woman. "I didn't know about your fucking loony tunes habit before my call, so, no, that's not the reason for my fucking call."

"Oh-kay." She was completely nonplussed. "So, what's the reason?"

Clenching my fists as tight as I could manage without causing serious injury, I worked to steady my words. "The article."

"What article?"

Oh my God. I was going to strangle a woman for the first time in my life. In fact, I'd never even considered it before now. But for Harlow Paige, I was willing to get dressed, take a cab, climb whatever fucking flights of stairs I had to, and bang on her door in order to do it.

"You know what article."

"Is it about you?"

"Of course it's about me!" My voice felt scratchy as Beverly came to a sliding stop around the corner. I waved her off with a wildly gesticulating arm.

"Well, geez. I didn't know. Maybe you really love Sia, and you're mad about the piece I did on her hair. What do I know?"

I closed my eyes tightly and took a deep breath. "Harlow."

"Okay, fine. *Which* article about you?"

"Harlow!"

"Well, there are two. Be realistic here. I'm not a mind reader!"

"I talked to you. I cooperated. I gave you plenty of juicy, true material to use for those photos. And yet, I read the fucking article, and not one word of it was what I actually told you."

"I had another inside source."

"One better than me?"

"Yes, if you must know. You're biased."

"I'm biased," I repeated.

"Yep. You like to sugarcoat things about yourself, obviously. So I had to talk to another inside source."

"And that person would be?"

"I can't tell you that. But if I get permission from them, I will." She paused and I sighed, deep and beleaguered.

"Okay," she relented. "I got permission."

I furrowed my brow in confusion. "Just now?"

"Yep. I'm the inside source."

"How the fuck are *you* the inside source? I've never met you."

"Ah, see, that isn't something my source is comfortable divulging."

"Your source, meaning you." My temples throbbed with my now heavy pulse.

"Exactly."

"Harlow—"

"Listen, Scott, I've really gotta go. But it was nice chatting, okay?"

"No, it's not okay—"

"Talk to you soon."

Click.

I stared down at the screen of my phone, a deep, piercing frustration making my eye twitch.

Goddamn this infuriating woman. I was half tempted to track this columnist down and give her a piece of my mind in person.

Because seriously... Who in the fuck is this Harlow Paige?

CHAPTER*seven*

Harlow

"TELL ME YOU'RE EXCITED, LOW."

Internally, I sighed. "I'm excited, Dad."

He scrutinized me with his gaze and one heavy brow slanted in disapproval.

"What?" I questioned. "I said I'm excited."

"You're not acting excited."

"How many times do you think we've said excited in the past two minutes?" I asked, hoping that I could redirect the focus away from my *lack* of excitement to see yet another Broadway show with my father. Don't get me wrong, I've always loved them, but this was the third show in the span of three weeks that he'd begged—and all but forced—me to see with him.

And since my mother and Jean-Pierre had never been big fans of musicals, I was my Dad's go-to gal for everything bright lights and show tunes.

My mother and father—a complete anomaly—were literally the happiest divorced couple on the planet. They'd thrown in the towel on their marriage when I was eight years old, and they'd been best buds ever since.

Hell, my father often tagged along on trips with my mother and her second husband of sixteen years.

My stepdad, Jean-Pierre, was an American transplant from Paris and the apple of my mother's eye. Yes, he did have an accent. And, yes, it probably did sound extremely sexy to any American woman who wasn't his stepdaughter.

The only downfall of my parents' divorce and my mother's marriage to Jean-Pierre was that they weren't fans of musicals.

Thanks for nothing, guys.

"Don't act so crabby, Low," my dad remarked. "*Kinky Boots* has won every major Best Musical award, including a Tony. Anyone sitting in your seat right now would be excited."

"Don't forget the Laurence Olivier Award," I added sarcastically. I'd heard more about *Kinky Boots* from Dad over the past week than most of the cast probably even knew, and they acted out the show six nights a fucking week.

"Exactly," he agreed with a giant grin. It was safe to say his sarcasm radar was off-kilter. *Blame it on the* Kinky Boots, I guessed.

He glanced down at his watch, and his smile grew wider. "Only thirty minutes until show time."

My dad had always been one of those people who arrived everywhere way ahead of schedule, and it was a serious pain in my ass, especially tonight. I understood getting somewhere on time, or even five to ten minutes early, but holy mother of egg rolls, no one needs to get anywhere with an hour's worth of time to spare.

Mmm…egg rolls…those would be so perfect right now…

I glanced inside my giant purse—which probably wouldn't fit the dimension requirements for carry-on luggage with Delta—and rummaged through my snack pocket. *Fuck yes! A small bag of M&Ms and a snack-size bag of Lay's potato chips.* I knew exactly what I would be doing for the next thirty minutes. It definitely wasn't egg rolls, but it would do.

My father glared the second my fingers touched the chip bag, the edgy rustle of plastic like a gunshot in the relatively quiet room. It sounded like heaven in the form of snack food to me, but obviously, my father thought otherwise. His gaze tracked down the source of the noise like a goddamn homing device.

"Low," he chastised.

"What?" I whispered back. "I'm hungry, and it's not like the show has started. We have at least another thirty minutes before the lights dim and someone starts belting out show tunes."

"It's not show tunes, Harlow. It's Broadway," he added on a sigh. "And do you remember who helped write this award-winning show?"

"Cyndi Lauper," I answered. With the way my dad had beat that information into my brain, there was zero possibility of me forgetting it.

"Exactly."

The words *Girls Just Wanna Have Fun and Eat Potato Chips* were on the tip of my tongue, but I decided to take it easy on him. The man enjoyed his Broadway shows, and even though I'd always had a tendency to bitch and moan when I got dragged along, I loved my dad. Seeing his smiling face during the shows and hearing his excited chatter afterward was always worth it.

I wasn't always a hard-ass. Just on occasion. Most of the time I was a real fucking softie at heart, especially when it came to the important people in my life.

"No snacks until intermission." My dad gave me the look. You know, the one parents give their eight-year-old kids when they meant business.

"You do realize that I'm twenty-nine, right?" I questioned, and he smirked.

"Yeah, but you'll always be my little girl, Low," he responded. "And right now, I refuse to sit by and watch you disgrace this theater with greasy potato chips."

I bet Cyndi Lauper's dad would let her eat potato chips before the show...

It was in moments like this I'd wished my parents would've stayed married longer and at least birthed me a sibling to share the brunt of their meddling. Some days, being the only child was a real pain in my ass. Other days, it was fantastic, but days like this, when all I wanted to do was eat potato chips before *Kinky Boots,* it was a real drag.

"Excuse me," a sophisticated older woman whispered toward us. "Do you mind if I slide in?" she asked and held up her tickets. "My son and I have those two seats in the middle."

"Of course," my father answered immediately and hopped to his feet to let her pass through the small aisle. I followed his lead, albeit a little less gallantly, as I shoved my potato chips back in my purse and awkwardly stood out of her way with my bag pressed to my abdomen.

"Thank you," she said with a soft smile and sat down in the empty seat beside my father. "I had hoped to get here earlier, but my son is always running a few minutes behind."

My father glanced at the empty seat beside her, and she chuckled nervously.

"He's answering a quick work call outside the doors," she explained. "I swear, my Scotty doesn't get a minute's rest with his job."

"I feel the same about my little Harlow," my dad said with a soft smile. "It's like pulling teeth to get her to go to a Broadway show with her dad."

Little Harlow? Jesus Christ.

"Considering this is the third Broadway show we've seen in the past three weeks, I call baloney, Dad," I chimed in. He chuckled, but his eyes never left the woman sitting beside him, and oddly enough, her gaze never left him either.

I glanced back and forth between them while they made small talk about the weather and then moved the conversation along to their favorite Broadway shows. Seeing as they didn't know each other from Adam, I was a bit shocked by how easily their conversation flowed, and the fact that my father was actually showing interest in chatting up a woman.

For the past decade, the man had seemed content to stick to his routine, never once seeking out female companionship, apart from his time with my mother and Jean-Pierre.

"I'm Nicole, by the way," she said with a shy smile, and my father grinned in response.

"It's nice to meet you, Nicole. I'm Bill."

Surprisingly, the next twenty minutes continued that way. The two of them chatted, while I sat back in my seat, daydreamed about my goddamn potato chips, and counted the lines of the ornate ceiling mindlessly.

It was only the sudden movement of Nicole hopping to her feet that pulled my attention away from my snack fixation. If you ever want someone to want something so badly they can hardly breathe, tell them they can't have it.

"Oh! Scotty! Over here!" she whisper-yelled toward the main aisle, and my gaze followed her line of sight.

A tall, dark, and handsome drink of a man—at least that was how he appeared from my current shoulder, back, and tight ass view—stood a few feet away from my seat scanning the room across from us. The sound of Nicole's voice did as she intended, though, grabbing his attention and turning it—and his body—toward us. Familiar chocolate brown eyes flashed with recognition when he finally spotted Nicole, and I nearly fell out of my seat.

Holy shit. It's Scott Shepard.

What were the fucking odds?

"Scotty," Nicole whispered again, for what purpose, I didn't know and didn't care. I was too busy hyperventilating. Dr. Erotic grinned as he strode toward our aisle.

The chances were fifty-fifty, whether he would give us his back or his front for the theater aisle shuffle, but as he got close, turning to the side and rearranging his feet to slide in, I knew I'd lost the odds. *Fuck. He's giving us the face.*

Holy moly, I could not *believe* Scott Shepard's mother was the one who'd been chatting with my father for the past twenty minutes.

I should have bought a fucking lottery ticket.

I did my best to shield my face with my hand, but my father was no help. Nudging me to stand up and let Scott into our row, he had no idea what a terrible fucking job he was doing of covering for me until it was too late. Even then, he didn't really know what a cluster-fuck he'd created. But I knew. Boy, did I know.

"Excuse me," Scott said as the front of his body got close enough to heat the front of mine. It was nothing more than a polite statement to apologize for such an intimate position, but when his eyes locked with mine, recognition instantly set in. It took a moment for his mind to catch up with his eyes, but when it did, a slow, easy smirk kissed his lips. I wasn't sure if it was all in my head, but it felt like it took him a tremendously long time to move on from me to the empty spot beside his mother.

"Scott," his mother said the second his extremely fine ass touched his seat. "We have the best seat mates tonight." She tossed a soft smile directly at my father.

"It appears that way," he responded with a grin and a brief, and surprisingly not violent, glance in my direction.

Relief set in when it appeared that he might have just recognized me from my stint in his ER and hadn't yet realized I was, in fact, the gossip columnist who'd written a few, and slightly embellished, articles about him.

Okay. This can work, Harlow. Just play it cool and avoid saying your name at all costs.

But that hope only lasted for all of ten seconds.

"I'm Bill Paige, by the way," my dad introduced himself and shook Scott's hand. "And this is my daughter, Harlow."

Ah, fuck.

It was a real fucking shame Scott was such a smart guy. If he'd been stupid, it might at least have taken him a little longer to make the connection that was sure to ruin my night.

"*Harlow* Paige? As in *the* Harlow Paige from the *Gossip* column?" he questioned.

Goddammit…

"Yep," my dad answered proudly. All I could think was *uh-oh.* "That's my Harlow. Are you familiar with her work?"

"It's *you?*" Scott's—now glistening—eyes never left me. "I thought your name was Frances?"

How in the fuck did he know my first name?

My eyes all but bugged out of my head. *My chart.* "You said you weren't going to look at my name."

"I *accidentally* saw your name, you know, when I was signing off on your file," he responded cynically. "It's kind of a job hazard, *Frances.* Or should I call you Harlow? It's kind of hard to keep up."

"Frances is her first name, but she doesn't go by it," my father kindly explained for me, somehow not catching on to the underlying animosity. "She hated that name as a kid, and by the time she turned ten, she would only answer to her middle name—*Harlow.*" My father's expression turned puzzled as he glanced back and forth between us. "Wait…*signing off on your file?* How do you two know each other?"

"We met a few weeks ago." Scott's mouth morphed into a cocky fucking smirk, and I wanted to strangle him. "HIPAA violations prevent *me* from being able to give the details, but Harlow could explain the situation that introduced us," he added, and I could hear the amusement in his voice. "That is, if she wants to."

Oh yeah, I'd love to tell my father a head laceration that occurred during sex was the reason I'd met Scott. What a fucking asshole.

"Oh! Did the two of you meet at the hospital?" Nicole asked innocuously. She couldn't see the patch of thorns she was wading into for all the blinding love for her "do-gooder" son.

"Violations?" The vein in the center of my father's forehead started to make its debut. "What is he talking about, Low?"

I sighed. "Calm down, Dad. It's nothing to get worked up about."

"It sounds like a big deal!" my father said on a near shout, and concern for what would happen next made my heart rate double. "Were you arrested?"

"Jesus, no," I answered on a whisper. "You remember the stitches on my forehead?" I asked and he nodded.

"From the bicycle injury in Central Park?" he asked, and fucking Scott Shepard cleared his throat and chuckled softly to himself.

Yes, I did tell my dad a little bit of a lie about my head injury. Just a minor story about a crazy man on a bicycle who ran into me in Central Park that caused me to fall down and hit my head on a rock. Just a tiny little white lie.
But seriously, who would tell their father the real story if they were in my shoes?

"Was he the man who was riding when you got injured, Low?" he questioned, and I internally groaned at his ironic choice in words.

The man who was riding? Good Lord, that sounded terrible. *And a little too close to the actual scenario...*

"No, sir," Scott answered, and if the strain in his throat was any indication, he was one breath away from losing himself to laughter. "I was, in fact, not doing *the riding* when your daughter got injured."

My father looked at me. "If he wasn't the one riding, then how do you two know each other?"

Fucking fiddlesticks, I needed everyone to stop saying riding before I fainted from discomfort.

"He was my ER doctor, Dad," I explained, and this time when he looked at Scott, his mouth was curved in appreciation.

"You took care of my Harlow after she got injured by that rider?"

"I sure did," Scott answered helpfully, an amused smirk all but sewn on to his face. "I sutured her after *the riding* incident."

"Who got hurt while riding, Scotty?" Nicole asked, her voice carrying a bit too nicely. *Goddamn theater acoustics.* I was torn between smacking Scott in the face or finding a way to dig a hole into the theater floor in order to migrate to China. *Perhaps I can use my stiletto.*

Apparently, as an outsider, it was hard to follow along with us as we talked in code.

"Harlow," Scott answered and nodded toward me. "That's how I met her. I had to suture her riding injury."

I was going to kill him before *Kinky Boots* even started if he kept saying riding.

"How did she look afterward?" my father asked. "I bet she was a bit shaken up from that reckless rider."

Scott grinned shamelessly, his cheeks coming to life with a rosy flush as he basked in my embarrassment. "She did look a little shaken up. Mostly just angry, though."

"You were angry?" my father questioned and looked at me. "I really wish you would have gotten that rider's name. I'd love to call him and give him a piece of my mind. No one should be that reckless."

"I agree," Scott piped up again. I wanted to smack him. "People should ride responsibly."

"You're right." His mother nodded in agreement. "People *should* ride responsibly. Otherwise, they shouldn't be allowed to ride at all."

Now, although I was internally dying a slow death, given the circumstances that led to this very humiliation, it was hard not to agree with that. Barron the Bore should've had his riding rights revoked immediately after he rode my ass straight into the ER. Although, in Barron's pathetic defense, a few days after his bed had sliced my head opened, he did send me an apology in the form of a nice bouquet of flowers. I appreciated the sentiment, but no contact with Barron for the next one thousand years was still the plan.

"So, you didn't get the man's name?" Scott questioned, childishly continuing this farce of a conversation for nothing more than his enjoyment, and I fought the urge to roll my eyes.

"Nope."

"Really? I would've thought you would've at least gotten a name or phone number...something..."

"I didn't," I snapped.

My dad sighed heavily. "You really should have gotten that rider's name, Low," he added in disappointment, but thanks to the dimming lights, both my view of his disappointment and the time for speaking began to fade.

And for once in my life, as the curtain started to lift, a Broadway show was my favorite fucking thing on the planet.

My least favorite thing? Scott fucking Shepard.

CHAPTER *eight*

H ARLOW PAIGE.
Frances Harlow Paige.
Harlow fucking Paige, the *Gossip* columnist, was *Bleeding Woman.*

Bleeding Woman was Frances.

And *Frances,* well, she was *Harlow Paige.*

I'd been running through the convoluted web—*okay, it's not that complicated, but the distorted reality I'd believed to be true made it feel like it*—of her identities as the actors on stage danced and sang for six full songs. Now, well entrenched in the seventh, a song about a woman who was always choosing the wrong guys, an intense burn had taken root in my stomach with the sting of reality.

Of course they were the same person.

In hindsight, I should have known. Sure, New York City has millions of people, and the chances of them being the same person were slim—statistically speaking—but life had a funny way of working out like this.

And the personalities matched up perfectly.

Challenging to the point of agitation, Harlow *Bleeding* Paige, held my attention. Both her visit to the ER and the witty exaggeration of her articles had seized a curious part of me in a nagging, torturous way I hadn't been able to forget. Day after day, I'd wondered about the woman I'd sutured and the woman who wrote passive-aggressive columns about me that bled a little too close to the line, and everything that'd been muddled and smudged by uncertainty of who and why now felt clear in my mind.

One complicated woman was at the center of it all. Glancing past my mother, I scoured the lines of Harlow's face for some sign of remorse or discomfort. A wrinkled brow. A minute frown. I moved on to her body. A clenched fist. A nervous fidget. Something.

But she gave me nothing.

Instead, her eyes were glassy, the shimmer of their moisture glinting in the glow of the stage lights as she worked at her bottom lip with the edge of her teeth. One hand rubbed at a tight-covered thigh, and the toe of her boot bobbed to the music. She seemed thoughtful without looking anxious, like each word of the song would expose some vulnerable part of her if she weren't careful.

As discreetly as possible, so as not to garner the ire of my musical-bopping mother, I pulled my phone from my pocket and fired off a text to a number I'd saved to my phonebook, like a normal person.

Me: So you're Bleeding Woman.

It wasn't exactly the most creative opening after thinking about it for six and a half songs, but it was the best my cynical mind could do, apparently. Not to mention, it wasn't like I could sit there and think on it as I typed while the light of the screen sent out a virtual distress call to any and all ushers in the area. Just like in a movie theater, they didn't like when you texted during the entertainment.

Harlow: Bleeding Woman?

Right. Of course, she wouldn't remember the thing she'd said that I'd remembered a million times since. It figured.

Me: Your sex victim name.

Harlow: Oh. Yeah. I guess that's me. But why act like you didn't creep my medical file to find my real name? You CLEARLY know it.

I leaned forward, just slightly, again trying to get a read off of her by inspecting her face, but she was completely out of view behind the bulk of her dad, like she'd become one with the seat. I'd just have to do my best to assess the situation without visual cues.

Me: I didn't do it on purpose.

Okay, that was a bit of a lie, but it wasn't like I was the only one sugarcoating the truth. I mean, she was also that fucking columnist from *Gossip.*

Harlow: Job hazards, right? Pffft.

Me: Listen, I tried not to look, but I had to sign off on your chart. And like you should talk. You're the Gossip columnist.

Harlow: Yep. That's me.

So fucking casual. My jaw ached from clenching it, and my pulse pounded in my ears. She had a way of getting under my skin like no other, but at least I was keeping it contained, eating away at me on the inside rather than causing a scene.

As if on cue, my mother turned to me with a hostile frown.

Okay, maybe I'm not keeping it on the inside.

A tiny fragment of our previous phone conversation struck me like lightning.

Me: Well…I guess you were right about being an inside source.

Harlow: I don't lie.

She doesn't lie? SHE DOESN'T LIE? Was she serious?

Me: …

What? I don't yell via text message or even out loud. Just in my head, usually.

Harlow: Okay, so I lie *sometimes*. But, whatever. It's a gossip column. What do you expect?

Me: Oh, I don't know. Some kind of truth in reporting…

Harlow: It's a GOSSIP column.

I started to type again when another message popped up from her.

Harlow: Can you stop messaging me now? I'm trying to watch Kinky Boots.

I scoffed, and my mom outright seethed in my direction. Bared teeth and a silent snarl, Nicole Shepard was five seconds away from tanning my thirty-five-year-old ass. *Shit.*

Me: You don't want to watch Kinky Boots. You want to avoid me and the consequences of your actions. The "freedom" of anonymity sure makes being out in the open even worse, huh?

Harlow: Stop. Messaging. Me.

Fine. She didn't want to talk via text? That was *just* fine.

"Oh, what the *fuck*? Are you *serious* right now?" Harlow shouted as she came out of the stall to find me leaning against the bathroom counter during intermission.

I wouldn't say it was my finest hour, but it felt like I'd been waiting for answers for forever, and I didn't feel like waiting anymore.

I'd lucked out, managing to clear out the other women and lock the door. I was actually surprised how willing they were to believe I was surprising my girlfriend with a wanted bathroom quickie.

If you're ever in this situation, please do a better job of looking out for
your fellow female friends' safety.
No random man should be let into the women's restroom under the
pretense of surprising his girlfriend with sex. Or for any fucking
reason, for that matter.

"You didn't want to text," I told her, crossing my arms over my chest and putting one ankle over the other.

"And you read that as *please stalk me like a pervert in the women's bathroom*?" She shouted a bark of laughter. "Christ, this is going to make one hell of a column. Let me know how the police interrogation goes."

Well aware of the boundaries I was pushing—*more like trampling all over*—I was careful to keep physical distance between us, shifting even farther away when she moved to the sink to wash her hands and keeping mine clearly to myself.

"You don't think I deserve some kind of closure?"

"Closure? What the hell do you need closure for? I was your patient, and then you had a couple of gossip rag columns written about you. Isn't that like a normal Tuesday for you, *Dr. Erotic*?"

I clenched my teeth and rolled my jaw, taking a moment to smother the building fire in my chest. She was trying to irritate me. Pushing all my buttons on purpose. I didn't know exactly what reaction she was looking for, but whatever it was, I didn't want her to have the satisfaction of getting it.

"Come on, Harlow," I teased. "Isn't *Kinky Boots* teaching you anything about friendship?"

She rolled her eyes and turned the tap to make the water hotter. Always a doctor, I surreptitiously checked out the healing gash on her forehead. It looked good, like she'd been taking care of it. Of course, I'd done a hell of a job on the sutures, so really, I was just admiring my work.

"Adversaries sometimes make the best of friends."

"We're not adversaries," she contested, drying her hands and unlocking the deadbolt on the bathroom door. "We're not anything."

Out the door and, I presumed, back to her seat, she left me there in the bathroom with absolutely nothing gained from our conversation other than determination.

She didn't want to be adversaries, friends, lovers…anything?

Sure sounds like a challenge to me…

God, I fucking loved a good challenge.

CHAPTER*nine*

Harlow

A
S *KINKY BOOTS* ENDED ON A MORE THAN PERFECT NOTE, LEAVING THE crowd tingly with happy thoughts, positive vibes, and hundreds of smiles, all a mile wide, I'd be a liar if I said it was awful. Despite the fact that Kinky Boots had led to an in-person meet-and-greet—and a side of bathroom stalking—with Scott fucking Shepard, the notes of friendship, adversity, and wacky fashion all won me over piece by piece. And, when I stopped feeling bitchy long enough to admit the truth, one thing was obvious: hands-down, it was one of the best Broadway shows I'd ever seen.

And let's face it, I'd seen a lot of Broadway over the past fifteen or so odd years.

Cyndi Lauper had created something magical with the musical genius she had injected into the show. It definitely had something, and I had a feeling my dad would be dragging me back to the Al Hirschfeld Theatre for another showing.

The crowd's applause, already a steady, rolling roar, increased ten-fold as the performers made their way back to the stage to take a bow. My dad hopped to his feet and wolf-whistled as the main cast members stepped out of the line and to the front of the stage. "Bravo! Bravo!"

I wouldn't be surprised if, when the house lights came up, I found a few fresh tear tracks on his face.

His enthusiasm urged a soft smile to my lips and made me grateful to the cast for making such an impact.

Broadway and Bill Paige. A match made in musical heaven. I often wondered if he had a past life as a performer.

"Wow," he said between claps as the cast took their final bows on stage. "What a great show." He glanced at me out of his periphery, just in case the actors made some last-minute enchanted statement. "Wasn't it fantastic, Low?"

"It was." I nodded, struggling to swipe the amused grin off my lips. "*Kinky Boots* was perfection." *Bill Paige is perfection.* Really, I had the best dad.

"It really was," Nicole added with awe in her voice, briefly reminding me of the person I'd been pretending I'd forgotten.

Whatever her devil spawn of a son's name is.

"It's been ages since I've seen a Broadway show, but wow, I need to change that. I'm missing out."

"You are," my dad agreed and gently grinned in her direction. "It's one of the perks of living near the city, Nicole."

"See?" She nudged Scott—*ugh*—with her elbow. "You should take your mother to Broadway shows more often."

Scott smirked and glanced around the theater dramatically. "Oh, shit. I thought that was what I was doing. Where am I? Am I hallucinating?"

"Smartass," she muttered on a laugh. "I mean, you need to do it *more*. Not just once every few years."

"Whenever I can fit it into my call schedule, I'll take you, Mom," he said, and she groaned.

"Ugh. So, basically, once every few years, then?"

Scott grinned. "Boy, you've gotten grumpy in your old age."

"I'm not old!" She smacked his shoulder, glancing briefly to my father with rosy cheeks. Scott laughed.

My dad cleared his throat and wrapped his arm around Nicole's shoulder.

Damn. Bill's got game.

"Consider it a standing offer. Anytime you want to go to a show, I'll gladly escort you."

"Okay." She smiled at him, and he smiled back at her and—Jesus Christ, these two were doing a lot of smiling.

"See?" Scott questioned with a hint of sarcasm in his voice. "Everything always works out in the end."

"Not with any help from you," Nicole muttered, but her eyes seemed welded to my father.

Holy moly, what was going on with these two? The last time I'd ever seen my dad look at a woman like this, I was five and he was still married to my mother—and I'd caught him with a Playboy in the bathroom.

Don't worry. His pants were on, and all of his parts were covered. Trust me, trauma like that and we'd probably be having a different conversation right now.

"Well." Scott glanced at me and then at our parents, who appeared to be having some sort of silent conversation no one else was privy to. "I think you should join us for a drink afterward."

He was talking to my dad, but at the same time, he *wasn't* talking to my dad. The sneaky bastard.

"That's a fantastic idea," Nicole agreed, squeezing my father's arm playfully. "Are you free to join us? We could exchange notes on the show. And maybe you could tell me a few of your favorite parts?"

"I'd love that." Bill nodded, all too eager to agree, and then glanced at me. I had one foot in the direction of the exit, but then he had to go and ruin it. "Doesn't that sound nice, Low?"

Fuck. *Don't remind everyone that I'm here, Dad.*

Just act natural and smile, I coached myself.

"Sounds like a great idea."

"Okay," Bill agreed with a proud smile. "We'd love to join you."

We? Hold the motherfucking train…

Hadn't Scott said you, meaning one, meaning just my father?

"Wait…uh?" I blurted out, eager to derail this sucker, but unsure what in the hell I was going to say to get out of spending more time with Scott. "I think—I might have plans—"

"You *might* have plans?" Scott asked with that cocky fucking grin of his. He knew exactly what he'd just done, and instead of being a gentleman and giving me an out, he sat patiently, waiting for me to say, explicitly and without assistance, that I did not want to hang out with a total asshole and his sweet mother for the evening.

His mom's big brown eyes looked dejected, almost tawny with disappointment. My father questioned, "I thought you said you wanted to go, Low?" His voice was soft, but the line of his body was firm. Bill Paige's version of *what the hell is going on, young lady?*

"I meant…*you* should go…and you still should," I stuttered. "But I think I might've already made plans with Amanda…" I tossed out and then instantly realized my mistake as his keen eyebrows danced into a suspicious tilt.

Obviously, I'd made a critical error. My best friend wasn't even in the country. And she wouldn't be in the States for the next month because she'd be busy traveling through Europe on a goddamn PR tour with her soon-to-be Spanish lover.

Fucking hell. *I wish I were in Europe right now with my soon-to-be Spanish lover.*

Wait. I don't want a lover. Boy toy? Yeah, that's much better.

"Didn't she just leave on that business trip?" my father questioned. "I thought Jean-Pierre had helped her book the hotels in France?"

Goddamn it. Was it hot in here? Bright? Had we teleported into a fucking interrogation room?

Scott quirked a brow. "Did you maybe get the dates confused, Harlow?"

Ugh. *Fuck you, Scott Shepard.*

"Hold on... Let me double-check my calendar..." I held up one finger and pretended to go through the calendar on my phone. Really, I was just scrolling back and forth from one end of my apps to the other. I didn't even keep a fucking calendar. Believe me, I'd tried numerous times to keep up with my schedule, but I always forgot to track dates after about a week of pretending to be organized. "Oh! It looks like I got the months confused," I lied with a relieved smile. "It's not until next month. I'm completely free tonight."

"Boy," Scott chimed in with an amused smirk, his body nearly quaking with unspent laughter. "That's a relief."

"I know, right?" I said in the fakest voice that had ever left my lips. Splenda had nothing on this shit. "It's like the stars have aligned tonight." *To make my life a living hell...*

"They definitely have. This really has turned out to be a fantastic night," my father said with a smile in Nicole's direction.

And, no surprise, she was smiling, too. And when I glanced at Scott in my periphery, he was also smiling. Most likely at my discomfort, but still, every-fucking-body was smiling.

Besides me.

"Where should we go, Low?" my father asked and then grinned proudly when he added, "My Harlow always knows the best places in the city to go for every occasion. I have a feeling it's from all of that column research she does."

"Well..." I started with a forced smile, scrambling to think of the worst place within a five-block radius and coming up empty. Goddamn, the last thing I wanted was to pick somewhere inviting. I'd never get rid of Scott.

"Maybe it would be a good idea if we stick to a bar close by. Something local and relaxed, though. No Times Square hot spots. You know, so it will be easy to chat about the show." *And hopefully, the wine will be cheap, and I can drown my misery in alcohol...*

"What a good idea," Scott interjected, but his voice reeked of sarcasm. "And who knows? Maybe Harlow will find some inspiration for one of her columns."

"Wouldn't that be great?" my dad agreed with a grin. "Kill two birds with one stone."

"Exactly." Scott winked in my direction, and I fought the urge to flip him off. "Well," he said and gestured toward the aisle with his hand, "let's continue this wonderful evening of getting to know one another."

A wonderful evening of getting to know Dr. ERotic?

Someone. Help. Me.

CHAPTER *ten*

"WHAT IS THIS PLACE?" HARLOW ASKED AS WE STEPPED INSIDE OF Mustang's, one of the best barely known gems in Manhattan.

Part dive bar, part think tank, the walls were lined with patron-created drinks written on cocktail napkins, envelopes, old newspapers, and the like. It was the only place I'd ever been to that didn't recognize standard drinks as common practice. Instead, you made up your own, tried it out, and if the bartender deemed it "sea-worthy"—or sellable—your concoction got tacked up on the wall after you gave it a name. If you didn't like whatever came from your experimental mind, you could try again or order someone else's proven success story by picking from the walls. It had to be at least slightly cost-ineffective, wasting liquor on unsuccessful samples, but somehow, they made it work.

Maybe that's where the dive bar part comes into play.

Instead of going into the details, I pushed Harlow toward the bar, my mom and Harlow's dad following closely behind. "You'll see."

78 · max monroe

Her dad had touted her as one of the best locals in New York, a real gal of the town who knew exactly where to go for the best atmosphere, but she'd fallen pretty spectacularly on her face when forced to come up with a place under pressure.

I had a feeling that was her mind and body's way of revolting against my presence more than anything, though.

"Have you never been here?" my mom asked Harlow excitedly. This was one of her favorite places ever, the two success stories she'd ever created, a Limeade Tequila Sunrise and a Drug Dealer—two parts Coca-Cola, one part cherry juice, and one part rum—her pride and joy.

I didn't have the heart to tell her that the second one was basically just a rum and Coke, and the bartender apparently didn't either. Still, I had to give her bonus points for creativity on the name.

Harlow shook her head before my mom directed the question to her dad. He shook his head too. "How'd you find this place?" Bill asked.

My mom laughed. "Scott, of course. He always brings me to the best places in the city."

Harlow's curious eyes shot to me before she could conceal them. *Ah, yes, little Harlow. You're not the only one who knows New York's secrets.*

Stepping close enough that the heat of her back radiated into my chest, I whispered in her ear. "That's not my only talent."

She turned slightly so she could body check me with her shoulder. I laughed and rubbed at the point of contact on my chest. It didn't hurt at all, but I definitely felt something. I just couldn't put my finger on what.

"Bill, you have got to try a Nipple Blaster!" my mom said on a near shout. Harlow's eyes rounded to the size of saucers.

"A Nipple Blaster, huh?" Bill asked, completely unfazed. Though, if I wasn't mistaken, there did seem to be a little carnal hunger in his wolf eyes.

"Yes! It's Scott's creation."

"Why am I not surprised?" Harlow muttered under her breath, and I laughed. She wasn't my biggest fan for whatever reason. *Okay, maybe it was holding her hostage in a painful conversation about how she'd ridden her way to stitches or haranguing her in the bathroom, but whatever.* Somehow, though, her dislike of me just made me like her even more.

"It's just a twist on a Buttery Nipple."

"What's the twist?" Harlow asked. Her body looked like it was stiff, fighting the whole idea of actually giving me any attention whatsoever, even if just to ask a question, but her curiosity got the best of her. I'd have to make a mental note of what needing information did to her willpower.

"A Fireball chaser."

"Let's all do one!" my mom cheered excitedly. The tiniest hint of a smirk curled the very tip of Harlow's lips.

"You in?" I asked her directly. She shrugged.

"I guess I can't be the downer."

Bill nearly shoved me out of the way to envelop her in a bear hug. "That's it, sweetheart. Perk up! You're the youngest one here." He glanced to me quickly. "At least, I assume."

"You're right, Bill. She's the youngest."

Harlow's eyes narrowed at the way I said it. *That's right, little miss columnist. I've been researching you.*

I signaled for the bartender's attention while Bill moved back out from in between his daughter and me and settled in to chat with my mom, and he gave me a chin lift that said I had it. "Four Nipple Blasters." The bartender gave me a nod and pulled out eight shot glasses.

Harlow shifted uncomfortably in front of me and crossed her arms over her chest. I bit into my lip as my mind went straight to the one sexy thing she could be trying to conceal. Was Harlow Paige getting a little hot and bothered every time I said the word nipple?

I leaned close, teasing the shell of her ear with my hot breath as I tested the theory. "Do you like Buttery Nipples, Harlow?"

She shivered, her shoulder jumping up to her ear just slightly before she tightened her arms. I smiled to myself. Yep. Harlow might not like me, but her nipples seemed to be liking me just fine.

One, two, three, four, the bartender lined up the shots on the bar in front of us, stacking the Fireball chasers directly behind each glass. I pulled a hundred-dollar bill from my pocket and handed it to him before Bill could get his wallet out of his pocket.

"On me," I told him.

"Thanks, Scott," he said with a thump on my shoulder and a smile for his daughter.

"I like this guy, Low."

She grumbled. "Of course you do, dad."

I laughed as I picked up a glass and handed it to Harlow, and Bill did the same for my mom. Then we both took our own and formed a circle to clink cheers before tossing it down the hatch and grabbing for the chaser. Mine went down easily enough, but Harlow's face was downright comical.

"Not a big drinker?" I asked as she set her empty glasses back on the bar.

"Not usually hard liquor," she admitted.

"I like that," I told her. And I did. I was all about a good time, but I liked the idea of someone who didn't need alcohol to have one. And Harlow Paige might be grumpy right now, but I could tell she was a good time when she was with people she admitted to liking—probably bordering on too good.

"I think I need to sit down," my mom said suddenly, and I turned to her with concern. Bill, of course, gentleman that he was, immediately grabbed her arm to offer support. And she fucking *winked* at me.

"Oh, don't worry, Bill. It's just this one hip. Gives me a little trouble if I stand for too long."

My eyes narrowed. She didn't have any hip problems.

"Let's go sit down then, Nicole."

"You don't mind?" she asked.

Poor sap. He didn't fucking mind at all. My mom looked over her shoulder and winked one more time as Harlow sank into a barstool, her head in her hands. Jesus Christ. My mom had just arranged alone time for me with Harlow. *My mom is helping me with dates now. This feels like a low point.*

Harlow didn't look up from her point of focus, a drop of water on the bartop, when she spoke. "Your mom is…well, she's something."

Hell on wheels. My mom was hell on goddamn wheels.

"Okay, yeah, she is," I laughed. "But I'm sure your parents are Ward and June Cleaver."

"Well…" She laughed, finally leaving the water droplet to its own fate and forcing her eyes to meet mine. "Not exactly. They're kind of like Ward and June Cleaver and Bill Johnson."

"What?" My face pinched in confusion, and laughter bubbled in my throat at the same time. "Who the hell is Bill Johnson?"

"He's my dad. Actually, Bill Paige is my dad." She rolled her eyes. "Obviously. But my mom, Karen, aka June, and her husband Jean-Pierre, aka Ward, are the perfect couple, and my dad is, crazy as it sounds, their perfect sidekick."

I tried to picture what she was describing. Her mom and Jean-Pierre—faceless bodies in my mind, of course—dressed as Batman and Catwoman with Bill in a Robin costume next to them. I tried to make four out of two-plus-two, but all I could compute was a very disturbing threesome.

I mean, my parents at least got along in a civil capacity—my mom was going to my dad and stepmom's anniversary party, for fuck's sake. But she was doing it with barely concealed disdain. The pieces of Harlow's perfect parent trio weren't quite lining up.

"So, what? They're like besties? Your mom, your stepdad, and your dad?"

She nodded enthusiastically, her face completely devoid of sarcasm. "Yeah. They're going on an Alaskan cruise together in a few months for my dad's birthday."

Finally, it all made sense. At least, an opportunity to tease Harlow mercilessly did.

I smirked. "So, they're a threesome."

"What?" she shrieked, covering her ears.

"A threesome. You know…double penetration?"

"No, they're not a fucking threesome, you pervert!" Her lips curled away from one another, and the normally tanned glow of her skin faded into a sallow white.

"You're the one who said they're all set to go on vacay together," I pushed, doing my best to keep my face straight. "Your dad doesn't have any other friends he'd rather celebrate with?"

"They're best friends!"

"Sounds like something else to me."

"Oh, eww! Stop! They're best friends."

"Who sleep together," I mumbled under my breath.

"Stop! They have separate rooms!"

"That's what they tell you, maybe."

Steely determination set in as she stared me down. "Oh, yeah? Then I guess your mom is about to make their fourth? How do you like that?"

Mentally, I cringed. But I fought it for the sake of winning our argument.

"Sounds kinky," I said, voice steady.

"Gross!" she shouted, but there was a hint of laughter in her voice. "You're gross!"

"You're just focusing on our differences, Harlow. You need to focus on our commonalities."

Her nose wrinkled, and she batted at me with a hand. "Oh, don't you school me using *Kinky Boots*."

"Why?" I argued. "Some good has to come out of seeing it."

She laughed. "I take it you didn't like it?"

"I thought it was fine."

"But…"

I shrugged. "I'm not big on musicals."

She rolled her eyes before admitting, "Neither am I. Though, I have to admit I didn't mind this one."

Both of us looked to our respective parents, and Harlow stood up to make our way over to them. We didn't even have to say anything. She just fell in step right in front of me as I guided her with a hand at the small of her back.

It was weird how natural it all felt.

When we got to their table and she greeted them, I pulled my hand away from the heat of her shirt and studied my palm. *Why is it tingling?*

"Isn't that a great idea, Scott?" my mom asked, pulling my attention away from my hand.

"What's that?" I asked, obviously having no idea what the topic of conversation was. I was kind of busy studying my sudden ability to conduct electricity.

"I was just asking Bill to be my date tomorrow night…for the party."

The party…?

Oh. My dad and Linda's anniversary party.

Ah Jesus. My mother.

"Well…" I looked into my mom's eyes, expecting to see some sort of game, but there was genuine hope there. She really liked Bill. Hell if I was going to be the one who ruined it.

"I think that's a great idea," I finished.

"Maybe Harlow could be your date," Bill suggested after a nudge from my mother. *They're in this together.* I just barely stopped myself from laughing.

"Dad!" Harlow protested. "You can't just invite us to stuff. There's probably a head count and menus and all sorts of important details. Plus, Scott probably already has a date."

Her objection, so detailed and full of conviction as it was, sealed it for me. Now, I had to make her go.

"Oh, no. Trust me, it'll be fine if you guys come. I was flying solo, but I'd love if you accompanied me, Harlow."

It was the damnedest thing. I could practically *hear* the litany of curse words she was running over my name in her head and *feel* the steam as it poured out of her. It was almost as if Harlow gave me heightened abilities.

I've always wanted to be a superhero.

"Perfect!" my mom squealed.

I smiled at Harlow. "It's a date."

CHAPTER *eleven*

Harlow

ALL IT TOOK WAS A SINGLE GLANCE TO THE WALL CLOCK IN MY KITCHEN TO make my chest tighten. It was already noon, and I'd yet to write a single goddamn word.

Jesus, where did the time go?

Probably lost on mentally flipping Scott Shepard off...

He'd really pulled a fast one on me last night. Somehow, directing the conversation in a way that ended in me having to see him twice in a twenty-four-hour period.

"I'd love if you accompanied me, Harlow."

Asshole. I groaned out loud as I replayed his words.

"It's a date."

Fucking hell. I had a date with the devil, otherwise known as Scott assface Shepard.

Although, he does have quite an attractive face and one hell of a tight ass...

Oh God. Get it together, Harlow! Do not think good thoughts about the enemy!

Was I really mentally sparring with myself right now because of a cocky bastard of a man?

Sigh.

Where had my life gone wrong? And how did I keep ending up with these awful dates?

Double sigh.

As a realist—*my friend Amanda would argue I'm more pessimist, but she's a French-frolicking traitor right now*—my outlook on tonight was the opposite of good. I mean, if Barron the Bore landed me in the ER after what was supposed to be a simple night of dinner, what did Dr. Erotic have the power to do?

Maybe give us a real orgasm, my vagina chimed in.

Shut up, Vagina. You're the one who got me in trouble with Barron in the first place.

Another cursory glance at the clock made me wince.

Shit! How is it twelve fifteen now? I've done nothing!

I forced my focus away from mentally flipping off Scott Shepard and read through my notes on various column ideas for the fifteenth time. I groaned. I needed something better than which Hemsworth brother looked better naked. Sure, those Aussies were the apples of a lot of women's eyes—including my own *because, hello? Have you seen Thor?*—but I wanted and needed something with substance versus the trite, cliché crap that filled most gossip-based columns. I wasn't going for the next Great American Novel, but something better than which Kardashian had the biggest ass wouldn't be off base.

Hmm. Maybe I can do an article about which Hemsworth has the biggest ass…

Before I could brainstorm more ideas—as I desperately needed to—my phone buzzed with a text message. I sighed in annoyance. I knew who it was before I even checked the screen.

Dad: Which shirt should I wear?

He'd been at it all day with the text messages. Five messages ago, it was which shoes. Ten messages ago, it was hairstyle, which was ridiculous because my dad was partially balding. The hairstyle question had all of one option—the same fucking hairstyle he'd been sporting for the past twenty years.

It didn't take a rocket scientist to figure out from the one million text messages that Bill Paige was bristling with anxious energy because of that stupid anniversary party Nicole Shepard had invited him to. And, yeah, with Scott's underhanded trickery, I'd gotten dragged into the shindig as well.

Although, ironically, it had appeared that my *dad* was trying to play matchmaker last night at Mustang's and set me up with a man who had been dubbed *Dr. Erotic*. So it wasn't like Scott hadn't had any help.

I made a mental note to ask my dad if he'd ever seen Scott's show. I had a feeling he didn't really know the kind of reputation that man had built for himself. Unless you were Hugh Hefner, it wasn't exactly the norm to spend your nights out surrounded by twenty-something popstars and busty swimsuit models.

Needless to say, it felt like I was going on some kind of weird double date with my father. And it only felt weirder when I thought about the fact that our pseudo-dates were mother and son. This was some serious Jerry Springer kind of shit. But if I was being honest, there was a small part of me—the columnist side—that secretly wanted to go. My readers had shown a huge interest in the pieces I'd written about Dr. Erotic, and I was praying tonight I'd discover even more dirt to dish.

My phone buzzed with yet another text message from my father.

Dad: Hello? Low? I need help here. Which shirt should I wear?

I smiled at his impatience and looked through the numerous picture messages he'd sent. All of them were the same exact collared, long-sleeved, button-up dress shirt, just different colors—lilac, sky blue, black, white, and about ten other color options.

Bill Paige, back in the game. If I weren't trying to fit in a little writing time for Monday's column, I'd find it more adorable than annoying.

Me: The blue one. It brings out your eyes.

My dad had a killer set of blue eyes I'd spent half my life watching women react to shamelessly. He just never reacted back. I honestly wasn't even sure if he knew the effect he had on the opposite sex, but tonight, once I finished up this column, I'd do my best to make damn sure he had the confidence boost he needed to be ready for a night of schmoozing Nicole Shepard.

Dad: Will you come over a little early and help me get ready?

Me: I thought that's what we were doing with all of these text messages?

Dad: Low.

Me: Fine. But I need to finish this column first.

Dad: Can you get here by 4?

Me: That's 3 hours before the party, Dad. That seems like way more time than we need. Unless you're wanting me to do your nails before we go...

Dad: Shit. Do you think I need to get a manicure?

Good Lord, he was nervous. Even too amped up to realize I was being a total smartass and teasing him. As I started to type out another text message, I silently wondered if I should lay off the sarcasm and give him a break.

Nah.

Me: When's the last time you had one?

Dad: I've never had one. God, is that bad?

He was proverbially crawling up the walls over this party tonight. The thought made me laugh, so I typed out a message.

Me: Will I find claw marks on your walls like in Jurassic World when I get over there?

Dad: What? No.

Me: Then, no. You don't need a fucking manicure, Dad. Just take a breath and relax. Everything will be great. I promise.

Dad: This is nerve-racking. Is this what dating is always like?

Well, sometimes it's a lot fucking worse, I thought to myself. *Especially when your date has a bed made out of shards of glass.*

Me: Sometimes, but considering it's been like thirty years since you went on a date... I think it's safe to say you're a little more nervous than most.

Dad: Goddammit, Low. Don't remind me.

Me: LOL. Relax, Pops. Everything will be perfect. I'll come over in a little bit and make sure you're looking like a silver fox. Nicole will be putty in your hands.

Dad: Silver fox??? I don't have that much gray hair, Low!

Before I could explain that silver fox was actually a good thing—a simple saying referring to handsome older men—he fired off another panicked message.

Dad: *Do you think I need to dye the gray out of my hair before the party?*

Help. Me. It was only half past noon, and my dad had already considered getting a manicure and dyeing his hair. This was going to be one long fucking day…

Me: *Silver fox = Handsome and distinguished older man.*

Dad: *So it's a good thing?*

Jesus Christ.

Me: *Yes. It's the nice way of saying sexy. But I refuse to use that word in the same sentence in which I'm talking about my father.*

Dad: *Do you think Nicole thinks I'm a silver fox?*

Me: *Yes. And before you ask me anything else, I'm ending this conversation because it is about to reach awkward places. Call Mom or Jean-Pierre if you want to continue it further.*

Dad: *Love you, Low.*

Me: *Love you too, Dad.*

I set my phone back on the table and prepared to dive back into work, but my phone buzzed again with a message.

Dad: *See you at 3?*

Me: I thought you said 4?

Dad: No, I said 3.

I loved my dad, but holy hell, he was driving me crazy.

Me: Dad. I can scroll back through the messages and see that you said 4. So, yes, I'll see you at 4. Now, leave me alone until then so I can work for a little bit.

Dad: Do you want me to help you pick out your outfit for tonight, sweetheart?

Oh, for fuck's sake.

Me: I'm fine, Dad. I've got it.

Dad: Are you sure? I think it might be good if you wear that cute pink dress with the white bow.

Me: You mean the same dress I wore at my high school graduation?

Dad: Was it that long ago?

Me: Uh, yeah. And since I'm 29, I'm pretty sure I no longer have that dress.

Dad: What about the purple dress with the ruffly things at the bottom?

Holy hell. Now he was referring to my junior prom dress.

Me: Bye, Dad.

Before he could send back any more texts, I turned my phone off. A daughter could only handle so much of helping her father get ready for a date.

I was also going to be attending my father's date, as the date for his date's son—who also happened to be a man I pretty much despised.

Good Lord, tonight is probably going to be a clusterfuck of epic proportions.

CHAPTER *twelve*

"THEY'LL BE HERE SOON," I TOLD MY MOM AS SHE PACED A TINY TWO-FOOT line in front of me, doing her best to wear a hole through the floor of Tavern on Park, the quaint but opulent banquet hall.

My dad and Linda were already out and mingling, and hors d'oeuvres passed every few moments on silver trays. They'd gone all out for their fifteen-year celebration, and I didn't blame them. Linda and my father were the perfect couple my mom and dad had never been. A yin and yang of sorts, but quiet and loving—two qualities my parents together had never been.

Still, my mom was a woman scorned, even if she knew she wasn't right for my dad and that he wasn't right for her. I personally think she'd just wanted to be the person to leave rather than the one to be left. But after nearly two decades, the facts weren't changing.

"We should have picked them up."

"Mom, this is New York. Picking people up is nice and all, but it's about ten times the trouble. They wanted to meet us here. They'll be here soon."

"Fine," she grumbled. "I just wanted to shock Linda."

I nodded. I knew that's what she wanted.

"Of course, you ruined it anyway." She cocked her head and narrowed her eyes to emphasize how unhappy with me she was.

"Mom, I had to tell Linda we were bringing people. Don't you want our dates to have chairs to sit in? That'd be kind of awkward, wouldn't it?"

She clamped her mouth shut and shot lasers out of her eyes—her standard move for knowing I was right but not wanting to admit it. Obviously, I came by my stubbornness naturally.

"But if it makes you feel any better, the additions were so last-minute, the venue is probably making them pay out the nose. They like to have a head count further in advance than this," I consoled, hoping to diffuse the situation rather than escalate it.

She shrugged. "That does make me feel slightly better, thank you."

I laughed. "You're welcome."

I lifted my eyes from my mother to the door, and all laughter cut off abruptly as the air left my lungs.

Holy shit. Struggling to compose myself, I patted at the button of my suit coat and then lifted my hands to straighten my already straight tie. My mom noticed my fumbling and turned to look.

With soft curled hair, tucked behind one ear, and plum-red lips, Harlow was stunning. Her eyes skated up from the ground to meet mine and caught.

I didn't know exactly what I looked like, but I knew it wasn't collected. Transfixed, maybe. The sleek, tanned skin of a stiletto-tipped leg winked at me from the thigh-high split in her long black dress, and the deep V in the front went nearly to her navel. And still, somehow, I'd never seen a more classically beautiful woman. She didn't look cheap or like she was trying too hard.

She looked goddamn breathtaking.

I watched, immobile, as she crossed the room to me like she was floating. She was graceful and composed, and Christ, I felt like we were the only two people in the room.

"Hi, Harlow," I greeted softly when she made it to me.

"Hi, Scott," she whispered back.

Like it had a mind of its own, my hand started to move, toward her arm, her shoulder, something—just anything to feel my skin on her skin.

"Your beard looks like it's eating your face alive. I thought you'd at least shave for a fancy shindig like this," she commented, and thank God, really. The derisive note in her voice was the only thing that made room for my sanity to return. I shook off my episode of fascination and focused on what we did best—laying carefully concealed barbs within normal conversation and amusing one another.

"It's a Beards for Babies thing that Will Cummings is doing."

"Will Cummings? You mean, Dr. Obscene?"

I shook my head as a bark of laughter escaped my throat. "You know, he'd just love to know you're more familiar with his nickname than his real name. Truly, he'd be honored."

"I take it he doesn't covet the celeb life quite as much as you, *Dr. Erotic*?"

"No, he doesn't." My eyes narrowed. "That's why you're going to keep him out of the limelight, right?"

"Hey, I'm just—"

"An opportunist."

With a perfectly manicured hand to her chest, she feigned discomfort. "You wound me."

"Bullshit. You're not offended in the slightest. And you shouldn't be. I, for one, find it blindingly attractive."

She rolled her eyes.

"But keep the stories to me, okay? Leave the other two alone."

"Ohh," she cooed, her eyes lighting up. "I'd almost forgotten about the third. What's his name? What's his deal? When do his episodes air?"

"Harlow."

"What? I'm just trying to be informed."

"He's got a kid. Drop it."

"Wow, a beard for the babies and defensiveness for the child of the third mysterious doctor of *The Doctor Is In*. Are kids a weakness for you, Scott?"

"Yes. They are. And quite frankly, they should be for everyone."

Her face softened ever so slightly. Not enough to change the shape, and not enough to make me step closer, but enough to know she didn't have a heart of stone locked in there behind all that armor.

"Shall we?" I asked, offering her my elbow as the band music softened and they instructed everyone to make their way to their seats.

She looked at my arm closely for several moments before taking it, and I noticed for the first time that my mother had moved on to Bill. I'd completely forgotten about her. *Does that make me a shitty son?*

"So what's the deal with your parents?" Harlow asked as we walked, securing my full attention once again. "I told you about mine."

I nodded and pulled her in closer so I could whisper. *God, she smells good.*

"Ah, yes. Nicole and Tanner Shepard divorced when I was seventeen years old after nearly twenty years of unhappy marriage. They both knew they weren't meant for each other probably five years in, but I was a toddler. And while my mom is the stubbornest woman on the planet, my dad is the nicest man. No way he was going to leave her and me during those formidable years. When they finally separated, my mom held a grudge. Still does, quite frankly. But not because she actually loves him or anything."

"Kind of like a kid with a toy?"

"Exactly like that," I agreed. "Anyway, he met Linda a couple years later, and they married nearly immediately. Now, *they* are soul mates. The real, written-in-the-stars kind. Somehow, they manage passion without disagreement. I hadn't even thought that was possible until the two of them."

"Wow."

I nodded, pulling out her chair for her. Her eyes followed me over her shoulder. I was nearly lost in them again when my dad's voice rang out through the microphone. "Scott, could you sit down, son?"

The whole audience of partygoers laughed as I gave him a wave, shook off the lusty power of Harlow's eyes, and tucked myself into my seat.

"Thanks, Dr. Erotic," my dad commented. Once again, the crowd laughed. Even Harlow.

"Yeah, yeah," I grumbled with a shake of my head. I never lost my smile, though. Only parents like mine could find ways to tease about something like this rather than criticize. They were both my biggest supporters—no matter what.

"My son, everyone," my dad boasted proudly.

See?

"Linda, honey," he called, shielding his eyes from the light so he could find her. "Can you come up here?" The spotlight found her greeting guests at a table across the room and followed her as she made her way to my dad with a sweet blush on her face.

As soon as she was within touching distance, he pulled her close with an arm around her waist and placed a kiss on her cheek. The room let out a collective sigh as they looked on. Normally, my mom would have had some kind of smart comment, so I turned briefly to get a read on her, but she was too busy whispering quiet words with Bill in their seats across the table.

I smiled. Maybe the time Nicole Shepard let it all go had finally come.

I returned my attention back to the front to listen as my dad spoke. "I just want to thank everyone for coming tonight." He turned to his wife to address her directly. "Linda, we've only been married for fifteen short years, and they've absolutely flown by. Every year, I think maybe I'll finally feel like it's enough, like I've had a satisfying amount of time with you, but every year I get hungrier. It'll never be enough. Even at sixty years, I'll be wishing for sixty more. I love you."

"Good God," Harlow muttered, drawing my attention. She was pulling a tissue from her purse and dabbing her eyes.

I nodded and she scoffed. "They're the real deal," I confirmed.

She shook her head. "I didn't believe you."

I smiled. "No one ever does until they see it for themselves."

I tuned back in to the room around me as everyone else was raising their glass. Harlow and I jumped to do the same, clinking our glasses together.

"To love!" everyone shouted at once. Harlow's eyes widened like she'd just been cursed, and I laughed.

"Don't worry, Low." A tiny crease formed between her eyebrows at my use of her nickname. "I don't think a cheers is the same as a contract in blood."

Harlow was quiet as they served dinner, listening to the rest of the people at our table chitchat. I watched carefully as she picked through everything on her plate, one item at a time in an effort to pass more time innocuously.

Her timing couldn't have been worse, though, as she placed the last morsel between her plump lips. The soft, welcoming beat of Sara Bareilles "I Choose You" filled the room, and couples trickled in to fill the dance floor. At the same time, Linda and my dad made it to our table to say hello.

"Scotty," Linda said as I stood up out of my chair and pulled her into a soft hug.

"You look gorgeous as always, Linda."

My dad scoffed and pulled her from my arms and into his own. "Tanner!" she squealed adorably.

"He's trying to steal you," my dad teased, and Linda blushed.

I shrugged. "I know a good woman when I see one."

"Must be from all the practice," Harlow said—unsuccessfully— under her breath.

Linda's eyes widened, but both my mom and dad laughed outright.

Harlow flushed with embarrassment. "I'm so sorry, Mr. Shepard—"

"No, no, dear," my dad comforted, pulling her to her feet and giving her a once-over from top to toe. "All you've done is prove my son right."

She blushed an even deeper hue of red as my father gave her a nudge into my arms.

"Come on, son. Join us out there for a dance with your good one," Tanner Shepard said with a wink.

Harlow was visibly uncomfortable, and I clung to it. Normally, an insinuation of a serious relationship on my father's part would have made my teeth ache in discomfort, but somehow, knowing Harlow wasn't clinging to hope at every syllable made me feel completely at ease.

"Yeah, doll," I said, pulling Harlow's front flush to my own. She glared. "Let's dance."

Skimming slowly down her arms from top to bottom, I linked my hands with hers and pulled them up to settle on my shoulders. A deep crevice of a wrinkle formed between her eyebrows, like a canyon carved by an angry river, but with so many bystanders nearby, she didn't fight me physically or verbally.

Once her hands were settled, I moved mine back down the sides of her dress, smiling as an unconcealed tremor ran through her at the sensation of my touch, and clamped them tightly to her hips.

Just about boiling over, she opened her mouth to speak, but I was too quick, spinning her rapidly around and around as we traveled to the center of the floor.

Her fingers dug in on instinct, hoping to keep herself steady, and I smiled as I slowed us to a stop and changed direction into a gentle sway, pulling our bodies even closer together. She pushed against my shoulders to fight it, but as the song faded to a close and Etta James "At Last" built in its place, her body melted.

It wasn't me—at least, the dislike on her face didn't suggest it was—but the song. Something about it made you give in. I could feel it in my body too, instinctively pushing closer to hers on its own accord.

Soft, warm, and willing, Harlow's body was everything her mind refused to be around me.

She leaned in even closer as I spun us, softly this time. Light flickered as it filtered through the other couples on the floor, and my hands tightened on her hips like a reflex.

She feels good. Christ, maybe too good.

We moved in perfect time with one another, and her eyes held mine like she could read all of my secrets—my past and present, my hopes and dreams…even things I didn't know about myself.

So lost in it all as the song came to a close, I jolted as she separated our bodies, almost violently, as the last note struck. As if it was Cinderella's clock on the last chime of midnight, she left the dance floor at a near jog.

Not once looking back, Harlow was careful to leave nothing behind for me to hold on to—not even a shoe.

CHAPTER *thirteen*

Harlow

GOD, HE FEELS SO GOOD, I THOUGHT TO MYSELF AS I NESTLED EVEN DEEPER into Scott's arms while we danced. It'd been a long time since I'd actually let my defenses down and enjoyed the simple touch of a man.

Sure, I'd willingly gone on a date with Barron, and even let him engage in the world's most traumatic oral foreplay, but I'd done that under the pretense of wanting no-strings-attached sex.

But, *this*, dancing with Scott, actually savoring his skin against my skin, wasn't the same type of scenario. This was different. This felt like…something more.

His grip tightened as his fingers rubbed soft circles against my skin through the thin material of my dress. I shivered. And, surprisingly, found myself fighting the urge to moan out loud.

I wanted to stay wrapped up in this moment forever.

And as I looked across the dance floor to find Tanner and Linda wrapped up in one another's arms as they slowly swayed to the music, I found myself wondering what it would be like to be in a loving and committed relationship like theirs. Not the kind of relationship I'd had with my ex, but one where there was a solid foundation of trust, mutual respect, and admiration. The kind of relationship that stood the test of time, both people willingly and happily sacrificing silly personal wants for another.

I think I want an amazing relationship like that…

Oh my God, had I really just thought that?

I'd made a promise to myself a long time ago that I'd never get into another long-term relationship. I'd attempted that once in my life, and I'd found out that I was better off on my own, doing my own thing, and only relying on myself. My last—*and final*—long-term relationship taught me one thing: Never trust anyone too much. For myself, for my happiness, I had to stay strong in that mind-set… *right?*

Christ, until now, I'd been absolutely certain singledom was what I wanted.

Until now.

God, what was happening to me?

My chest grew tight with the initial sensations of panic. This moment on this dance floor was now officially emotional overload, and I wasn't equipped enough to understand all of these foreign things I was feeling.

I have to get the fuck out of here.

I didn't know what was happening to me, but I knew I didn't like the direction of my brain's thoughts. I needed to get somewhere safe—preferably, not inside of Scott's arms—and find a moment of peace from this fucked-up emotional roller coaster I'd managed to hop on.

As the last notes of the too romantic song filtered into the room, the urge to push up onto my toes, meld my breasts to Scott's chest, and touch my lips to the perfect pink of his became consuming.

Instantly, I released my hold on his shoulders and put some much-needed distance between us. Before I could second-guess myself, and without any warning or words to explain my sudden mood change, I turned away from Scott and moved off the dance floor as quickly as my stilettos would let me.

I had no idea where I was headed or what excuses I'd give my father, but every cell in my body was telling me to just get the fuck out of that party as soon as physically possible.

I grabbed my purse and jacket from our table and walked over toward my dad—who was currently charming the pants off of Nicole—to say my goodbyes. I made a mental note that since it was Saturday night, a simple excuse of meeting friends for drinks wasn't too risky an explanation for my sudden departure.

Bill's smile was warm as I approached, but the ends of his mouth turned down slightly once he noted the purse and jacket in my hands.

"Are you leaving?"

"Yeah. I'm supposed to meet some friends for drinks," I lied and hugged him tight. "Be careful getting home, Daddy," I said and kissed his cheek.

Luckily, Nicole squeezed his shoulder, pulling his gaze from mine to hers and completely distracting him from questioning me further.

"You too, sweetheart," he said with an easy smile.

I smiled at Nicole. "Thank you so much for tonight. I had an amazing time."

"Thanks for coming." She pulled me into a quick embrace. "And call me if you ever need some juicy gossip about my son," she whispered teasingly into my ear. I could literally hear the smile in her voice.

Man, I loved a mother who doubled as a ballbuster.

I laughed. "An inside source?"

She nodded and winked. "I'm hoping one day he'll learn that he shouldn't waste his time with women who are only after one thing."

I quirked a brow in confusion.

Sex? Surely, they're after sex.

"Money," she answered helpfully.

Oh. Money.

104 · max monroe

"Ah," I responded with an understanding nod. "The illustrious gold diggers."

"Exactly," she said with a grin. "My son deserves better than gold diggers."

I wanted to say that *gold diggers or not, your son appeared pretty fucking happy surrounded by all of the beautiful women he tends to keep in his company*, but I bit my tongue and breathed past the stinging pain in my chest. Holy fuck, what was that? There was no way I was jealous of Scott's revolving door of dates…*right?*

Good Lord, this party had morphed into some kind of alternate universe where relationships sounded like a good idea and I actually *liked* Scott Shepard. Had Linda and Tanner put drugs in the punch or something? Cripes. I needed to leave before I started thinking about marriage or kids or something else that was equally terrifying.

"He'll learn one day," Nicole added. "I'm just hoping it's sooner rather than later that he finds a nice, pretty girl like you and settles down."

My eyes popped wide open in shock. *Nice, pretty girl like me? Settling down?* Did she think I was good enough?

Oh Jesus, Harlow! Not the fucking point.

Yeah, I need to leave. Now. Before I have to resort to self-inflicted violence.

"I'm sure Scott will find his perfect girl, Mrs. Shepard," I reassured while mentally adding, *but it definitely isn't me.*

"Well, I better head out." I quickly changed the subject toward my exit. Because, yeah, this anniversary party was a mindfuck, and I was better off anywhere but here. "Have a good night, you two. I'll call you tomorrow, Daddy," I said, and I didn't give them time to say anything else as I shuffled through the partygoers and headed for the door.

The instant the cool air of the New York City night hit my face, I breathed a sigh of relief. I glanced down at my phone to check the time. Ten p.m. glowed into the darkness, and I decided even though I didn't necessarily have a plan, I'd rather walk the city than take the subway or a call a cab.

Hopefully, the walk will do me good. Lord knows, my brain needs some time to think about all the bullshit she's been putting me through tonight.

But the reprieve lasted not even ten minutes before my phone chimed in my purse with a text message from Scott. I hated that there was a part of me that felt excited about it.

Sexy AF Doc: Where are you headed off to?

Okay, yeah. I might have nicknamed him in my phone during a moment of weakness while thinking about how perfect his ass is.

I quickly typed out a response while thinking, *God, he is a nosy bastard.*

Me: None of your business.

Not even a minute later, he sent another message.

Sexy AF Doc: You should take a right at the next block. There's a perfect bar called The Library.

Seriously? Who named a bar The Library? It sounded like a sad place where men or women went to cheat on their spouses…*Whoa. Whoa. Whoa. Hold up. Did he say take a right at the next block?*

How did he know where I was?

I stopped in my tracks and stared down at my phone for a brief second, before slowly turning around to find Scott standing a mere fifty feet behind me, grinning like a cocky son of a bitch. I responded to his message while shooting mental spears at him across the short expanse.

Me: Are you stalking me?

He smirked. I watched as he looked down at his phone and typed out another response.

Sexy AF Doc: *Just following you a little to make sure you're okay. You left pretty abruptly back there.*

He was right. I'd left the party like a total lunatic. No explanation, nothing. Just up and walked away from him on the dance floor. But I kind of felt like he was being a bit of a lunatic, too, by following me.

He's a lunatic. I'm a lunatic. Maybe we are the perfect match?
Clearly, my brain needed to shut up.

Me: *Just following? And that's somehow better than stalking?*

Sexy AF Doc: *It's less creepy.*

Me: *It feels CREEPIER. Like I should get a restraining order kind of creepy.*

Sexy AF Doc: *No restraining order needed. Just come have a drink with me, Harlow.*

Have a drink with Scott Shepard?
This is probably a bad idea, Harlow, I thought to myself.
But that lasted all of two seconds before my fingers typed out another response.

Me: *Are you buying?*

He took a few steps forward until we were nearly standing side by side, and his eyes only briefly left mine as he typed out a quick response.

Sexy AF Doc: Yes.

Me: Fine. But I'm choosing.

Sexy AF Doc: Perfect.

I read his message and glanced up to meet his rich gaze—right there. *He looks even better up close.* Seriously, if his eyes were candy, they'd be that delicious, specially made chocolate you could only get from exotic locations like Paris or Brussels.

"Sexy as fuck Doc?" he questioned with a smirk.

I rolled my eyes. "Tame your ego, cocky. I never save contacts in my phone as their actual names," I explained on a lie. He was literally the only person I'd ever nicknamed in my phone.

"Yeah," he added, and his smirk got bigger. "But you didn't nickname me Ugly Doc, now did you?"

"I'm about to change it to Creepy Doc."

"You think I'm sexy," he declared. "Harlow Paige thinks I'm sexy *as fuck.*"

"How do women stand you?"

He winked. "Most women find me charming."

"I guess I'm in the minority, then."

Liar, liar, pants on fire, Harlow...

He chuckled. "You're so full of shit."

"And you're full of yourself."

"Nah," he refuted. "I'm just aware of the effect I have on women."

"Are you going to buy me a drink, or are we just going to stand around and talk about how amazing you think you are?"

Scott's chocolate eyes sparkled with intrigue. "Goddamn, you're a feisty little thing, aren't you?"

"I'm just me." I shrugged. I honestly didn't know any other way to be. I knew I could come across as opinionated—or bitchy—to some people, but it was just my nature to say how I felt and not beat around the bush with niceties. Hell, I often envied the people who could sugarcoat things to prevent hurting someone's feelings.

"I think I like you, Harlow," he said with a smirk.

Obviously, no matter how badly I wished I could deny it, Scott Shepard was starting to grow on me too. I liked his cocky smiles and witty banter. And don't even get me started on his muscular body or goddamn eyes. Jesus Christ, I could spend hours swimming through those chocolate orbs.

But instead of letting him know the real effect he had on me, I quickly redirected the subject. "Well, if you want to stay in my good graces, you should recall that you offered to buy me a drink…"

He grinned. "You're in luck. Remembering things is yet another talent of mine."

CHAPTER *fourteen*

DIDN'T KNOW HOW I'D GOTTEN HERE, HOLDING THE DOOR OPEN TO A BAR I almost never told anyone about for fear that its secret special something would get out—and instantly turn popular—while Harlow scooted inside ahead of me. It was like my body was acting on its own, without permission from my brain.

But as I'd watched her say quick goodbyes to everyone but me and scoot out of the party after leaving me aroused and emotionally twisted on the dance floor, I hadn't been able to stop myself from following her.

And I still was.

We made our way through the crowd in The Library, an ironical-ly named establishment with loud, pounding bass and a heavy beat. With Harlow leading the way, we ended up at the bar, where she ordered two shots of tequila.

The bartender set them both on the bartop, and I pulled money out of my pocket to pay as she slammed the first one back and then picked up the second.

"Uh…" I laughed and leaned in to speak closely enough that she'd be able to hear. "Isn't one of those for me?"

"No," she said, just before she tipped the second glass back and swallowed the liquid whole with ease. My eyes dilated as they zoomed in on her throat and lost all real focus. The glass knocked as she slammed it back to the bar surface, and my eyes jumped back to hers. "Order your own."

"I thought you didn't drink much hard liquor," I said, watching her eyes turn almost immediately hazy with the fresh buzz.

She smiled, looser already, and plopped onto the stool to her left. "I don't. Trust me, with those two shots, the edge is officially gone."

"Well, then," I said with a laugh, taking the seat to her right and signaling the bartender for two more. "I guess I better catch up."

We didn't say anything else as the bartender prepared my shots, placed them on the counter, and took my payment.

Something was going on inside of Harlow's head, but I wasn't the guy to try to figure it out. I didn't spend my time musing over complicated women and wondering about the things that made them that way. I was out to entertain and be entertained, and at the end of the day, if both of us got physical gratification out of it, all the better.

I'll admit I had to fight the urge to wonder—and ask—with Harlow, though. An urge that had never before existed.

I tamped it down and swallowed both shots one after the other as she looked on. The heavy, seductive beat of the music pulsed inside my chest, but a part of me still thought this wasn't a good idea.

Immediately, I ordered two more. I had a higher tolerance than she did, and if the way she was smiling at me was any indication of things to come, far be it for me to let her have a good time all on her own.

Rinse and repeat, the same routine with the bartender, the same routine with the shots, and a high buzzed in my veins.

"There," she shouted over the music before reaching out and grabbing me by the tie almost violently. "Now we can dance."

I followed her lead once more, the hold she had on my tie not giving me much choice as she dragged me out onto the dance floor and plastered her body to my own.

I still had one working brain cell that was trying to reject her flipped switch—a fast transformation from objection to demand in the area of physical contact—but the combination of alcohol and her breasts against my chest did a pretty good job of turning it off.

"Get ready, Scott," she taunted. "You may have some fancy foot-work at fancy parties, but I'm gonna teach you how to really dance."

Selena Gomez's "Good for You" filtered through the speakers as she pushed back away from my body and swayed, running her hands across her own chest and down to her hips, until they were inside the slit on her dress and against the perfect skin of her tanned thighs.

I swallowed thickly and swayed, enthralled as she turned her back to me and let her head drop back.

My lingering groan slid perfectly into the rhythm of the song. *Why is she so fucking sexy?*

Reaching out, I grabbed onto her hips and pulled her ass against me. She went with it, settling her head onto my shoulder and moan-ing at the obvious sign of my excitement.

Good Christ.

The salty, sweet taste of her skin as her throat hit the tip of my tongue was the last thing I remembered from the inside of that bar.

Stumbling, bumbling, fucking fumbling, I pulled at the zipper on the back of her dress as she unbuckled my belt and the button on my pants and shoved them down off of my hips.

The door of my apartment shutting behind us rang out like a gunshot, but neither one of us slowed down. Her throat was highly addictive, like sugar on a tart strawberry, and I couldn't stop going back for more.

"God, Low," I hummed against her skin, *still* fighting with her fucking zipper. She pulled back out of my arms, and the swollen, well-used state of her lips made my dick jump.

"Don't ruin this by talking, Scott," she teased, a sexy as hell smile on her face as she reached around her back to free herself from the demon-zipper dress on her own.

Thank fucking goodness.

She got it pretty easily, pulling it down and dropping the dress from her shoulders to bare her breasts before forcing it gently over the curve of her hips and stepping out of it.

Sweet Lucifer, her nipples were peaked and perfect, the rosy, brownish hue unlike any color I'd ever seen before—and I'd seen a lot of nipples. Christ, it was like I'd been color-blind my whole life, and Harlow had bought me the special glasses.

I hopped on one foot and chucked one shoe and then the other before shucking my own pants and ripping my already torn open shirt—compliments of Harlow—off and letting it fall to the ground.

She looked on hungrily, a little grin curving just the corner of her abused mouth, as she stood there in nothing more than a sheer black thong.

I attacked.

Forward in a flurry of motion, I grabbed her by the hips and lifted her until the length of her legs wrapped my waist tightly, and I carried her until her back bumped into the wall at the mouth of the one hallway in my apartment.

She grabbed and yanked at my hair, and the nerves stood on end. One breast and then the other, I feasted on everything they had to offer, nipping and sucking until mottled red rose to the surface of each.

More, more, more, give me all of it, Low.

Her hips rolled against mine, and my cock poked out of the top of my boxers in search of her sweet heat.

She weighed next to nothing, but holding her against the wall wasn't conducive to my best work.

I pulled her up, burying my face in between her perfect-handful-sized breasts one more time and licking.

Every inch of her skin tastes like perfect summer fruit.

Christ, I think I'm already addicted.

She let her head drop back, a soft, audible thud breaking the pants of our labored breathing as it made contact with the wall.

I put a hand to the drywall and pushed off before moving my lips to her sweet throat again and sucking there, stopping just shy of marking her skin, as I walked us back to my bedroom and dropped her in the middle of my king-size bed.

"Scott," she rasped, and my dick started to ache.

I lost the only clothing I had left, my boxers and socks, and followed her down, reaching up and to the side until my fingers met the knob on the top drawer of my nightstand.

It was on the tip of my tongue to ask her if she was sure if she wanted to do this, but I choked on the words as I sent them back down. If she didn't want to, she'd say it. And I'd respect it.

But until then, this was the best almost-sex I'd had in years—maybe ever—and I'd be damned if I was going to let being too polite ruin the moment.

Back to the task at hand, I opened the drawer and grabbed a condom before shifting to my knees between her legs and rolling it down my length.

She licked her lips and sat up, moving her hand on top of mine to assist, and just like that, any lingering doubt fled the building.

Urgency clawed at the line of my spine and robbed me of some of my finesse as I fell forward on top of her, our heavy, panting breaths the only thing filling the room, reached between us to pull the gusset of her panties to the side, and thrust myself in to the hilt.

Fire built in my back as she scored it with her fingernails and closed her eyes in ecstasy, the roll of her groan nearly guttural.

I could relate. I was feeling pretty fucking splendid myself.

One thrust led to two as I lost myself inside of her tight heat and moved my hands over every inch of her body. She moaned as I grasped at her hips, the thin material of her thong driving me crazy as I set a rhythm. Like a quick squeeze of a hand, her pussy clamped down on me and sucked at me until I'd lost any semblance of control.

I roared, I heard it ring in my own ears it was so loud, as I ripped the material on both sides of her hips clean through.

Bliss, pure and carnal, took hold of every last cell of my body as we climaxed together in a way I'd never ever fucking forget.

I might have been blind to the look on her face as she came thanks to my own pleasure, but I swore I could feel it bleeding in through the inky blackness behind my eyelids.

We'd hardly spoken, but the roughness of her cry and the sting of her teeth as they marked my shoulder as *hers* said all of the words— *maybe all of the words in existence*—for us.

CHAPTER *fifteen*

Harlow

SLOWLY AND RELUCTANTLY, I REMOVED MY ARM FROM MY FACE. I BLINKED, closed my eyes, and blinked again. Streaks of sunlight penetrated the unfamiliar window and damn near blinded me with its hot, white rays. A bit disoriented, I sat up and curiously scanned the bedroom that wasn't mine. The room was sleek yet personalized—king-sized bed, white sheets, white comforter, and a few pieces of perfectly selected art hanging on the walls.

Where in the hell am I?

Scooting to the edge of the bed, I dragged my feet off the mattress and rubbed my knuckles into my eyes. I stretched my arms above my head and yawned as I watched my legs dangle above the light hard-wood floors. The instant I stood up, my eyes caught my reflection in the floor-to-ceiling mirror beside the white armoire. *Cripes. I'm naked...*

Where in the hell were my clothes?

Across the bedroom toward the door, I scanned the space until I caught sight of my dress haphazardly strewn across the floor like it'd been dragged into the room by a stampede. Hazy—yet somehow very real—memories of last night filtered into my brain.

The party. Drinks with Scott. Dancing with Scott. *Sex* with Scott. Oh. My. God.

Last night, I'd had a crazy, slightly drunken, toe-curling, several orgasms, amazing-sex night. With Scott Shepard.

My eyes met my reflection in the mirror again, and I couldn't stop myself from laughing at the absurdity of the situation. I mean, I'd just had sex with someone I'd written *Gossip* columns about. I'd never done that. Hell, I'd made a point never to do that.

Blame it on the alcohol?

More like my vagina and the fact that you're really starting to like Scott…

I ignored the latter and focused on the first part. My horny vagina. Yeah, she was definitely to blame in this scenario. But, in her defense, Scott was walking, talking sex. After the Barron debacle, all she'd wanted was to feel good.

The longer I stood there staring at the wanton, slightly disheveled woman in the mirror, the easier it became to pick out the details. I wasn't just naked—I was *worked over.* Beard rash covered ninety-five percent of my skin, and two very large and obvious reddish-purple marks dappled my breasts. Each breast to be exact. *Hickeys? Seriously?*

It was like I was fifteen all over again and experiencing my first real hookup in the back of Jimmy Velvet's old pickup truck. Jesus Christ.

"Good morning," the perpetrator himself greeted me. I glanced up slowly, as if working my way through a murky pond, to find him standing in the doorway and fully dressed in a white, buttoned-up collared shirt and gray slacks.

His deep, baritone voice, his eyes, *him,* all of it brought a flood of memories back into my brain. The way we'd danced together at the party. How good it'd felt to be in his arms. The terrifying things it'd made me feel and think. The way I'd internally freaked the fuck out and left him on the dance floor. Yeah, it was safe to say, last night had been a bit of an emotional conundrum for me.

But it'd also been amazing, too.

Fucking hell, I'd be a liar if I didn't admit that I was secretly thankful Scott had followed me after I'd abruptly left the party.

What was happening to me?

You like him.

I mentally shook that thought off. Naked and in his bedroom, with a very handsome Scott standing behind me, was not the time for that kind of internal monologue.

I wasn't particularly modest or embarrassed by my body in its natural state, but standing completely naked, comfortably chatting with the man you didn't expect to hook up with last night was a challenge for even the most confident of women.

"Sleep well?" he asked with a soft smile, and I turned away from the mirror to face him.

I didn't miss the sparkle of enjoyment in his eye as he perused my naked and visibly hickey-fied body. And unfortunately for any chance I had at a display of self-righteousness, what I felt in response wasn't even close to embarrassment.

Man, I hated how good the renewed ache in my abdomen felt.

Quickly, before my vagina could take charge again, I redirected my focus.

"Did you seriously give me hickeys?" I questioned and pointed to both breasts.

His smile turned amused. "I thought those were called love bites?"

"Does it really matter what they're called?" I spat back. "I mean, what thirtysomething-year-old man gives a woman hickeys?"

He chuckled softly and shrugged. "I guess I got a little carried away."

"A little?" I pointed to the marks again. "There are two of these suckers."

"Personally, I quite like them there. And you seemed to like it when I was giving them."

"Is this how it works with the famous Dr. Erotic? You take women home, have insanely amazing sex with them, but before the night is through, you leave your mark?" I put a defiant hand to my bare hip, and he grinned.

"Insanely amazing sex?"

Oh, shit. Jesus, Harlow.

"You know what I mean."

He raised a cocky brow. "I'm not sure I do. I'd love to know which parts, specifically, were *insanely amazing*."

I rolled my eyes and ignored any and all land mines I was sure to step on if I delved into *that* conversation. "You gave me hickeys, Scott! I'm not going to stand around stroking your ego!"

"Oh, don't worry," he said with a smirk. "You stroked me enough last night to last a lifetime."

I groaned in annoyance. He was like an overgrown kid. "Are you always this annoying in the morning?"

"Probably." He shrugged. "No one has ever been around to let me know before."

I'm sorry...what? He didn't notice how momentous that statement was in my head, obviously. Because if he had, he wouldn't have kept fucking talking. "Does it help if I tell you I made breakfast?"

I schooled my face into neutrality as my mind whirled over the fact that Scott never kept women around until the morning, and yet, here I was. *In the morning.*

Just focus on the breakfast, Harlow. You like food. Focus on the food. I could think about the rest of it later—or never.

"That depends."

"On what?"

"What's for breakfast?"

"Scrambled eggs."

Eggs? Bo-ring. I yawned. "Meh."

"With bacon," he added, and I shrugged in indifference.

He smirked. "*And* pancakes."

Wait...pancakes?

I fought the urge to drool, and my eyes perked up of their own accord. "Just plain pancakes?" I questioned skeptically.

He shook his head with a smirk. "Blueberry."

Oh, hell fucking yes. Plain pancakes were one thing, but blueberry pancakes were a whole other level of *I can't resist them.*

"Coffee?" I questioned, and he nodded.

"Freshly brewed and ready."

"Fine," I agreed and strode toward the doorway with my shoulders and chin held high. "You've convinced me," I said generously as I came to a stop in front of him. "But I'm only agreeing to the breakfast for the pancakes and coffee. Not for the conversation."

He grinned and, without warning, wrapped his arms around my waist and pulled me toward his body. My feet stuttered to comply, but he didn't even give me time to refuse before his soft, full lips were pressed against mine. A soft lick later, I opened to him, and his mouth claimed me in a mind-altering kiss that knocked me straight off my game.

His hands followed suit, sliding up my bare back with a soft, seductive, *knowing* touch, and instantly, I shivered.

When his fingers slid into my hair, his tongue still dancing with mine, a moan left my throat before I could stop it. *God, this man can kiss.* My motherfucking toes curled into the plush carpet of his bedroom.

It's no wonder I let him give me hickeys and fuck me stupid last night.

His mouth moved from my lips to my jaw to my neck, a slow, perfect path to get his warm breath to my ear. Goose bumps skated across my skin. "I thought last night was insanely amazing, too, Low. *You* were insanely amazing," he whispered. "And just so you know, I've never given a woman hickeys before in my life. You're a first."

He pressed one last soft kiss to my still-wanting lips and then leaned back with a smirk. And before I could stop him, he snuck a quick spank to my bare ass and strode down the hall and toward the kitchen.

"Hey!" I shouted toward him, and he just chuckled.

"C'mon, feisty!" he called over his shoulder. "Let's eat some pancakes!"

Normally, I'd do the opposite when someone was trying to boss me around. Normally, I'd be stubborn and tell him to shove his breakfast food up his ass.

But pancakes.

Blueberry pancakes.

Yes, I was just doing it for the blueberry pancakes. For distraction.

Too bad him making me breakfast, as it turns out, is an even bigger deal for him than letting me stay until morning.

My asshole mind really knew how to bury the lead.

CHAPTER *sixteen*

I FINISHED CHANGING INTO MY SCRUBS AND TOSSING MY SHIT INTO MY LOCKER before pulling my iPad out and connecting to the internet.

Like it was old hat, I went straight to Harlow's column on the *Gossip* site with a click of my favorite bookmarks menu. I knew she'd published a new one today since that was the excuse she'd used when leaving my apartment right after pancakes yesterday morning.

It was all still a little weird to me, the fact that I'd cooked the pancakes in the first place, followed by her being the one to decide to leave. Normally, I was all for the escape act—actually, I was usually the one executing it—but the sex was never that good.

I wanted another round. Or twenty.

Still, I reminded myself. *There's time for that.*

I was so used to cramming all of the sex I wanted into one day to avoid a commitment. But Harlow seemed even less eager to settle down than I was, so in this case, I could probably keep the fling going longer.

I waited with a smile on my face while the page finished loading, only to have it melt off nearly instantly.

Ryan Reynolds Sets More than Blake on Fire

Well, shit. I'd have thought this one would be about me for sure. I had her fucking claw marks on my back as evidence that *I* set her on fire.

Did I not do a good enough job? Were her hickeys already fading? I hope not.

I didn't really understand what had drawn me to mark her so thoroughly, but whatever it was, the urge wasn't waning. If anything, the thought of them fading into oblivion made my collar feel tight and my chest feel heavy.

All of my unsubstantiated, unexpected frustration was cut short with a ping of my phone.

I pulled it out of my pocket, figuring it was a page from the floor, waiting for me to stop reading gossip articles and come to fucking work. But it wasn't.

It was a text message from Pamela Lockhead—a woman I'd had sex with, sure, but not the one I'd been thinking about.

God, you really are a manwhore, my mind taunted as I tucked my iPad back inside my locker and focused on my phone.

Pamela: I got a meeting with the mayor for you.

My eyebrows shot nearly to my hairline with both surprise and excitement.

Me: Holy hell! Seriously? I think I might be in love with you.

I winced when I hit send before thinking through my words carefully. *Jesus Christ, Scott. I might be in love with you? That's the worst fucking thing you could say to this woman.* She hadn't seemed clingy when I'd taken her home that night, but immediately after being intimate, she'd flipped the switch. I was still angry with myself for taking everything that far. On some deep, internal level, I'd known Pamela Lockhead wouldn't be happy with fucking once and moving on.

Pamela: It's in two weeks. I just emailed you all the details.

This time, I made sure my response didn't make me want to punch myself in the nuts quite so much.

Me: Thank you.

Pamela: We should get together between now and then. Have some fun.

See, Scott? Do you fucking see what you've done? She had clinginess written all over her. The more I would fuck her or consider fucking her, the more complicated my life was going to be. It was better to cut and run after the one time.

Not to mention, the thought of fucking Pam after fucking Harlow felt ruthlessly lackluster. And, surprisingly, made me feel oddly nauseous at the very thought.

Me: Sorry. I'm slammed with work the next two weeks.

Fucking hell, that was an awful cop-out. But I couldn't exactly tell her to fuck off given the fact that she'd just secured a meeting I'd spent months unsuccessfully attempting to land on my own.

Pamela: Maybe after then. ;)

Ah Christ.

Me: Yeah, we'll see.

Don't judge me. My mother may call me a heartbreaker, but I hate breaking fucking hearts. My real game is staying far enough away that I don't have to.

I tucked my phone back into my pocket before I could give it any more thought and slammed my locker closed. No doubt I was a good five minutes late for my shift now. But that was one perk of being the boss. I'd just tell Deb I was busy doing important shit, and she'd have no choice but to believe me.

Knowing they were working shorthanded without me, I shoved open the door and broke into a jog on my way to the floor.

Will Cummings was running the other direction with a sweating, panting pregnant woman on a gurney next to him.

He smiled and nodded in my direction. "I see you got a live one," I called after him, but he was too busy listening to the woman as she screamed in his ear. He really was one of the best doctors I'd ever seen, his bedside manner completely unparalleled. Not actually obscene in any way.

I, on the other hand, actually deserved my nickname. Hell, I probably deserved his. But the old saying was right: Nice guys finish last.

"Dr. Shepard!" Deb yelled just as I rounded the corner.

She had barely contained panic—the kind that only came with years of training—in her eyes.

"What's up, Deb?"

"You're just going to have to see it," she told me and turned in the other direction to break into a jog.

I followed her obediently, grabbing a pair of gloves from an empty bay on the way there. If this was anything like she was making it sound, time and protection were going to be of the essence.

She pulled the curtain back as the woman behind it cried out in hysterical agony, and it didn't take me long to figure out why.

"Jesus fucking Christ," I muttered just before jumping straight into action.

Visibly pregnant with a—

"Is that a curtain rod?" I asked, fucking horrified as I got a closer look at the pole sticking straight up and out of her protruding belly.

"Yes," Deb said, efficiently briefing me. "She's thirty-six weeks pregnant and was walking on 53rd when that struck her from above. Probably someone working in an apartment with the window open. The police are looking into it, but overall, it just seems like horrible timing."

"My baby!" the woman screamed, panting to catch her breath through the panic. "Somebody please tell me my baby is okay."

"What's your name?" I asked as calmly as possible, stepping forward to take her trembling hand in mine.

"Luc-y," she answered, a little sob hitching at the very end of the word.

I turned quickly to Deb. "Page Dr. Cummings. I just saw him headed to the OR with another patient, but I want him on this."

"You got it," she responded quickly while Sherry worked to get an IV going in Lucy.

I turned back to her and looked her in the eye. "Hi, Lucy. I'm Dr. Shepard—"

"Like on *Grey's Anatomy*?" she asked, horrified and curious at once. It was amazing what adrenaline could make you focus on.

"Sort of. But I promise there's less death around here."

She tried to smile, but the effort was completely in vain. I didn't blame her. Given the seriousness of her situation and the lingering Harlow-Pam clusterfuck, I didn't feel much like joking either.

"What's your baby's name? Have you picked out a name yet?"

She nodded, her face cracking as she started to fall apart.

My heart jumped into my throat for what *she* must be feeling, not what I was. Thanks to years of training and medical experience, I felt calm. "No, no, Lucy. You stay focused on me, okay? What's the baby's name?"

"Jacob."

"Jacob. That's a fucking great name. Strong. Sure," I coached her.

She nodded. "I might have chosen Scott, myself. But Jacob is really, really good." Sherry managed to work and roll her eyes at once. I was a great leader, giving my staff the skills to multitask like that.

Swift and efficient, I assessed the point of entry and put up a silent prayer that the rod's relatively small size, the low amount of bleeding at the site, and the fact that it was lodged slightly to the right of her abdomen versus the center, would be the reasons both the patient and her baby survived.

Quickly, I placed the fetal monitor on the heartbeat of Jacob, and all of us took a deep breath when his heartbeat filled the air, strong and sure, just as I'd said.

"See, Lucy. He's strong. Everything is going to be okay."

Still, I knew I couldn't do anything about removing the rod until Will was there to monitor and assess the baby.

"Vitals?" I asked Sherry, and she immediately rattled off the patient's heart rate, blood pressure, and oxygen saturation.

Her oxygen level was stable, which told me the rod hadn't impacted her diaphragm, or worse, her lungs, but her blood pressure showed a steady drop over the past five minutes. I needed to get her to the OR before mom's decrease in vitals started to affect the baby. Not to mention, the patient most likely had serious internal trauma that needed to be fixed stat.

I looked at the clock and noted another sixty seconds had passed.

We need to go. Now.

Deciding he was taking too long, I made a decision on the fly and rolled with it. Honestly, that was the brunt of what I did on a daily basis. If you can't make quick decisions, you don't belong at the head of an ED.

"Okay, we're moving. Tell Will to meet us in OR Three."

"Okay, Dr. Shepard," Deb called as I pulled the sides up on Lucy's bed and made use of the wheels.

"Let's go, Sherry. Scrub in."

She nodded, and we were off at a run.

Five hours of surgery and a safe delivery by C-section later, mom and baby had both managed to survive the trauma. Jacob was with his father—who managed to show up moments after we'd entered the OR—safe and secure in the nursery of the maternity ward. And Lucy was stable, but being monitored closely in the Intensive Care Unit.

I had no doubts she'd survive, but the amount of internal injuries I'd had to fix once I got inside made it certain that her road to recovery would be a little bumpy.

But Lucy was strong, and her baby was strong, and the amount of loved ones who'd congregated in the waiting room during surgery proved she had all of the love and support she'd need to get through it. I was confident, a few months down the road, Lucy and Jacob would be happily living their lives, and this unfortunate traumatic experience would only be a memory.

Needless to say, the five hours we'd spent inside that OR had been worth every second.

Will had done a hell of a job, and not to blow my own horn, but I wasn't so bad either.

But as I watched Will celebrate this success story with his girlfriend, Melody—after trusting her enough to call her up to assist from the clinic—I felt a twinge of loneliness I wasn't used to.

Unwilling to think too much about it, I texted Harlow.

Me: Have dinner with me.

Harlow: No.

A smile took over my face immediately. God, yes. This was what I'd needed—to spar. These days, life without challenge seemed boring.

Me: Have lunch with me.

Harlow: No.

My smile deepened even further as I sank into the wall behind me and moved my thumbs over the keyboard on my screen.

Me: Have sex with me.

Harlow: NO.

Me: You know, I read something somewhere about protesting too much. It's a defense mechanism to protect you from what you really want. With the way you shouted no like that, I'd say you really want to have sex with me again.

Harlow: Yet another guy who doesn't realize that no actually just means no.

And just like that, my smile was gone. I shoved away from the wall and swallowed the thick saliva in my throat. I respected women more than anything. I might not always show it perfectly, and I might push the boundaries sometimes, but *that* was a hard fucking boundary I never crossed.

Me: Wow. That's… I'm sorry.

Harlow: Fucking hell. That wasn't fair of me. You know that no means no. I know you know.

Everything suddenly felt too serious again, and a deep, clogging pressure filled my chest. I had to do something to break through it.

Me: So that's a yes to the sex?

Harlow: Haha. God, you are an ASSHOLE.

Seeing her laughter in those four little letters almost as well as I'd hear it if she were right in front of me, I finally felt lighter.

Me: Okay. I'll ask again tomorrow. ;)

CHAPTER *seventeen*

Harlow

"YOU BONED HIM!" AMANDA SHRIEKED INTO MY EAR. "YOU BONED DR. Erotic! This is almost too much to comprehend right now!"

"Would you stop yelling? I'm at work right now," I whisper-yelled into the phone as I hopped to my feet and quickly shut the door to my office. Well, my *shared* office with another *Gossip* columnist. Since, I did most of my work from home—w*ell, usually my favorite coffee shop up the street from my apartment*—I wasn't in the offices more than one or two days a week.

Thankfully, my office mate Fiona, was enjoying a nice reprieve in the Bahamas.

But it was more than clear I'd made a huge mistake on dishing the dirty details to Amanda while I was at *Gossip's* offices. The last thing I needed was for my coworkers to hear I'd been rendezvousing with Scott Shepard. It was one thing to work with nosy people, but it was a whole other ball of wax when being nosy paid their fucking bills.

Unfortunately, it was either now or a six a.m. phone call East

Coast time, thanks to the six-hour time difference my stupid jet-setting friend had created. And Lord knows, I was not a fan of waking up before the sun rose.

"Like, in your office at work?" she asked. "Or just sitting around in your underwear inside of your apartment at work?"

"In my office, smartass."

"Are you wearing pants?"

"Obviously," I muttered. "My boss would stab me in the vagina with her stiletto if I was just strolling around the offices flashing my beave to everyone."

"So you're a crotchless panties kind of gal?" my best friend questioned with a smile in her voice. "Go figure. I never would've guessed."

"Oh, yeah," I retorted. "I just love wearing underwear that literally serve no purpose. It's my favorite."

She laughed. "I still don't understand the point in them. Like, either just be naked or wear underwear. Why do the halfway thing?"

"For some reason, a lot of guys dig it."

"Mateo would just want me bare."

Wait…what? Did she just say Mateo?

"I mean…" she stuttered. "I'm pretty sure Mateo is the kind of guy who doesn't—"

"Who doesn't what, Amanda?" I questioned. "He's the kind of guy who doesn't like fucking you when you're wearing crotchless panties? Because you're totally boning your client and you said you'd never do it, but you totally are having sex with that Spanish piece of meat! Oh my God! You little floozy! Why didn't you tell me?"

"Fuck," she muttered. "I just… It just kind of happened…"

I grinned. I'd fucking called this one since before she'd left to run Spanish Adonis's PR tour. "Is this the point in the conversation where I say I told you so?"

"Like you should talk," she snarked. "Two words. Scott motherfucking Shepard."

"Pretty sure that's three words."

"Whatever," she retorted. "And I'd say it looks like we're both having an *I told you so moment*, huh?"

She had a point. "Touché."

"But in all seriousness, this whole thing with…yeah…with *him*…it needs to stay on the down low, okay? Like, no one else can know it happened or else I could lose my job with the firm."

"I'm not going to say a word. Promise." I might've been a gossip columnist, but I had boundaries, and my best friend's life was definitely a hard limit for me.

She sighed. "Sometimes it's a little unnerving that my best friend writes a goddamn gossip column."

I laughed. "You mean, it's unnerving when you're actually in the middle of something completely hot that is totally gossip-worthy, but that I would never in a million years write about?"

"Exactly," she responded, amused. "Okay, I gotta go now, but you bet your sweet ass we are revisiting the whole *you having sex with Dr. Erotic* conversation later. I need to know details. Lots and lots of dirty details."

"Ditto. I've heard Spanish guys are really good with their rhythm, and I really need you to confirm that it isn't a case of stereotyping. And I sure *as fuck* would love to know if you're ever going to come back home or if you intend to run away with your new boyfriend."

It felt like it had been a year since I'd last seen my best friend. Sure, it'd only been about a month, and the PR tour that was supposed to be a month had only been extended to two, but still. I was half tempted to catch a flight to Europe just to make sure she was okay and not living against her will in a random cult inside of a remote village.

She scoffed. "He's not my boyfriend, Low. And I'm not sure of the exact date I'll be back. The PR tour is prolonged because Mateo is getting such an amazing response everywhere he goes."

"Okay. Fine. Your Spanish *lover*," I corrected. "And by amazing response do you specifically mean the response he receives from your vagina?"

She snorted. "Shut up."

"Give your Spanish lover a tongue kiss for me. Loveyoubye!" And before she could toss out a sarcastic retort, I ended the call and got back to work.

And by work, I meant research.

And by research, I meant browsing the internet for funny GIFs and taking BuzzFeed quizzes.

In my defense, though, sometimes it's these very GIFs that inspire the next column.
Generally, it's the GIFs where hot male celebrities are shirtless, but still.
Inspiration is inspiration, right?
And in my opinion, nothing says inspiration like Ryan Reynolds and Chris Pratt shirtless…

"Harlow," my boss's voice pulled my attention from my laptop. In all of her power-suit glory, with the door now opened, she stood inside of the doorway of my office space.

I cleared my throat. "Yes, Stella?" I asked as I quickly clicked out of the BuzzFeed quiz I was taking and sat up straight in my chair.

She strode across the hardwood floor, her stilettos click-clacking with each step until she reached my desk. Stella McCarthy—my boss and the editor in chief of *Gossip*—was a real-life doppelgänger of Miranda Priestly from *The Devil Wears Prada*. When she said jump, everyone in the office asked how high. And when she actually took the time to stop by your office, you'd better make damn sure you weren't fucking around.

I took a quick glance at my laptop screen to make sure only my Word doc was visible. The last thing I needed was for Stella to see me taking a *Guess My Age Based on My Olive Garden Selection* quiz.

"I need you to cover an extra piece this week."

Goddammit, Cruella de Vil. I've already taken on two extra pieces this week!

"Okay." I forced a smile. "What's the piece?"

"That popstar, Smiley Walrus."

Not only was Stella a pain in the ass to work for, the woman never got celebrity names right. Like, ever. It was honestly a fucking conundrum considering she was the editor in chief for a gossip rag.

"Do you mean Miley Cyrus?" I asked, and she raised a pointed brow in my direction.

Another thing about Stella, the woman refused to admit any mistakes or faults. She was literally the world's worst human being to work for.

"That's what I said, isn't it?" she questioned in irritation.

Um. No. I'm pretty sure you said Smiley Walrus…

"Yep," I lied.

"I want a piece about her budding relationship with that Holmsmore brother," she instructed, and I had the urge to say, *Hemsworth brother*, but I bit my tongue. The last thing I needed was Stella's wrath on a Tuesday morning.

Generally, if you got on her bad side for the week, she'd take pleasure in giving you a month's worth of work with a deadline of twenty-four hours. And the sickest part of all was that most of the time, she didn't even use the extra assignments.

"Okay." I forced a neutral expression even though the urge to glare was strong as a motherfucker. "No problem."

"Finish it by tomorrow so it can go on the site by Friday."

Ugh.

"I'll start working on it now," I said, and she strode back out of my office without another word. When the sound of her stilettos click-clacking down the hall disappeared completely, I sagged into my desk chair on a deep and heavy sigh.

It was times like these that I wondered how I'd gotten so off track in my life. When I'd started my freshman term of college at NYU, I began the year with the intention of going pre-med. And by the time I'd reached my junior year, I'd been ahead and finished all of my prerequisites. Hell, I'd even been accepted for a summer internship with one of the country's top specialized surgeons.

But then, I'd met Brent. And my life had taken an abrupt turn and headed in the exact opposite direction of where I'd intended.

I'd lost a lot during that relationship. I'd lost myself. I'd lost my priorities. I'd lost some of my closest friends. I'd lost everything that was important to me. And it would always be the one example—*the most important reminder*—of why another long-term relationship was not something I'd ever try again.

Unless I happened to have already met the right person.

Good God, not this thought process again…

No. No relationships. Not with Scott or any other man for that matter. I'd promised myself that, and I was sticking to that fucking promise. I loved myself too much to let myself get lost again like I had with my ex.

Before the painful memories of my relationship with Brent—or the ridiculous and scarily recurrent thoughts I'd been having about Scott—could find their way inside my head, I moved my focus to my laptop. I was on a deadline, for fuck's sake. I didn't have time for bullshit. I had to find my goddamn center and finish this feel-good column about current celebrity relationships that overcame all of the odds—for a couple years, at least—along with the added piece about Smiley Walrus and her Holmsmore fiancé.

Sigh. Just find your writing mojo, Harlow…

Twenty minutes later and my brain was void of depressing thoughts and solely focused on my work tasks. Writing gossip columns wasn't exactly my dream job, but it paid the bills, and often, I did enjoy making *Gossip* readers laugh with witty one-liners and quirky anecdotes.

"Knock. Knock." The unexpected voice stopped my fingers' progress across the keys and pulled my gaze away from my laptop screen. A young guy, probably college age, stood in the doorway holding a brown paper sack in his hands. "I have a delivery for you."

"A delivery? For me?" I questioned in surprise. I wasn't expecting any deliveries.

"You're Harlow Paige, right?"

"Yeah." I nodded. "That's me."

"Yep," he said and walked into the office. "This delivery is definitely for you, then."

"Do you know who it's from?"

"Uh…" He set the brown paper sack on my desk and scanned the Blackberry in his hand. "It's from a Dr. Hickey?"

"Dr. Hickey?" I asked, horrified. Of course, I knew the sender's real identity.

Scott Shepard. *Only a self-righteous, sarcastic bastard like him would go to the trouble of calling himself something horrendous like Dr. Hickey.*

I bit my lip to fight my smile, but it was a lost cause. My cheeks stung from their abrupt, puffed-out, happy state.

Jesus. Why am I smiling like a lunatic?

It was a mindfuck, to be honest. Scott Shepard should have annoyed me, not made me goddamn giddy and grinning like I was one antidepressant away from stripping off my clothes and dancing naked in a field of daisies.

"Just sign here," the delivery guy said and held out his iPad and stylus pen.

I followed his instructions and quickly scribbled my electronic signature across the device.

"Have a nice day," he said with a wave and left my office.

As I unrolled the top of the brown paper bag, goodness assaulted me. *Mmm.* Sweet and sugary, there was no mistaking the scent of maple syrup. *Food.* Tasty, high-calorie food was inside this bag.

I pulled the white takeout box out of the bag and popped it open to find a large serving of the most irresistible looking pancakes I'd ever seen in my life. Nutella, bananas, whipped cream—Jesus Christ, it was heaven in a box.

I was all set to dive in face first, when I spotted the small envelope attached to the back of the bag. My name was written neatly across the front, and inside sat a little note.

I know you can't resist these. Or me.
Enjoy.
Dr. Hickey

I shook my head.

That cocky bastard.

Why I was smiling was still a mystery, but I decided to blame it on the pancakes. I mean, no human being in their right mind could frown when looking down at this pile of sugary goodness. Before I ate myself into a carb coma, I pulled my cell phone out of my purse and called the pancake culprit.

"Harlow," he greeted on the second ring, a smile apparent in his voice.

"Dr. Hickey?" I asked, and he chuckled shamelessly.

"Did you taste them?"

"Hell no." I feigned annoyance. "I never eat food sent over by people I don't know. I trashed them."

"You're so full of shit," he refuted. "I bet you've got a greedy fork within an inch of digging into them right now."

I totally did.

Wow. I don't even remember pulling that fork out of the plastic.

But he didn't need to fucking know that.

"Nope," I lied. "I had the delivery guy reroute them to the dumpster behind the building."

"You know what's crazy?"

"What?"

"I just got off the phone with Tim, *the delivery guy*, and he said you accepted the delivery."

Fucking Tim.

Wait…how did he know the delivery guy's name?

I raised a skeptical brow. Something was fishy about this scenario, and it wasn't the fucking pancakes. "How in the hell do you know the delivery guy?"

"He's actually one of the techs in the ER," he explained. "I gave him some extra cash to act like a delivery guy."

"What the hell?" I all but shouted. "He even had a fucking iPad and made me sign for the goddamn pancakes."

Tim was a total con man and almost as big of an asshole as Scott.

Too bad you don't really think Scott's an asshole…

Ugh. *Stop with the friendly thoughts!*

Scott chuckled softly in response, but he didn't say anything further about Tim the Trickster. "Take a bite, Harlow," he demanded, and every cell in my body agreed that it was the best idea they'd ever heard.

But despite the drool at the corner of my lips, I stayed strong. "No," I spat. "Not doing it."

"Just take a bite," he whispered. "You know you want to."

"Nope."

"Do it, Harlow."

But God, they look so good… I couldn't stop my tongue from licking across my lips in anticipation.

"Will you leave me alone, then?"

"Sure."

"Fine," I agreed and dug in with my "at-the-ready" plastic cutlery. My taste buds danced with the delicious flavors of freshly made pancakes covered in the world's best ingredients.

Holy Moses, they were amazing. I moaned before I could stop myself.

"That good?" Scott's amused voice filled my ear.

"Shut up," I retorted over a mouthful of pancakes and Nutella.

"God," he purred into my ear. "I fucking love that moan of yours."

"I'm not having phone sex with you."

A barking laugh left his lips. "Have real sex with me, then."

"Nope," I refuted, even though, for some insane reason, I secretly wanted to shout, *Hell yes, fuck me stupid, and then feed me these pancakes again in the morning!*

"Go on a date with me," he demanded—something he'd been doing more and more since the day after penetration.

"Nope."

"Come on, Harlow," he cajoled.

"I don't date."

"Just one date," he persisted.

"Not happening."

"Dr. Shepard!" A panicked voice filled the background. "We need you in exam room eight!"

My brow furrowed. "Uh… That sounds important… I better let you go…"

"Nope," he refuted. "You have to agree to a date with me first."

"Dr. Shepard!" the voice called again, even more anxious this time.

"Holy hell, Scott!" I shouted into the phone. "Now is not the time to talk about dates! Go to exam room eight!"

"Dr. Shepard!"

"A man's life is on the line here, Harlow," Scott added. "You should probably just agree to the date so I can go save his life."

"This is so fucking dirty!"

"Uh-oh…" Scott whispered, and my eyes went wide.

"What?"

"Nothing…" He paused and then a shocked gasp left his lips. "Oh God, that doesn't look good…"

Holy hell.

"Jesus Christ! I'll go on a date with you!" I yelled into the phone. "Just go help that man!"

"Fantastic," he responded immediately. "Tomorrow night at seven."

"Fine," I said through gritted teeth.

"Where do you want to eat?"

"Oh. My. God!" I shouted in exasperation. "I'm hanging up. Go save that guy's life."

"Am I done?" a voice whispered in the background, and Scott responded back to whoever it was with ease. "Yep. Thanks, Cal."

And miraculously, the earlier panic and chaos completely

disappeared from the background.

"Wait a minute…" My jaw dropped in shock. "What's going on, Scott?"

The line stayed quiet.

"*Scott.*"

"Yeah, Harlow?"

"You owe me, dude." The voice was in the background again, and just like before, Scott responded to him, "Eighteen holes next week-end? I'll buy?"

"Hell yeah," the voice agreed.

That motherfucker.

I pulled the phone away from my ear and sent a FaceTime video request Scott's way.

Within seconds, his handsome face filled my screen.

"Miss me that much?" he asked with a sexy smirk.

"Where's the emergency?" I questioned while my eyes scruti-nized his current location. There was no hustle and bustle, no noth-ing. Just a fridge and a microwave sitting behind him.

The jerk had been sitting in a goddamn break room the whole time.

"Oh. My. God. Did you have someone pretend to be dying just so I would agree to a date with you?" I questioned, and he nodded without shame.

"See you tomorrow night, Harlow," he said, and I flipped him the bird before hanging up the phone.

Too bad, after I'd hung up the phone, my entire fucking face was smiling.

CHAPTER *eighteen*

"OH NO," SHE GROANED AS I OPENED THE DOOR TO THE SLIPPER ROOM, a little place I'd been a couple of times on the Lower East Side, and ushered Harlow inside.

It'd only taken eighteen offers and blackmail in the form of a fake dying man, but she'd finally agreed to a date with me. She wasn't exactly calling it a date, but I was, and obviously, as she was a gossip columnist, I was more in touch with reality. Right?

It said something about her, though, that she hadn't backed out of the date after she knew I'd coerced her into it under false pretenses.

What it said, I wasn't sure, but whatever it was seemed positive. But I guessed the evening was still young. I'd have to be on the lookout for poisoned offerings.

Somebody let me know if you see an apple in her purse.

The lights of the Slipper Room were a rosy red, and a completely mischievous glow enveloped the place as soon as you stepped inside.

The only thing in front of us was a lone, tall set of stairs leading to the unknown.

"This is a sex club, isn't it?" Harlow asked, apropos of nothing.

I coughed a startled bark of laughter and gave her hip an affectionate squeeze. "Not quite."

The truth was, as soon as I'd picked her up in a cab from the corner of 42nd and Fifth Avenue a little over forty minutes ago—she'd been adamant that I not know where she actually lived—I'd been wishing a sex club was what I'd planned for the evening. A night in at my place. An overnight at a hotel. Fucking anything that would lead to being able to remove the tiny black skirt she'd donned so I could see what lay underneath it.

Good Christ, the amount of skin her legs had out to play made her look two feet taller than she actually was.

Her nose wrinkled, and her eyes turned down at the corners. I had a feeling she was shooting for plain disbelief, but her features betrayed her. Disappointment lived under the surface. I had to laugh. "A letdown, huh?"

"No!" she snapped. My waning laughter renewed.

"Okay, Harlow. Whatever you say," I relented, guiding her toward the stairs, putting my hand to her back, and leaning in to whisper in her ear. "Don't worry. I'll punish your pussy later."

She tripped, a simple misstep due to clumsiness, I'd have thought—if it weren't for the timing.

I smirked to myself and moved my hands to her hips to steady her. "Would you like that, Low? Do you want to be punished?"

She shivered and tightened her hold on the railing. I'd been hoping to make her trip again, but the tremor would have to do. I'd lost the element of surprise, after all.

We walked in silence up the rest of the stairs until we reached the front desk and handed over the tickets I'd pre-purchased online.

"What is this place?" she asked again, albeit in different words.

"It's a variety club," I explained, pushing her deeper into the room so that she could see the stage. I felt a little bad, like I was always pushing her places, but honestly, half the time she moved like her feet were encased in cement.

It was frustrating. Of course, the hell of it was, it was also alluring, so different from the eager bounce of most women I spent my time with.

Complicated. That word had never sounded so good until Harlow.

"They opened nearly twenty years ago. Burlesque, drag, you name it, they were doing it. From the way I hear it, they used to open it up to pretty much anything and everything. The raunchier, the better."

Her eyes lit with interest. "Really?"

"Oh yeah. Some of the performances are still pretty borderline when it comes to societal appropriateness."

"That sounds like so much fun," she breathed excitedly.

I laughed. "It does, doesn't it? The couple of times I've been here, I've thoroughly enjoyed myself."

Her eyes narrowed ever so slightly. "A regular date spot?"

I shook my head with a smirk. "Never." The truth was, both times I'd come, I'd been by myself. It'd never even occurred to me to bring a woman here before.

I pulled her toward a table in the back, still close to the stage since it wasn't possible to be far away—the room itself was no more than fifty feet deep—and pulled out her chair for her.

She murmured her thanks and sat down quickly. I followed the line of her legs, hoping the hem of her skirt would fail to protect her. Unfortunately, it remained in place.

"I have to write a column about this place," she mused.

"Feel free," I offered magnanimously, even though I had no actual say in the matter. "But keep in mind that as soon as you're writing about it, it's bound to lose some of its mysterious allure."

"Hmmm..." She frowned thoughtfully. "Maybe I won't write about it."

I shrugged. "Watch the show and decide. You've got to be getting pretty tired of writing about Dr. Erotic." I rolled my eyes.

She laughed. "He has been pretty boring lately."

"Really?" I teased. "I heard he's sleeping with his inside source. Seems like a juicy story to me."

"Ah, see. That's…yeah. How do I put this?"

I looked on with wide eyes as she stuttered.

She took a deep breath and started again. "Let's just say that story is a little too real for *Gossip*." She lowered her voice to a mutter. "And me."

I smiled. "What was that last bit?"

The house lights started to dim, and a spotlight shone on the stage. She winced and pointed to the stage. "Sorry. Can't talk. The show's starting."

I shook my head but surrendered. That was fine with me. I didn't really want to talk anyway.

Grabbing the side of her chair, I pulled her toward me with a rough yank, and she gasped.

I winked, draping my arm around the back of her chair to twirl her hair and then bringing it back so I could rest my hand on her thigh.

"Just wanted to sit close."

"Why?"

I smiled. "It took a lot of work to get this date. You better believe I'm going to milk it."

She rolled her eyes and sat back, facing the stage again. When the lights went out completely and the first note of music rang out as a woman in pasties and a G-string took the stage, I leaned over and whispered the rest.

"Plus, I'll need to be close to finger your cunt. Tell me, Low. Are you wet for me already?"

She squirmed in her seat and crossed her legs, trapping my hand in between them. It took everything I had to follow through with the rest of my plan.

Just words, Scott. No touching.

Well, no touching until later when she was naked and sprawled out across my bed.

To encourage myself, I recited the reasoning behind my strategy.

Anticipation strengthens desire. Anticipation strengthens desire.

By the time we leave here tonight, Harlow's pretty little pussy will be dripping wet, and I won't have lifted a finger.

CHAPTER*nineteen*

Harlow

TWO STEPS INTO SCOTT'S APARTMENT AND MY CLOTHES WERE ALREADY FLYING. Between one breath and the next, my blouse, bra, skirt, and underwear were tossed haphazardly across the hardwood floor of his living room. I kicked off my stilettos a second later.

I knew he'd done this on purpose—getting me riled up to the point of insanity by teasing me with his hot and dirty words. Strategically, what started out as hot little comments whispered into my ear during the show, evolved into all out dirty—and quite promising—verbal foreplay that left me throbbing and wet in anticipation. I felt crazy. Horny kind of crazy. And if Scott didn't start fucking me soon, I'd probably have to resort to violence.

Good Lord, I want him.

Luckily, Scott had followed my "we don't need any fucking clothes" lead and stood gloriously naked before me. I took my time, appreciating the sight of him, and raked my eyes down his body—his big biceps, his flat stomach, the trim hips that led into a V—until I stopped at his cock. Thick. Hard. Ready.

I licked my lips. When it came to Scott naked, *especially his cock*, I was a fucking fan.

"You like what you see?" he asked, slowly, *erotically* stroking his hand up and down his length.

Every journey from the base to tip and back again enforced what I'd already been feeling tenfold. I wanted to taste him. Suck him. Kiss him. Feel him inside of me. I wanted everything, and I wanted it all right now. I clenched my thighs together, the sticky evidence of my arousal blatantly painting my skin.

"Yes," I whispered. "But I'd like it better if you were inside of me."

"Fuck, Harlow." Scott stared at me for a brief second before his big body moved into action, striding toward me. His hands gripped my ass, spanning the entirety of each cheek they were so large, and lifted me up. I obediently wrapped my legs around his waist.

"I wanted to take this slow, but I can't," he breathed into my ear, and then his tongue sneaked out and licked along the edge softly. "I need to be inside of your tight little cunt."

God, yes. I moaned.

Without hesitation and with me in his arms, Scott strode toward his bedroom. With every determined step, his cock slid against my already sensitized skin.

I felt delirious. Insane. Every cell craving, wanting, needing, fucking anticipating the moment he finally slid inside of me. Tunnel vision set in, and my body could only focus on the way his skin felt against mine, the way his breath sounded in my ear, the way it felt against my neck, the way his hands gripped my ass...*him*...us...all of it.

"Hurry," I whimpered into his ear, and his length jerked against me in response.

"Fuck," he groaned and pushed my back against the wall of his bedroom, directly beside the nightstand, his mouth capturing my lips in a hot and heady kiss. With his free hand, the one not gripping my ass, he haphazardly rummaged through the drawer until he snagged a condom.

He held it up to my lips, and I bit my teeth down on the foil while his fingers pulled it in the opposite direction. It tore easily, and with Scott's apparent practiced efficiency in this area, the condom was in place in no time. Both of his hands free to grip my ass again, he moved us toward the bed with three lengthy strides.

"Hold on tight, Harlow," he said roughly, and like a good, horny girl, I fucking listened.

My arms wrapped around his neck, and my legs clenched tighter around his waist as he crawled onto the mattress until my back was pressed against it.

And, without warning or hesitation, Scott drove inside of me, pressing himself to the hilt.

"*Yes,*" I moaned, my eyes rolling back of their own accord.

Good Lord, it felt good. *He* felt so fucking good.

The sexy setting of our outing, the foreplay, the anticipation, *all of it*, had built my need so high that one simple thrust had my pussy clenching around him. Stars were practically dancing behind my eyes from the intense pleasure.

"Fuck, you're wet," Scott groaned into my ear as he started into a deep and powerful rhythm. In and out, in and out, his cock worked the inside of my pussy with precision, building my climax up with each thrust. Most men would need a goddamn map to find the treasure Scott had located on the first stroke.

Covetous and greedy for one another after that, our lips and tongues continued to dance as our hands hungrily ran across each other's skin—scratching, feeling, rubbing.

Time blurred or stood still or fucking passed at lightning speed as the journey to my orgasm peaked. I honestly didn't know which, but I knew sex with Scott was unlike anything I'd ever experienced, and if ever there was an instance where time could be manipulated to do everything all at once, my climax with his cock inside me was it.

"God, you're so close," he whispered directly into my ear, his breath hot and erratic from the exertion, and a guttural moan left my lungs. "I can feel that tight pussy gripping me. Fuck, you feel so good, Low. So. Fucking. Good. I don't want it to end." He groaned as his thrusts became faster, uninhibited, fucking deeper, and even if I wanted to, I couldn't stop myself from falling over the edge.

The rhythm of my orgasm took me by surprise, starting out quick and intense, and then hovering in a slow afterburn that enveloped my entire being and suspended it. My vision blurred, and my heart beat like a kick drum inside my chest. I struggled to remember how to breathe.

I felt high from it. High from him.

Lost in the abyss of mind-altering pleasure, moans, whimpers, fucking noises I'd never heard leaving my lips, I barely heard Scott's grunt in response as my pussy rippled around him.

"Fuck. *Yes*," he moaned loud enough to shake me from my trance. His thrusts became faster and erratic as he rode out his climax inside of me.

And as we lay there on his bed, our bodies strewn across one another while we worked to catch our breaths and slowly come back to reality, my mind—finally freed from its pleasure chains—took off at a run.

I'd never in my life experienced an orgasm like that before.

This is, like, more than sex...

I internally sighed. *Not this thought process again...*

Before I could get lost in a mental sparring match with myself, Scott moved onto his back and removed the condom, quickly tossing it into a small trash can beside the bed. His big warm body was back beside mine a moment later.

"Go on another date with me tomorrow night," he whispered into my ear, and I couldn't stop myself from giggling.

"You're just saying that because, for some reason, our dates always end up with sex."

"That's definitely a positive." He grinned and wrapped his arms around my bare body and pulled me into his side. "But it's not the only reason."

"What are the other reasons, then?" I asked and moved my gaze up to meet his eyes. "I mean, you know that I don't date, and I definitely don't do long-term relationships."

"I'm curious," he stated and quirked a brow. "Is there a reason you don't do long-term relationships? Or have you always felt like that?"

I shrugged. "I had a long-term relationship a while back, and let's just say, it didn't end so well. I learned a lot from that relationship, specifically the fact that I'm just not a relationship kind of girl."

"Mind if I ask what happened?"

"I lost myself," I answered honestly, and for some insane reason, I found myself giving even more details. "It wasn't a healthy relationship. I gave, and my ex took, and before I knew it, my entire life path had changed because I was always putting him and his priorities first. I'm sure you'd be surprised to find out that I was actually pre-med in college. I had big dreams of being a pediatrician."

"You would be an amazing pediatrician."

I studied his resolute gaze. "You really think so?"

"I know so," he answered without hesitation. "You're extremely intelligent. You're easy to talk to when you're not trying to read me the riot act," he teased, and I laughed. "And I can imagine you're amazing with kids."

I sighed. "Well, too bad there's no going back on that one."

"No going back?" he questioned. "You're not even thirty yet, Low. If becoming a physician is something you're passionate about, you can still do it."

"Pretty sure that's a dream I need to let die," I muttered. "Anyway, now I'm curious," I announced because, hell, I needed to change the subject. We were talking about me way too much. "Why do you want to keep going on dates with me? I mean, you're not exactly a relationship kind of guy."

"Because I like spending time with you," he answered, and his words dripped of genuine honesty. "And deep down, I know you like spending time with me, too."

I scoffed and laughed at the same time. "God, you're so full of yourself."

He grinned again. "You know you like hanging out with me," he retorted, and even though he was right, there was no way in hell I was going to give in to his argument. "We have fun together."

"*Naked* fun," I corrected. "The parts where we're both dressed is usually just kind of *meh.*"

He chuckled and tickled my rib cage. I tried to squirm out of his hold, but he just held on tighter.

"Admit it," he said. "You like spending time with me."

"I like having sex with you."

"And spending time with me."

"I like when you cook me pancakes."

"And spending time with me."

I stayed silent, and he tickled my stomach this time.

"Jesus Christ, stop it!" I said once the tickles became too much.

"Say, *I like spending time with you, Scott,* and I'll stop."

"Never," I said through panting and giggling breaths. "Stop it!" I shouted and tried to wiggle myself out of his arms, but his biceps flexed tighter.

"Say it, Harlow."

"No!"

He didn't say anything after that. Instead, he flipped me onto my back with ease and straddled my hips with his naked body. He grinned down at me while his strong hands held my wrists gently to the bed.

"You know what I think it's time for?" he asked, and I rolled my eyes.

"For you to let me go?"

"Nope." He shook his head.

"Sexy times?"

He chuckled. "Not that either."

"Then what?" I asked and tested his hold on my wrists with a few impatient tugs.

His charming smirk urged a smile to my lips, and my reaction only made his smirk grow wider with amusement.

Sexy bastard.

"I think Dr. Hickey needs to make the rounds."

"No. No. No." My eyes went wide. "Dr. Hickey needs to leave my skin the fuck alone."

Scott shook his head. "He definitely needs to check a few spots. See how things are looking…"

I tried to buck his body off of mine with a few upward thrusts of my hips, but it was useless. Not only was Scott Shepard's body sculpted like a fucking Greek god, but those drool-worthy muscles served a purpose. The man was strong.

His lips moved down my jaw to my neck until they reached the spot between my breasts. His mouth sucked a little at the skin there, and I squirmed under his hold.

"Do not give me another fucking hickey," I demanded, and he grinned up at me.

"You know…" he started but paused to suck gently at the skin of my left breast. "I could maybe be convinced to stop if you…"

"If I what?"

"If you admitted something…"

"Not happening." I shook my head. "I know you think the sun rises and sets on your cocky ass, but that is not how it works."

"Okay." He shrugged. "If you insist…" he whispered, and his lips found the top of my right breast. His tongue sneaked out and tasted my skin before his mouth formed a gentle suction on the now sensitive skin.

My thighs clenched in response.

Jesus Christ, this is making me horny again…

He sucked harder, and I knew if I didn't put an end to it soon, I'd be gifted hickey number three in a matter of seconds.

"Fine!" I shouted, and he immediately pulled away. "I'll admit it! Just stop giving me fucking hickeys."

He leaned back and quirked a persistent brow in my direction.

"God, you drive me crazy," I muttered, and he smirked.

"Are you going to say it, or should I continue my mouth's perusal of your delicious skin?"

"Ugh." I groaned. "Fine. I like spending time with you."

He grinned down at me. "Aw, thanks, Low. I like spending time with you, too."

I rolled my eyes.

"You know what sounds good right now?"

"What?"

He rubbed his nose up my jaw and stopped at my ear to whisper, "Eating out."

Yes. Yes. Yes.

"Keep going…"

"Specifically, my mouth on you, sucking out all the juice you can handle. Does that sound like something you'd enjoy?"

Holy hell.

"I'm definitely…intrigued."

"I thought you might like the sound of it."

I nodded, and he moved down my body until his face was mere inches from the apex of my thighs.

"God, this cunt," he whispered, his warm breath brushing across my heated and aching skin. "I fucking love this cunt."

His gaze met mine as he slowly, gently, licked his tongue against me.

"You taste so fucking good, Harlow," he moaned into my skin, and his lips found my clit, sucking me into his mouth and flicking his tongue against the sensitive bud in rhythmic waves.

I moaned, everything inside of me vibrating with anticipation all over again, and my hips jackknifed toward his mouth on their own accord.

"First, you're going to come on my tongue," he demanded and tasted me again with his persistent tongue. "And then, you're going to come on my cock."

Yes. Please.

CHAPTER *twenty*

THE DAY HAD FINALLY COME: I WAS BECOMING A MAN.

No, I'm kidding.

It was the day of my meeting with the mayor—the one I'd weaseled my way into by sleeping with a woman. Though it hadn't been my original intent, I'd taken it all the way. Flirting had led to kissing and kissing had led to undressing and her grabbing me by the dick had led to…well, you know. My Dr. Erotic reputation had gotten the best of me.

I'd like to say it was a low point for me, but to be honest, it wasn't even close. I'd done some very questionable things in my tenure, and having a little sex with a consenting adult wasn't all that high up on my list of offenses.

Of course, it didn't feel all that great right now, knowing I was going to have to deal with the consequences during this meeting—a meeting Pamela had made expressly clear in her email she'd be attending.

But, whatever. I'd try to do better from this point forward and shit. That was really all any of us could do. Right?

I pulled my phone from my pocket and walked a block away from St. Luke's. I'd just come off of an overnight shift, and I was a little tired, but it wasn't anything I hadn't done before.

I put my hand in the air to hail a cab and typed out a quick message to Harlow. It'd only been a month since I'd first met my new favorite woman, and yet, with the way I wanted to integrate her into every aspect of my life, it felt like I'd known her longer.

Me: I have a meeting in an hour at Jane in SoHo. It shouldn't take more than an hour.

Harlow: Uh… Good for you?

Me: Smartass. Meet me there in two hours, and we can walk around and shop afterward.

Harlow: Why does walk around and shop feel like code for something?

Me: Probably because you're smart, and you know that I'm not asking you to shop because I like to shop.

Harlow: You're asking me to shop because you like the sex.

Me: Yes.

I loved the sex, wanted the sex…would even go so far as to say I *needed* the sex with Harlow. I had a huge knot of tension taking over my body piece by piece, and the kind of orgasm I had with her was the only cure for it. Trust me, I knew. I'd tried jerking off multiple times in between our dalliances without satisfaction.

Harlow: Lucky for you, I like the shopping and the sex. I'll meet you there in two and A HALF hours. I'm not gonna be dropping in on some stupid medical meeting.

Some stupid medical meeting. I didn't bother correcting her.

Me: Fine. 2.5 hours. Jane. See you there.

Harlow: Order me some crepes to go.

I laughed as I sank into the seat of the cab. The driver looked back at me with distrust. Apparently, I'd laughed loudly.

"It's just the text message," I explained for some asinine reason. "It was funny."

The cab driver said nothing.

Okay, then.

Me: You just got me in trouble with the cab driver.

Harlow: Me? What'd I do?

Me: Apparently, infected my laugh with the spirit of the devil.

Harlow: Wow. And from all the way uptown. I'm talented.

Me: So your apartment is uptown?

Harlow: No. Shut up.

Me: I'm going to find out where you live eventually. Why don't you just invite me back there today?

Harlow: I'm not at home. I'm…out buying cheese.

Me: I'd wager you do your cheese buying close to your apartment.

Harlow: Go away.

I barked a shout of laughter, and the cabbie glared at me again. *Geez. Rough crowd.*

"I was just messaging with my..." I cleared my throat, expecting to choke on the word, but it came out altogether too easily. "Girlfriend."

I'd never used that word before. Not in my entire life. I'd expected it would feel more traumatizing. Instead, I found myself smiling.

And then, frowning.

Christ, is she my girlfriend?

Not really.

Would she want to be?

Probably not. She felt more like a hostage than anything. Arm-twisted, coerced, and blindfolded into my company.

Though, she did seem to like my company once she was in it.

Me: Do you actually like me?

Harlow: This is a weird question.

Me: I mean, am I annoying?

Harlow: Okay, now you're really asking two separate questions. Because, yeah. I guess I like you most of the time. But, yeah, you're definitely annoying.

Me: I don't know what to think about that.

Harlow: Well...then I guess that's fair, Scotty. Because most of the time, I don't know what to think about you.

Christ, that felt like a major admission. But maybe I'd read that wrong...

Harlow: Bleeding all over your text message here...

Okay. Maybe I didn't read it wrong.

Me: I don't know what to make of you either. I do know I keep coming back for more.

Harlow: Sigh...ditto.

I put my phone back in my pocket and leaned back into the sticky leather of the disgusting cab seat. And then I tried not to think about how disgusting the seat was. Luckily, with all the swirling thoughts in my mind about Harlow, it wasn't too hard to distract myself.

I felt out of my depth. I'd never felt this kind of draw to a woman before, and quite frankly, had never expected I would. But I'd definitely figured that if I were to eventually like someone with any real interest one day, they'd feel the same way back.

The uncertainty about how she felt about me was torture.

The cabbie blew his horn sharply, and my head flew up from its resting place to see that we'd stopped.

"We're here," he said, once again impatient. I was starting to wonder what I'd done to this guy. Taxi drivers in New York weren't exactly the friendliest best friends ever, but rarely, if ever, did I annoy them this much.

Maybe because you're turning into the same mindless guy who gets lost in thought about a woman constantly instead of keeping his fucking shit together.

I glanced two storefronts up to see that we were, indeed, there. Hopping out quickly, I tossed him the fare plus a little tip—smaller than usual because, yeah, thanks for nothing, asshole—and jogged through the drizzle to get inside.

Hopefully, the weather cleared up in a couple of hours like it was supposed to so that Harlow and I could enjoy our walk.

As soon as I made it inside the door, I hit bodies. The place was packed as always, but the food was worth it. Not to mention, they still actually took reservations, something I couldn't say for very many good places in the city.

Pushing gently through the crowd until I made it to the hostess station, I lowered my voice. "I'm meeting Pamela Lockhead, plus one more."

I almost rolled my eyes at all of this cloak-and-dagger stuff, but she'd given me specific instructions that they didn't use the mayor's name on reservations for obvious reasons.

I just couldn't believe I, Scott Shepard, had reason to be meeting with someone important enough to have a hidden identity.

"Of course," the hostess said, her eyes flashing with recognition for *me*—another thing I'd never get completely used to. "Right this way."

We stepped away from the podium and weaved our way through tight tables to the back of the space behind an almost partition that gave at least the illusion of privacy. But the truth was, the whole restaurant was no more than fifteen hundred square feet at most, and probably every fucking body in there would be able to hear every word we spoke—if they wanted to.

"Here we are," the hostess said as we made it to the table and both Pam and the mayor stood to shake my hand. I reached to take the mayor's first just to avoid awkward physical contact with Pamela for as long as possible, when the hostess put a soft hand to my arm and interrupted.

I turned my gaze directly to her as she spoke. "I'm so sorry to in- terrupt. I just wanted to say, Dr. Er...Dr. Shepard...that...I love you on the show." She blushed a little. "You're always so much fun, but I can really tell you're invested in the patients too."

I smiled. Sometimes I forgot the last episodes of the show were still airing. I'd stopped watching around the fifth one. I knew all I needed to about how they were trying to portray me, and I didn't have anyone to prove anything to.

Though, it'd be nice if the mayor took me seriously today.

Trying to speed things up, I did my best to be gracious but brief. "Thanks. I'm really glad you're enjoying it. Never hesitate to say hello if you see me out in the city."

She giggled. "Oh, you bet. I definitely will."

"Thanks, Alyssa," the mayor said, clearly knowing her by name and clearly dismissing her. My eyebrows pulled together, but I shook it off and took his still extended hand.

"Scott," he greeted. "Nice to finally meet you."

"You too, Mr. Mayor."

He laughed, a little haughty, but mostly warm. It was a completely odd combination. "Call me Brent."

"Okay."

Quickly, I turned to Pam and shook her hand. "Nice to see you, Pam."

She smiled and blushed, and I tried not to cringe. "Scott."

I wasn't usually one for regrets, but man, the taste of it was bitter in my mouth when it came to Pam.

"Well, let's sit down," Brent instructed. "Get started." He took his seat again.

"Pam was telling me some of the details of why you wanted this meeting, but I'd rather hear it from you. What can I do to help you, Scott?"

It was weird listening to him speak as though rehearsed. When I actually looked at him, something I'd never really done while he was on TV, I realized he had to be a couple of years younger than me, but he never looked it because of all of the authority he not only had, but wielded effortlessly.

I took my seat and dropped my napkin in my lap, trying to gather my thoughts and get started. "Well, as you probably know, I'm head of the Emergency Department at St. Luke's Hospital."

"I'm familiar," he interrupted. "Dr. Erotic, right?"

His tone didn't sound outright derogatory, but there was a hint of something there I didn't know if I liked. Though, his face was open and friendly, so I decided not to focus on it.

"Well, I've got ten years in on the floor there, and I've seen some of the craziest stuff you can imagine. Not only everyday stuff, but I've actually been on shift for almost every major casualty event since I started, and one thing has always been the same. The protocol for managing the care of victims in such an event *and* the structure with which patients are explicitly outlined for next-of-care is horrendously impractical. I understand the urgency in triaging and treating the victims of mass casualty events, but we don't have enough funding or enough staff to properly prioritize both patients from the event and those with outside injuries. And the current policy we're working from makes us choose." I tilted my head and admitted, "Actually, it chooses for us. No trauma—even a gunshot wound to the chest—according to what's written in your current health policy, is as high priority as any and all victims of a terrorist attack. I imagine the intent is in no way malicious and strongly built to assure the citizens of the city's commitment to public safety, but not only does it put patients at risk needlessly, it downplays any and all need for patient care that arises from a cause outside of said 'event.'"

"Oh, is that all?" he asked jokingly. I barely even cracked a smile because, quite frankly, no, that wasn't all.

"Not exactly. There's also a serious lack of training—"

"I'd think that would be on you, as the head of the department, wouldn't it?"

"Of course," I agreed, even though I didn't like what he was insinuating. "But it's also on you. Without funding and detailed written changes to the actual public health policy in place, I have very little opportunity and resources to do my job efficiently."

"Again, that sounds like something within the hospital."

"Well, then, with all due respect, you're not listening," I argued, and I watched as his jaw clenched. "St. Luke's, along with ninety percent of the other hospitals in the city, are municipally funded hospitals. I've spoken with the heads of department at nearly all of their emergency rooms, and they all have the same concerns I do."

"So what do you want from me?"

"To consult with me and other highly skilled and respected local physicians to restructure the public health policy, and to put your feather in the fight to actually get it passed and in place."

He nodded thoughtfully. I held his eyes until he looked away, wanting to have one up on him, and then glanced to Pam, who was taking furious notes at our side.

"You get all that, Pam?" he asked suddenly, and she nodded.

"Good. Then let's eat."

Let's eat? That was it?

"Relax, Scott," he appeased, apparently seeing my look of *what the fuck?* "I need time to digest everything you said. Plus, if you really want to be involved in building a new policy, you're going to have to be patient. None of this stuff happens overnight."

I nodded. I guessed that was fair enough.

Food arrived at our table, and my eyebrows shot together. I hadn't ordered.

The mayor laughed at my expression again. "Pam here ordered for you." He smirked. "She said you like waffles."

My eyes jerked to Pam and back again, put off by how pleased he was to have knowledge of our intimacy. I wasn't pleased at fucking all, and I wanted to know why he knew in the first place.

Pam, of course, said nothing. Come to think of it, she hadn't said anything the whole time. Just a lot of smiles and nods. She'd also implied knowledge of me that she didn't really have. We hadn't shared breakfast. We hadn't shared anything more than a dance, a fuck, and some text messages.

But all of that was way too complicated to drag into a meeting like this, so instead, I went with it. "Sure. I like waffles."

Brunch passed quickly enough, filled mostly by the sounds of us eating and polite small talk. Brent had asked a couple of seemingly probing personal questions, but I'd managed to avoid most of them.

I glanced to my watch as we stood up to leave and realized we'd run over by nearly half an hour. I guessed it was good Harlow waited two and *a half* hours.

The three of us moved as a group toward the door, but I picked up speed when I spotted Harlow lurking just inside the entrance. I didn't think, didn't hesitate, didn't consider anything; I just went.

Straight to her and into a hug.

The sweet smell of strawberry jam radiated from her damp head. *It's got to be her shampoo.*

The mayor cleared his throat behind us. I pulled back, keeping my arm around Harlow, and looking back to see his smile. There was something in it I didn't like.

Pam looked jealous. And I didn't like that either.

"Brent…" I paused, not knowing if Harlow knew he was the mayor or not—we hadn't discussed politics. "Uh, Mayor, this is Harlow Paige, my…" I struggled for the appropriate word to use, but finally settled on, "friend." It sounded all sorts of wrong.

Brent's eyes, however, danced at its use.

Mine narrowed before glancing to Harlow. She looked almost panicked, recognition stark in her voice. "Brent?"

"Nice to see you, Harlow," he said with way too much fucking familiarity. So much, it bordered on intimacy. Stepping right in front of me, he leaned down and touched his lips to her cheek, right at the corner of her mouth.

Fucking on her mouth, for shit's sake.

CHAPTER *twenty-one*

'D ONLY WAITED INSIDE OF THE RESTAURANT FOR SCOTT FOR A MINUTE OR TWO before he found me and enveloped me in a tight, warm hug. All had appeared normal until he'd released me and I realized that his lunch company stood behind him.

The instant my gaze met all too familiar eyes, my heart dropped into my stomach like a rock.

Brent is here?

And who in the hell is this woman standing beside Brent?

With stiff posture and narrowed eyes aimed directly at me, she was the hunter, and if I wasn't mistaken, I was her prey. I honestly had no idea why I was on the receiving end of her ire, but I didn't have the brain capacity to figure it out. The oil was hot and ready, and I had a whole bucket of other fish to fry. Scott had obviously had lunch with Brent—my ex, Brent. The fucking mayor, Brent.

Jesus Christ. *What is happening? What business does a goddamn reality show doctor have wining and dining the mayor of New York City?*

Shocked and nearly at a loss for words, his name shot off my tongue before I could stop it. *"Brent?"*

Always a fucking smarmy bastard, Brent flashed his notorious smile directly at me like we didn't have a ten-ton pile of shitty past between us. It was the smile that had fooled everyone into believing he was a man of character and morals. The smile that had led his political career toward success. That stupid politician's smile that had gotten him elected mayor of one of the greatest cities in the world.

"Nice to see you, Harlow," he said. His words oozed friendly cheer, but I knew his soul, and it was too fucking black for real pleasantries. Past lover or not, he was no friend of mine.

I watched as Brent leaned in and in, coming toward me like an out-of-control car. I used every mental voodoo trick I knew to pump the fucking brakes, but even that failed. Twisted wreckage and the hollow sound of a rolling rim were the only things I could hear as he pressed his lips to my skin at the intimate place where my lips met my cheek.

Hell, he might as well have just stuck his tongue down my throat.

I wondered immediately what he was trying to prove. Or screw up. Brent didn't know how to make an uncalculated move.

In case you haven't been paying attention, Brent was the ex. The one who made me realize long-term commitments were not for me.

He had a long-standing record of fucking up my life—our relationship was proof of that. He had started out as my college boyfriend, the man I'd once considered sweet and kind, the man I'd counted on, the man I'd *loved*, and he had turned into someone who wanted control over me, over every aspect of my life, over *everything*.

Somewhere along the line, when I was busy trying to make something of myself, secure a future worth something, he had changed from someone I'd admired to someone I despised. *Still* despise, actually.

The instant Brent's lips left my skin, nausea burrowed itself inside my stomach and shot up my esophagus like a fucking rocket. It took all of my mental strength to fight the urge to vomit onto everyone's shoes and across the floor of Jane.

Fuck, is it hot in here?

Discreetly, I fanned my heated cheeks and stepped away from Brent. I needed distance. And space. And possibly, a getaway car.

With Scott's eyes watching me the entire time, and the unknown woman practically seething in her stilettos, there was enough awkwardness and tension in the room to choke everyone in the restaurant.

God, I could imagine the way Brent had shown affection toward me only proved that, at one awful point in my life, we'd known each other on a more than just friends level. It most likely appeared pretty fucking god-awful to an outsider, especially Scott.

"How have you been, Low?" Brent asked and reached out with one of his slimy hands to rub down my arm. Instantly, I flinched away from his touch.

"I'm fine," I said with a brittle smile and then met Scott's eyes for the second time since I'd stepped into Jane. He looked irritated, and I would've had to have been blind to miss the rigidity in his posture and the stress lines creasing the corners of his normally relaxed and jovial eyes.

"You don't want to ask me how I'm doing?" Brent asked, and my eyes met his again. Cocky, confident, and fucking manipulative. That was all I saw when I looked at this man.

"How are you, Mr. Mayor?" I questioned without one ounce of care in my voice. Because I didn't care. This man was the absolute last person on earth that I cared about. And I'd always considered hate a strong word, one I generally tried to avoid, but my feelings toward him felt a hell of a lot like hate.

He grinned. "I've been really good."

Of course, he likes me calling him Mr. Mayor. I'd done it mockingly.

As always, he was confidently at ease with himself and the situation despite my visible discomfort. *What a fucking narcissist.* "Although, I do think it's been too long, LoLo," he added, the sound of his nickname for me sparking a renewed roil of nausea. "We need to catch up soon."

"That's great," I answered and ignored his suggestion—*or was it a demand?*—that the two of us engage in a friendly powwow like we were just the best of buddies and our relationship hadn't ended disastrously.

God, he was still a prick. Which was exactly why I needed to get the fuck out of Jane and this awful situation as soon as possible.

"Well, it was great seeing you, Brent, but…" I paused and looked toward Scott. "We better roll out of here or else we'll be late," I lied, and Scott's brow furrowed in confusion. "For that thing with my dad," I added. I honestly had no real excuse for why we needed to leave, but I just knew we *needed to fucking leave.*

"Oh, how is your dad, LoLo?"

Fucking LoLo. I ground my teeth. If we didn't get out of here soon, I wasn't going to have any molars left.

"He's good," I said and wrapped my arm around Scott's bicep. "Sorry to rush out of here, but you know how my dad is about punctuality. He's not too tolerant with tardiness."

Brent quirked a questioning brow in my direction, but I just smiled back at him like I wasn't the world's worst liar at that moment. We both knew I was lying. My dad might have been a stickler for being on time, but I had never in my life made it a point to comply. I rolled on my own schedule, Bill Paige's wrath or not.

I gripped Scott's bicep tighter and turned our bodies toward an exit route. He glanced down at me in confusion, but I ignored it and said, "Bye Brent," over my shoulder with a half-assed wave.

A few minutes later, both of my hands were shoved into my pockets, and Scott and I were walking side by side in total silence, only the busy sounds of New York City foot traffic filling the otherwise dead air between us.

I glanced at him out of my periphery, and I noted the firm, hard line of his jaw and the rigid way he held his shoulders. Something was up with him, that was for fucking sure.

By the time Jane was no longer in sight, I couldn't take it anymore and stopped in the middle of the sidewalk. "What's going on?"

I questioned, realizing he was probably wondering the same thing about me.

The instant Scott realized I was no longer walking beside him, he stopped and turned toward me, and his brown eyes were still creased with the same stress and irritation they'd held inside the restaurant.

"Seriously, Scott," I shouted. "What in the fuck is going on?"

His long strides ate up the pavement as he closed the distance between us. "Why don't you tell me? You're the one who appeared very friendly with the fucking mayor back there."

"*What?*" My jaw dropped in surprise. "Are you kidding me right now?"

"No," he spat through gritted teeth. "How do you know the mayor? I mean, he appeared quite fucking friendly with you."

"Before I give you an explanation, I want to make damn sure you realize how you're coming across right now," I challenged. "You're acting like a jealous boyfriend, and it's way out of line."

He scoffed. "No, I'm not."

"Oh yes, you fucking are." I stared at him, my gaze unrelenting. "And seeing as we are not in a relationship, I definitely don't owe you an explanation about my past relationships."

"You dated that guy?" His brown eyes went wide with surprise. "You used to date the fucking mayor?"

A long, heavy sigh left my lungs, but before I could respond to his question, a lady with both arms full of shopping bags bumped into my hip as she passed me. I glanced around the crowded sidewalk and realized this was definitely not the time or place to have an all-out discussion about my past relationship with the goddamn mayor of the city.

Brent had friends in all kinds of places—high, low, even *dirty*—and the last thing I needed was for a scumbag like him to get the idea that I made a point of telling other people what happened during our relationship.

I stepped toward Scott and gripped his elbow with my hand and led him toward a small alleyway void of any possible eavesdroppers.

"Yes," I said in a low, defeated voice. "At one point in my life, I did date him," I explained. "But that was a long time ago. Like, before his political career had really started."

Scott nodded in understanding, and even though I'd just told him he had absolutely no right to be in the know about my past relationships, I found myself telling him anyway.

"He's not someone I like to have contact with," I added. "Our relationship was a really low point in my life."

"Is he *the* ex?" he questioned and I nodded.

"Yes. I don't like to think about it. I don't like to talk about it. Most days, I pretend it never even happened. I've told you more about it than most people, to be honest."

"Leave the past in the past kind of thing?" His gaze met mine, and he flashed a soft smile.

"Exactly like that."

Without hesitation, he wrapped his big arms around my shoulders and pulled me in for a tight hug. "I'm sorry I acted like a jealous boyfriend," he whispered into my ear. "It just took me by surprise is all. And I met the mayor today because I'm trying to get him onboard with making much needed changes to the city's current public health policy."

Well, I couldn't deny it sounded like a good reason to have lunch with the devil. Even quite noble when I really thought about it.

"That's okay," I whispered back. "But next time you try to get all territorial and piss circles around me, I'm kicking you right in the dick."

He barked out a laugh. "I'll remember that next time," he said and then added, "Although, I think you enjoy *the sex* too much to kick me in the dick."

I fought the urge to giggle. "Shut up."

He was totally right, though.

I liked his dick too much to actually go through with a threat like that.

CHAPTER *twenty-two*

"**A**RE YOU ALREADY OUT OF MONEY FOR THE CLINIC?" I TEASED WILL Cummings's sweet girlfriend Melody as I gave her a hello hug at the Benefit for Bab(i)es.

She'd been the brain trust behind this charity event with the goal of raising money for the Women's Clinic of St. Luke's Hospital—a clinic that had her name in the title as it were—which just so happened to be Melody's passion and purpose.

I thought the name of the event was cute, Babes and Babies combined, and tonight was the reason I'd been growing a beard for the last two months.

Apparently, at some point during the festivities, they were going to take me up in front of the room and shave it. There was some kind of system where people would bid money on something about it too, but I didn't have a fucking clue what. I guessed I'd find out while it was happening.

Melody and I had seen each other in the hospital a handful of times, but we were really only acquaintances. Still, I was very impressed with her drive to help the underserved women in New York, and I commended both her and Will for making the Melody Marco Women's Clinic of St. Luke's happen.

It hadn't been an easy feat, and they'd both worked tirelessly until her dream and passion had turned into reality. And because of that, they'd achieved something amazing for the community.

Of course, it didn't hurt that Will knew people with insane wells of money to tap into, but still, the thought was there. I could be impressed with the thought even if he didn't have to be quite as resourceful as someone without a billionaire brother-in-law.

She shook her head and rolled her eyes, as Will pulled her back to his front, wrapped his arms around her shoulders, and answered me. "It's a free clinic, Scott. The costs are constant. Benefits like this are standard practice to keep them running."

Will hadn't quite lost his antagonism toward me since I'd made a few jabs at him while he was suffering in the spotlight as Dr. Obscene. But, at this point, I'd done such a good job of pulling the attention from him, putting it on myself, and altogether basking in it, I thought he'd be thanking me by now.

"Easy, Cummings. I was just teasing."

"Yeah, Will. Lighten up," Melody encouraged, and I smiled— which, incidentally, didn't make Will like me more. Go figure.

"Ah, that's all right, Mel," I said, figuring it was better to bridge the gap of our differences rather than let them erode even more. "He's right to be a little aggravated with me. I've done a pretty good job of being an asshole these last few months."

"These last few months?" Will questioned disbelievingly. But a genuine smile replaced his grinding jaw.

"Okay," I admitted. "I'm always a little bit of an asshole. But particularly while *The Doctor Is In* has been on."

"Ah," Melanie breathed. "Yeah, the show's a little bit of a sore spot. For both of us, honestly."

I nodded in understanding, apologizing again. At the end of Will's run on the show, he'd been caught fucking a nurse named

Emily in the on-call room. Secretly, I'd been impressed by his ability to seal the deal with no more than a look and few quiet laughs—at least, as it appeared on camera—but I could see how it maybe hadn't earned him any points with his girlfriend. "Really, I'm sorry."

She smiled then. "It seems to be working out pretty well for you, though, huh?"

Will groaned. "Can you even fucking believe it? This guy gets into more trouble on his best day than I do on my worst, and he looks like a god on the show."

A few chuckles left my lips. "Wow, Will. Glad to hear you approve."

"Shut up, dude. You know you lucked out."

I nodded again, knowing I definitely had. But also knowing some of my moves had been calculated. "I also paid attention to the cameras," I said good-naturedly. But I really had. I'd been perfectly well-behaved for the first time in my life to make sure nothing horrible showed up on national television. My parents were completely open and supportive, but they didn't need me out there throwing that in their face. My flirty, sarcastic nature on the ER floor was enough.

"Yeah, that was good thinking—"

"Baby brother!" Georgia Brooks, Will's sister, shouted as she practically jumped on his back like a monkey.

Melody stumbled as Will fell back with Georgia's unexpected weight, so I reached out and caught her by the arms. She smiled gratefully while Will pulled off his kin accessory.

"I'm your older brother, Gigi," Will said with a laugh, steadying her on her feet. "How much have you already had to drink?"

"You're not my mother!" she snapped softly, just as her husband, a now harried-looking Kline, came skidding to a stop behind her.

"It's her first *adult* night out since Evie was born," Kline explained with a roll of his eyes. "She's, and I quote, *living it up.*"

"Where'd Winnie go, Big Dick?" she asked, and I choked on my saliva. *Big Dick?*

Kline chuckled and pulled Georgia close to whisper in her ear.

Unfortunately, I was just close enough to hear him anyway. "This is your final warning, baby. Call me Big Dick in public again, and we're going to go fuck in the bathroom."

Her eyes glazed over and her cheeks pinked, but she licked her lips like she was considering saying it again right then.

And, hell, I was with her. I didn't understand the threat at all. If Harlow were here, and circumstances were reversed, I'd have had her in the bathroom already.

Christ. Harlow.

This was the fifth time I'd thought of her since I'd arrived, wondering if I should have made a couple calls, tried to get her added to the guest list as my date last minute. I'd RSVPed before I even knew she existed.

I also didn't know if she'd have even considered coming with me anyway. After the run in with *Brent* earlier today, she'd made it pretty clear that we weren't anything more than people who fucked, and I'd gone along with it. Partly to keep the peace, I guessed, but also partly because it was what I always did.

Casual was my thing. I'd never wondered if I wanted more, if it was even a possibility for me. Women chased me, and I tried to let them down easy. This thing with Harlow felt like the exact fucking opposite, and I wasn't sure I liked it.

If I was honest, the more I thought about it, the surer I was that I didn't like it. Not one fucking bit.

Unwelcome, red rage surged in my chest at the memory of Brent's lips on hers and the so very obvious intimacy they'd once shared. They'd had a relationship—one I'd known about even before she admitted it during our argument on the sidewalk. I could tell by the way he looked at her like he knew everything about her, and even that was an unwelcome surprise. Harlow had implied she was a wandering soul like me.

At least if that were true, it made sense that we wouldn't have a traditional relationship where she would call me hers and I had the privilege of calling her mine.

"Scott? Earth to Scott. Helllllloooo."

I shook my head to clear it and rubbed my eyes. Holy hell, I was turning into someone I didn't even know.

Winnie Winslow, my old coworker and good friend, was waiting with a smile on her face when I finished. Her husband, Wes Lancaster, stood at her side with a casual arm around her waist.

That. That's what I want, I thought automatically.

The rest of the people I knew were gone. How long had I zoned out?

"You okay?"

"Yeah. Just…the last twenty-four hours have been pretty long. I worked night shift last night," I half lied. I mean, the facts were true, but I'd been awake for more than twenty-four hours more times in my life than I could even keep track of. That shit had nothing to do with my current wandering mind.

"No date tonight?" Winnie asked with a smirk.

"You know I never bring a date to this shit. Unless it's you."

Wes shook his head with a laugh, but he pulled Winnie even tighter into his side with his arm at her hip.

I put both hands up in defense and laughed. "Don't worry, Wes. Not at all interested."

Wes smiled, but Winnie leaned forward and hit me. "And what's wrong with me exactly?"

I laughed again. "I don't think I can win right now, so I'm just going to shut up."

Wes leaned back out of Winnie's sight line and mouthed one word to me. "Smart."

Will tapped on the microphone at the front of the ballroom, and Winnie dropped her voice to a whisper. "Shit. I think that means we're supposed to sit down. What table are you at?"

I pulled the little place card from my breast pocket and flipped it open to see.

"Eight."

"Same as us!" she cheered softly. "Come on."

Wes just shook his head as Winnie grabbed my hand and pulled me. I smiled. I actually missed my friend. It was good to see her.

"Hey, everybody!" Winnie called as we made it to the table and Wes held out her chair for her. "Does anyone not know Scott Shepard from St. Luke's?"

I scanned the faces of those I knew: Kline, Georgia, Wes, Winnie, Nick Raines—another doctor at St. Luke's and Winnie's ex, who looked more miserable than even me, by the way—and then stopped when I got to a couple I'd heard about but never actually met.

"We don't," the huge guy said, offering me his hand. "Thatcher Kelly. And this is my wife, Cassie."

"Hi," Cassie greeted, holding out her own hand and then keeping it.

Uhh…

"You're hot."

I glanced around the table, a little fucking panicked at this point. Her husband was really fucking big. But he just winked at me. "She's right. You're pretty fucking attractive."

I glanced to Winnie for help, but she shrugged.

Actually, as I looked around the table, everyone looked pretty unfazed.

When my eyes finally made their way back to Thatcher, he was smiling big and broad. "Yep. This is how we always are. Nice to meet you."

I laughed a little, thinking, as weird as they seemed, I liked them immediately. There was just something about them. And if I wasn't mistaken, Cassie Kelly was sans bra, and I didn't really mind that either. "Nice to meet you too."

"Uh, hi everyone," Melody's voice said over the speakers cautiously. I turned my attention to the front just in time to see Will give her an encouraging nod. I guessed public speaking wasn't exactly her thing.

"First, let me just tell you how thankful I am to all of you who you came tonight. You have no idea how many deserving women you're helping by being here and donating your time and money.

"But I know, and they know, and trust me, we'll never forget."

Georgia put her fingers to her lips and wolf-whistled through a giggle before an ever-patient Kline pulled her fingers from her mouth and kissed them.

"Obviously," Melody went on, "dinner will be served soon. But before that, we've had nearly forty of you who grew beards for the babies, and we're gonna kick this thing off with the shave-a-thon. In case you don't know how it works, our forty patient, kind volunteers will be up here in these chairs—" she pointed to the group in front of her "—while ten barbers get to work giving them professional shaves. We've got a silent auction set up in the back, and the bidding will be open for the entirety of the time it takes the ten of them to shave for-ty men."

That was actually awesome. Huh. Well, I was glad I'd gotten in-volved even without knowing what the fuck was going on. In all hon-esty, it was pretty nice not having to shave for a couple of months.

"So, please, without further ado, get a drink, check out the priz-es, and, fellas…" She scanned the crowd for bearded men such as my-self. "Make your way to the front and have a seat, please."

Every guy at my table stood up, and for the first time that night, I noticed that they were all bearded like myself.

I know what you're thinking. I'm just now noticing all the beards? But whether or not the guy we're talking to has facial hair is not really something most men tend to focus on.

It didn't take long to make my way to a chair and take a seat, and as a member of the front row, I was one of the first to get shaved.

My very last thought before the razor met my skin?

I sure hope Harlow likes me without a beard.

CHAPTER *twenty-three*

Harlow

"**H**OLY HELL... *AGAIN?* ARE YOU EVER COMING HOME?" I MUTTERED INTO THE receiver as I hopped onto the L train and headed toward my mother's apartment.

"Is it bad that I have no idea?" Amanda giggled. "All I know is that I want to spend more time with him."

It was official, folks. My best friend was in love with Mateo Cruz. Although the fact that she was now on her second extension of her European PR trip, it didn't exactly come as a surprise.

"You're totally hooked," I said, and honestly, I felt nothing but happiness for her. "You're in l-o-v-e *love* with him, and you're going to marry him and have all of his adorable Spanish babies."

"And what's going to happen with you and Scott?" she asked. "With as much time as you seem to spend together, pretty sure you're on the path toward an actual rela—"

"Don't say it," I demanded. "We're literally just friends."

"Who have sex," she added and I grinned.

"Well, yeah, that, too."

"You know what I think?' she asked but didn't give me any time to respond. "I think it sounds like someone has a case of avoidance…" she singsonged into my ear.

"Uh-oh…" I muttered in the receiver and started making crackling and whooshing sounds. "Amanda? Hello?"

"Harlow, don't you dare act like you're losing cell service right now!"

"Amanda? Hellooo?"

"Frances Harlow Paige!" she shouted, but her use of my first name did the complete opposite of her intention, only making it easier for me to tap the little red phone icon and end the call.

I received a text message from her no less than thirty seconds later.

Amanda: Oh, hey, asshole…Call me back when you get some balls and admit to yourself that you're actually starting to really like Dr. Erotic.

Goddamn her. I started to type out a sarcastic text in response, but before my fingers hit the keypad, I stopped myself. No way in hell was I taking the bait on this one. Plus, I didn't have time to talk about Scott with Amanda. My day was already fully booked, most likely with my mother's inquisition.

As I hopped off the subway, I decided I'd deal with Amanda later, but for now, I'd use the five-block walk to my mother's apartment to mentally prepare myself for her nosy and often overenthusiastic questions.

Lord knows, I'd need it.

My father and Nicole's blossoming relationship was still growing by the day, and ever since he'd laid eyes on his lady love, he'd been way too eager with text messages and phone calls and oversharing of his happy, lovey-dovey feelings.

Dad: Nicole agreed to another date with me!

Dad: Nicole is so funny, Low. And beautiful. God, she's beautiful.

Dad: Just out of curiosity, what is the average number of dates someone goes on before taking things to the "next level"?

And so on.

And there was no doubt in my mind that oversharing had most likely spilled over into my life, meaning he'd probably kept my mother and Jean-Pierre in the loop on *everything*, including Scott.

"Harlow!" my mother greeted the instant she opened the door to her apartment. "I'm going to overlook the fact that I'm a little peeved at you for waiting so long to visit and focus on the fact that you're actually here."

It was Saturday morning, and with the giant smile and giddy steps of my mother's bare feet, it appeared I'd be spending the majority of the day with her and Jean-Pierre.

"I just saw you a few weeks ago, Mom," I retorted with a knowing smile, and she rolled her eyes in response. *"And,"* I continued, "I talk to you on the phone nearly every day."

"I don't want to hear your excuses," she said and ushered me inside her and Jean-Pierre's loft style apartment. "I will only accept you promising to stop by for lunch at least once a week."

"Fine," I agreed and shrugged out of my jacket. "Lunch once a week."

"At least once a week."

"Do you want me to just move back home?" I teased. "I can quit my job at *Gossip* and mooch off of you and Jean-Pierre."

She smiled wide and nodded. "Yes, please."

I laughed. "You're so weird."

"Just consider it," she said, and I followed her lead through the entryway and into the living room. "We can have coffee together every morning while Jean-Pierre cooks us breakfast."

Crazily enough, my mother was one hundred percent serious. She'd love for me to be living back home, and my stepfather wouldn't bat an eye over it either. He was a good man and did, in fact, do most of the cooking in their relationship. His European flair for food ensured everything cooked inside their kitchen was nothing less than delicious.

The aroma of fresh bread wafting past my nose was proof of that. I glanced around the living room and toward the kitchen to find Jean-Pierre standing at the counter chopping up fresh pineapple.

"Harlow!" he greeted with a huge grin. "How are you?"

"I'm good, but I'm confused why you're cooking," I questioned and glanced between the two of them. "I thought we were going out to lunch?"

"We are," my mom answered with a soft smile. "But I know you're terrible about eating breakfast in the morning, so I figured we'd have a little breakfast first, and then, we can eat a light lunch at Hot House in a few hours."

"So, basically, you're trying to extend this lunch into a twelve-hour ordeal?"

"Yep," she answered with a proud smile.

"I should've known when you tried to get me here at nine this morning and wouldn't budge past ten thirty."

She smirked. "What can I say? I've missed my little Harlow."

"What have my favorite girls been gabbing about since you stepped in the door?" Jean-Pierre asked as he set the fruit onto a platter.

"Oh, you know, the usual," I said with an annoyed sigh. "Mom is trying to get me to move back in with you guys, and I'm trying to explain to her that I'm too old to move back home," I teased, and my mom laughed in response.

"She'll never stop asking until you do it," he responded through a chuckle, and my mother flashed a glare in his direction, which only made him laugh more. "Don't shoot the messenger," he added with a cheeky grin. "I'm merely telling her the truth. And you know that I'd love for Harlow to come live with us again."

"See?" My mother's eyes met mine. "Even your stepfather thinks it's a good idea."

"That's because he knows it would make you happy, and we both know that man lives to make you happy."

"You're right," he chimed in and glanced at my mother with his heart in his eyes. "Your mother is my world."

She giggled as she walked toward him and wrapped her arms around his shoulders. "Love you," she whispered and he grinned.

While they had their typical little lovey-dovey moment in the kitchen, I walked around their apartment, taking in the place I used to call my full-time home.

Their SoHo pad was gorgeous, and extremely spacious for New York City's standards, and it had always been a place I adored. Large, floor-to-ceiling windows highlighted the open floor plan, and the space was filled with midcentury modern décor and various paintings they'd collected over the years.

It was one hundred percent my mother and her European husband.

She'd always been a painter at heart, and after she'd divorced my father, she'd run a gallery in Manhattan. And it was where she'd met Jean-Pierre. He loved art and she sold art and, well, the rest was history.

Her eccentricity and his open-mindedness about life had connected them, and it was their love of art that had started the foundation of their relationship. Hell, the entire wall above the sleek, white sectional sofa showcased over fifty vintage paintings from various artists they loved, including a few of my mother's paintings.

As I continued to look around their home, my fingers found a small marble nude sculpture of a shapely woman and traced the clean lines of her stone figure.

Art was life for them. It was in their blood.

And I often found myself a little envious that they'd created a life for themselves that revolved around their passion.

Deep down, I wanted that kind of life for myself. The kind of life that didn't revolve around writing gossip columns, but doing something that gave me purpose.

Medicine.

I internally scoffed at my brain's detour toward my past aspirations. Sure, becoming a pediatrician had been my original life goal, but the time to accomplish that had long since passed.

God, how had my life gotten so off track from where I'd originally thought it would go?

Brent, my mind whispered, and I sighed internally. I hated blaming my life's choices on someone else. My ex hadn't exactly helped me achieve what I'd wanted out of life, but ultimately, I'd been the one to make the decision not to go to medical school right after graduation. I'd been the one who'd given up the internship opportunity that would have most likely set me up for a successful path into med school, not to mention an even more successful career as a physician. Now I spent most of my time blathering about which male celebrity gave the best oral based on his eye color and a random groupie named Candy.

Fucking hell, I hated dwelling on the past.

"Breakfast is ready, Harlow," my mother yelled, thankfully pulling me from my depressing thoughts. "Come sit down and eat," she said as she finished setting the dining room table with white plates.

Grateful for the reprieve from my internal monologue, I made my way to the table and sat down beside my mom and watched as Jean-Pierre set the last plate of food onto the table.

"I hope you're hungry," he said with a grin and sat down across from me.

My eyes turned into saucers as they took in the numerous platters of delicious food sitting in front of me—fresh croissants and strawberry jam, crepes with bananas and Nutella and homemade whipped cream, and enough cut-up fruit to feed an army.

Jesus Christ. Between breakfast here and lunch at Hot House, I wasn't finishing off this day without packing on a few extra pounds.

"Holy moly, this is a lot of food. Do you think maybe we should skip lunch at Hot House?"

"Nope," my mother responded without hesitation, and before I could stop her, she grabbed my plate and started filling it up with a more than healthy serving of everything.

"Whoa. Whoa. Whoa. That's enough, crazy food lady." I took my plate from her busy hands before she could dish out crepe number three for me. "I'd like to be able to get into my apartment tonight without needing a crane to get my ass into the elevator."

"Don't be ridiculous, sweetheart." She scoffed. "You're nearly too thin as it is. A few extra pounds would do you good."

I sighed, and Jean-Pierre grinned at me from across the table.

"So, what's new with you, Harlow?" he asked in an attempt to steer the conversation away from my mother trying to overfeed me.

"Not too much." I shrugged. "I saw *Kinky Boots* with Dad a few weeks ago."

"Was that the show he met Nicole at?" my mother asked.

"Yep." I took a bite of Nutella and whipped cream and crepe goodness and moaned out loud. "Jesus, these are good. My compliments to the chef," I said with a raise of my fork toward Jean-Pierre, and he grinned.

"Thank you. I'm happy you like them."

"Do you want another, sweetheart?" my mom asked, and I rolled my eyes.

"Uh, no. I think I'm still good with the one and half I have left on my plate."

"Tell me more about Scott," my mother demanded, and my brow furrowed in confusion.

"Scott?"

"Yes." She nodded. "Your father told me a little bit about him, but I want all of the juicy details."

"There are no juicy details."

Well, I guess there were some juicy details…

I mean, we'd been hanging out a lot lately and obviously having sex on the regular. There was no denying that sex with Scott was off the charts, but no fucking way was I going to tell my mother about that. She might've been quirky as hell and oftentimes too open-minded, but I had boundaries I refused to cross.

"We're just friends," I said, and the instant the words left my lips, they felt like total bullshit, not to mention the pointed look my mom flashed in my direction basically called me on that very fact.

"What?" I questioned. "We're just friends. Nothing more."

Well, friends who had a lot of sex. Friends who spent a lot of time together. But, yeah, other than that, we were friends. Scott and I were just friends...*right?*

She pointed her fork in my direction. "I don't believe you."

"You know I don't do long-term relationships."

She sighed. "I think you say you don't do them, but deep down, one day, you will when you find the right guy."

"I wouldn't hold your breath on that one."

She rolled her eyes. "You get your stubbornness from your father."

Jean-Pierre chuckled, and my mother glanced at him in confusion.

"What?" she asked, and he just grinned.

"She actually gets her stubbornness from you."

"No, she doesn't."

"Yeah." He nodded, and his eyes shone with amusement. "She definitely does."

Before I could start on crepe number two, my cell phone chimed in my pocket with a message. I pulled it out and glanced at the screen to find a text from Scott.

Scott: What's your address?

Me: Not telling you.

Somehow, we'd gotten started playing this game where I refused to tell him where I lived. I wasn't sure why I was holding on so strong, but I think it was mostly the fact that he'd shown an early interest in stalking.

Or that stubbornness your mom and Jean-Pierre are talking about.

Scott: What if I wanted to send you flowers?

Me: I don't want flowers.

Scott: What if I wanted to send you balloons or a teddy bear or one of those cute boxes of chocolates?

Me: I don't want any of those either.

Scott: What if I wanted to send you pancakes?

Me: I don't need pancakes today. I'm currently eating crepes with Nutella and whipped cream at my mom's place.

Scott: What about tomorrow? I bet you'll want pancakes tomorrow...

The tricky bastard. He was trying to play dirty.

Me: Probably not. I'll probably have leftover crepes to tide me over. :)

Take that, buddy.
Which it was actually the truth. No doubt, my mother had probably already packed up a to-go box for me before we even sat down to eat.

Scott: You're impossible. Can I see you today?

Me: Are you in need of the sex?

Scott: I always need the sex.

"Are you in need of the sex?" My mother's voice pulled my attention from my phone, and I hadn't even realized she'd been reading the entire conversation.

Holy hell.

"Why are you reading my text messages?" I asked. She was less than concerned with the fact that she was a little sneaky eavesdropper.

And she ignored my question completely. "Just friends, huh?" She grinned. "It looks like a little more than *just friends* to me…"

"Fine," I said on an exasperated sigh. "We're friends with benefits. You know, where we're friends and we do the sex, but we're not committed to one another."

"So, technically, you could have sex with someone else if you wanted to?"

"Yes," I answered, even though the idea of having sex with someone who wasn't Scott sounded about as appealing as going on another first date with Barron the Bore.

"And so could he?"

Oh God. Scott having sex with someone else?

I hated how much I hated that thought.

"Uh…" I swallowed the discomfort down and forced the word, "Yes," from my lips.

She quirked a brow. "And you'd be okay with that?"

No.

"Yes."

"Are you sure about that, Harlow?"

"Uh-huh," I muttered and shoved another bite of food into my mouth before she could shoot another uncomfortable question my way. Avoidance felt like the very best tactic in this scenario. Especially since I had no fucking clue what was going on inside my own head.

I didn't want a long-term relationship. I didn't want to be tied down to anyone. And I definitely shouldn't have cared about the fact that, technically, Scott could have sex with someone else. Anytime he wanted, actually.

He probably is. He knows every fucking vagina in the city.

But what I should've been okay with, and what I felt actually okay with, were two very different things.

What in the hell was happening to me?

I had to get away from the relationship inquisition that was my mother before I had a fucking panic attack. "I'm stuffed," I muttered and slid my chair out from under the table and stood. "What time are we eating at Hot House?"

"Reservations are at one," Jean-Pierre answered.

"Then I'm definitely going to need to nap off these crepes if there's any hope of getting my appetite back by then." I patted my stomach and grinned.

"I think someone is trying to avoid the whole Scott and friends with benefits topic..." my mother singsonged, and I rolled my eyes.

"Obviously."

She laughed at my response, and, after I'd taken my dirty dishes into the kitchen, I made my way back into the living room. I slipped my shoes off, plopped my lazy ass onto their cozy sofa, and flipped on the television while I finished out a quick text conversation with Scott. He wanted to meet up at some point today, which I was more than open to, but when he sent the last message of *How about your apartment?* I chose to send back *I'm ignoring you now.*

The nosy bastard was determined to figure out where I lived, but I wasn't ready to cave on it.

Oh, but you can let him inside your vagina all the time?

My brain really needed to shut the fuck up for a little bit.

While I mindlessly watched a rerun of *The Office*, doing my best to fall into a Nutella coma, my phone buzzed with an email. It was a notification for the latest *Celebrity News* articles that had just gone live. I scrolled through the new headlines but stopped abruptly on the third one from the top.

DATING NEWS: Dr. ER might be off the market, ladies.

What the what?

As I clicked on the article's link and scanned through another columnist's words, I was mostly wondering why in the hell I didn't get this exclusive.

I mean, I was having the sex with him, not Kimmie Marie from fucking *Celebrity News.*

But as I continued to read the article itself, something else took high priority in my mind.

Kimmie prattled on about Scott attending an event called Benefit for Bab(i)es, and apparently, when he was asked about his ongoing status of never bringing a date to events, he'd answered, ***"Not tonight, but maybe soon."***

Not tonight, but maybe soon?

What in the ever-loving fuck was that supposed to mean?

Was he talking about me?

CHAPTER *twenty-four*

OUTSIDE ON THE SIDEWALK, THE SUN BEATING DOWN ON MY HEAVY shoulders, I stared down at the text message exchange I'd had with Harlow earlier that morning.

Me: Can I see you?

Harlow: Are you in need of the sex?

My lungs still burned as I thought of how she'd react when I fully explained what I really wanted. But then, in text message wasn't the time for it.

No, this is a conversation for in person.

Me: I always need the sex.

Harlow: LOL At least you're honest. My day is jam-packed, though. Breakfast at my mom's right now, and then we're apparently also eating lunch later in the city. I'll be as big as a whale by the end of the day.

Me: Ooh. What restaurant? Let me eat through you.

Harlow: LOL Hot House. I'll be free later this afternoon. I'll meet you somewhere, and you can eat through me, all right.

Me: Hot damn. How about your apartment?

Harlow: I'm ignoring you now.

She hadn't said anything then, and really, I think that was the starting point of my current semi-psychotic break. Realistically, she was probably just at lunch with her mom and practicing a little-known habit of actually paying attention to the person you were dining with rather than your phone.

But, yeah. All of this…all of these *emotions*—something I was horrifically unfamiliar with—were eating at me, and she'd been seemingly doing the dip on me when it came to her apartment since the day I'd met her.

And now, here I was, outside of Hot House, intentionally following Harlow.

Frustrated with what my life had come to, I leaned back against the warm bricks of the restaurant and sighed. I was crazy. I was fucking losing it. The apartment thing was just a running joke, and I was blowing it out of proportion.

Of course, just as I settled on going back to being sane, the door opened and, shading her eyes from the sun with one hand and digging in her monstrous bag for her sunglasses with the other, Harlow stepped out.

Quickly, I ducked around the corner of the building.

I cringed.

Oh Jesus, Scott. Time to reevaluate some things here.

Following a woman was fucking ridiculous, creepy, and highly illegal. Granted, she knew me and liked me, but yeah… *Holy hell, now I'm just rationalizing. That's what crazy people do.*

"Thanks for lunch, Mom." I heard her mom murmur something back before Jean-Pierre's French accent took over.

"It is always a pleasure, Harlow." His voice was genuine, heartfelt even, and I immediately liked him, sight unseen.

"Same. Thanks for listening, guys. Really. I know I unloaded a lot of stuff on you."

Stuff about me?

My ears perked up, and just like that, I forgot all about how crazy I was acting.

"Anytime," her mom answered sweetly before any and all sound faded away. I peeked around the corner to see them gone, Jean-Pierre and Harlow's mom crossing the street to the other side while Harlow neared the end of the block on this side.

I jumped into action, walking her direction quickly but casually and paying attention when she turned at the corner.

With her out of sight, I quickened my step to try to close some of the distance and then spotted the top of her head in the crowd up ahead as soon as I made it to the end of the block.

She only went about a block and a half before turning and jogging up the stairs of a brownstone style apartment building and inserting her key into the lock.

Honestly, I couldn't decide whether it was a good thing or not that the trip to her apartment had been so short. After all, I'd successfully completed my mission. But on the other hand, if I'd had more time, I might have circled around to the conclusion that this wasn't a good idea again.

The jig was up now, though, and I had to do something about it before I lost my nerve. With just one side of her hair pulled back and pinned, I could see the side of her face as she concentrated on what she was doing, and a rush of emotion hit me all at once.

This was it. *She* was it. I'd finally found a woman worth chasing.

Literally, my mind mocked mercilessly.

Breaking into a jog, I weaved my way through the people scattered on the sidewalk and bounded up the stairs behind her two at a time.

Her eyes widened, and her face grew longer before my eyes as her mouth did the same.

"Scott?"

"Hey, Low," I greeted casually. Far, far more casually than I felt, my heart beating so violently I thought it might jump straight out of my chest and land on the stoop in front of me.

"What are you doing here?"

I swallowed the thickness in my throat and concentrated on getting inside first. "I'm sorry to surprise you like this, but…can we talk? It's important."

Her face serious—seriously worried—she turned back to the lock and finished the job, pushing the door open and holding it for me. "Of course. Come in."

We walked in silence up two flights of stairs to what I presumed was her door. As she inserted another key into that lock and turned it, I immediately felt sick.

She pushed it open, and as soon as the light of the hall sliced into the small entry of her apartment, my admission poured unchecked from my lips.

"I followed you."

Her eyebrows pulled together as she stepped inside and I followed her, almost as if she hadn't heard me.

Strengthening my resolve to make sure it was all out in the open—every fucking last bit of it—I repeated myself. "I said, I followed you. Here. To your apartment."

"You fucking followed me? From where? How? I don't understand."

"Yes. From the restaurant. You told me where you were. Not understanding is definitely reasonable, and I'm sorry," I rattled off, addressing each of her questions as well as I could.

"But this was a conversation I needed to have in person." She didn't know what conversation I was talking about, but flustered, I rushed past that detail. "And you've been cagey about where you live for no reason, Harlow."

She glared and took three rapid steps to the end of the hall that led into her living room, but I kept on. "I know what I did today isn't healthy. I know it's fucking ridiculous, okay? But I put my dick in you on the regular! How can you not trust me enough to know where you live?"

"Whoops. Excuse us." Mystified, we both swiveled our heads immediately to the couch.

"Dad?" Harlow screamed just as I caught sight of my mom's bare breasts.

"Oh Jesus Christ," I cried.

"What are you doing here?" she shouted toward them—our parents, our fucking naked parents.

What was happening?

And more than that, it appeared everyone else knew where she lived to the point of using her place for conjugal fucking visits.

"I guess other people know where you live," I muttered softly, but she heard me. Oh, the death rays burning from her eyes were proof of that. Meanwhile, Bill was covering himself and *my mother* with a blanket.

"Scott," Harlow snapped. "Not now. Jesus Christ, one thing at a time, okay?"

And she was right, obviously. The naked parents on the couch took precedence, so I did my best to shut the fuck up.

"Dad," Harlow said again, gritting her teeth in search of patience. "What are you doing here? Naked? On my fucking couch?"

I reached out and squeezed her shoulder in support, but she shook it off.

I guessed that was fair too.

"We're supposed to meet your mother and Jean-Pierre soon. A stroll through Central Park."

"And?" Harlow put a demanding hand to her hip. "This situation definitely warrants an *and*, followed up by an actual explanation."

"And I got nervous," my mom piped up. I leaned over Harlow's shoulder to glare at her, but she pressed on, unfazed. "I know how important they are to your father, and well, I'd like to make a good impression."

Harlow sighed. "Still not seeing how this brings us here. With you guys naked in my apartment."

My mom shrugged. "Orgasms tend to calm me."

Oh Jesus Christ.

"Your apartment was close," Bill finished. "When we got here and it was empty, we figured we'd be quick."

"Good Lord, no more details, please," Harlow requested with her gaze firmly placed on the wall. "And I'm really regretting giving you that spare key, Dad."

I stepped in to assist. "Look, guys, we'll give you a minute to get dressed, but it's safe to say this isn't exactly appropriate."

Bill had the good grace to wince. My mother's stubbornness kicked in. "I don't know, son. Looks like this might be an example of the stalking pot calling the kettle inappropriate."

Count on Nicole fucking Shepard to call me on my shit.

"Gee, thanks, Mom." It was on the tip of my tongue to tell her that Linda wasn't always up in my shit, but even in the midst of her naked hijinks, that seemed like a low blow.

"Scott," Harlow interjected. "Let's go outside and talk."

I nodded, looking back at our parents one more time and allowing myself a little smile as I shook my head. I mean, Jesus. That deserved at least a little amusement.

I followed Harlow in silence, and we went back out her door, down the stairs, and outside, taking a seat on the stairs of the stoop.

She waited patiently while I worked up the nerve to explain myself.

It was completely unlike her and made me even more nervous.

"I'm sorry I stalked you."

"Yeah, that was a tad over the top," she replied immediately.

"I know," I admitted. "I talked myself out of it a couple of times, but then, yeah, it just happened anyway. I don't know how, but I can't change it now."

"Tell it to the cops," she teased. Or...God. I hoped she was teasing.

"Harlow—"

"What the hell, Scott?"

"I know," I said on a sigh. "But I guess I was feeling insecure."

"You? Dr. Erotic? *Insecure?*"

"See, that's the thing. I'm not *just* that guy. And, yeah, I guess sometimes, Scott Shepard isn't immune to getting insecure."

She scoffed and I nodded.

"I know, it surprised me too. I'm normally so awesome," I divulged, and she bit her lip just a tiny bit as she studied my face like a map, trying to get a read on me—and perhaps trying not to laugh at my obvious joke.

"And you were constantly dodging me about your apartment. I should know where you live, Low."

"Why?"

My eyebrows pulled together. "Why what?"

"Why should you know where I live? We're not in a relationship. We haven't made any promises to one another."

I took a deep breath in and blew it out while she watched. "Well...I guess that's the thing. There's something about you," I admitted with a shrug. "Something that makes it so I can't stop thinking about you, and you and me together, and that maybe...I don't know...maybe I *want* a relationship."

"So it was me you were talking about last night."

I felt my eyes pinch together. "Last night?"

"To the paparazzi. *Not tonight, but maybe soon*, I think you said."

"That comment was nothing. Jesus. Someone printed that?"

"Yep. Someone other than me, by the way. Which I considered castrating you for. But, given the circumstances, I guess that's the least of my problems."

"Problems?"

"We're not relationship people, Scott!"

Irritation crawled up my throat. "That's not true. You were in a relationship with Brent," I argued.

"Yeah. In *college*. And I told you that it didn't end well. I don't want to go there again!"

Instantly, I recognized talking about this shit wasn't going to get me much of anywhere. If I wanted more from Harlow—and I did—I was going to have to make it happen with actions. *Good thing I'm an action man.*

"All right. Calm down," I soothed. "I shouldn't have bombarded you with this. Let's start simple, okay?"

She looked skeptical, but she nodded her agreement. "Okay."

"You like me, right?"

"Scott..."

"It's an easy question. Do you like me or not?"

"Of course, I like you! I *let you stick your dick in me on the regular,* as you so eloquently put it."

I chuckled and winced at the same time. "Yeah, sorry about that."

She rolled her eyes. "So, yes. I like you."

"Then let's start there."

"I thought we already started!" she whined.

I laughed again. "Well, in a sense, yes. But this time, I mean with an open mind. Can you do that?"

She shook her head in the negative, but it wasn't because her answer was no. She was just scared. I'd have to figure out how to change that.

"Are we sleeping with other people while we keep an open mind and like each other?" she asked and scrutinized my face for a reaction.

Resolutely, and with nothing to hide, I held her gaze. "No," I admitted honestly. The truth was, I hadn't had sex with anyone but her since this whole crazy thing started. And more than that, I didn't want to.

She stayed quiet for a brief moment, and then, surprisingly, said, "Okay."

"Okay?"

"I said okay, fuckface. Move on," she demanded, and I couldn't stop myself from grinning.

She wanted to move on.

So, move on I did. Lips to hers in an instant, I pushed my tongue until the tip met hers and kissed her with enough certainty for both of us.

She broke away a few seconds in. "I just have one more question."

"Okay," I said hesitantly, unsure what else she wanted from my bloody, mangled heart.

"Where the fuck did your beard go?"

I guess she misses it.

Tomorrow's plan: start growing it back.

CHAPTER *twenty-five*

THE SOUND OF MY PHONE RINGING TOO LOUDLY STARTLED ME AWAKE. MY EYES caught sight of the barely risen sun peeking through my bedroom window, and I groaned. It couldn't have been past eight in the morning, and that left me wondering who in the hell was calling me at this god-awful hour.

I reached out from under my cozy comforter, and the cool air hit my skin, urging goose bumps onto my arms. I snagged my phone off the nightstand and slid my entire body, including my head, back under the warm cocoon of blankets. Even though the ringing had stopped, I tapped the home button and my phone came to life.

The numbers 7:45 glowed bright and blinding while a notification sat in the center of the screen.

3 missed calls Scott.

What the hell?

Before I had the time to send an angry message of ***Stop fucking calling me***, he sent a text message, making my phone ping loudly.

"Shit!" I yelled, bobbling it a little before getting it back under control.

Scott: Rise and shine, Harlow. Get ready. I'm taking you some-where special today.

Me: Are you on drugs? Do you have any idea what time it is?

Scott: Lol. No drugs. Just coffee.

Me: I'm not going anywhere right now. It's fucking Saturday morning and it's not even 8.

Scott: I'm on my way to your apartment.

He was on his way to my apartment? Was he joking with me right now?

Hell no. I didn't care how persistent he was. I wasn't going any-where but back to dreamland.

Me: I fucking knew it was a bad idea for you to have my address.

Two days of him having the information, and he was already us-ing it for outright evil purposes.

Scott: Get dressed, Harlow. I've got a surprise for you.

A surprise? Even though it was too goddamn early, I was in-trigued. I really fucking liked surprises.

Me: Does it include breakfast and coffee?

Scott: Yep. I just added it to the already awesome list of things I'm doing with Harlow today.

Ugh. There's a list of awesome? It shouldn't have been sounding better by the second, but *goddammit,* it was.

> **Me: I kind of hate you right now.**

> **Scott: No, you don't. And stop texting me. Get your cute ass out of bed. I'll be there in thirty minutes.**

> **Me: Thirty minutes?! Fucking hell.**

> **Scott: Less texting and more dressing.**

I giggled at the irony of his words and sat up in my bed and typed out another message.

> **Me: This is the first time you've ever encouraged me to put clothes on. It feels like a momentous occasion.**

> **Scott: Because today is important. And it's our first official date.**

> **Me: We've been on a date before.**

> **Scott: Um, no. I'm pretty sure you've blandly called everything we've done so far, outside of the sex, "hanging out."**

> **Me: That's a technicality. Besides, does it have to be at 8 in the morning?**

> **Scott: Yes. And I promise, you're going to have fun today.**

> **Me: What kind of fun? I mean, what if what you have planned isn't something I'd find fun? You should just tell me what it is, and then I'll decide if it's worth getting out of bed for.**

Scott: *Get dressed, Harlow.*

He wasn't giving in, and I couldn't stop my curiosity from getting the best of me. Goddammit. He was a genius. I sighed out loud and threw my comforter off of my legs and removed my ass from my mattress.

With my hands held above my head, I stretched out the kinks and creaks from my muscles, and, while drumming up the motivation to hop in the shower, I sent him one last text message.

Me: *Bossy bastard.*

Forty-five minutes later, I was showered, dressed, and riding the subway with Scott to an unknown location. His large frame—clad in a nice pair of dress slacks and a button-up, collared shirt—stood beside me as we careened through the dark tunnels of the city.

"Ready?" he asked with a grin. "We're almost there."

I glanced down at my skinny jeans and tank top and then back up at him. "I feel underdressed."

"You're perfect," he whispered and pressed a soft kiss to my cheek.

I quirked a brow in his direction, and instantly, he laughed. Probably because he already knew what my next question was before I even said it. "Where are we going?" I asked for the millionth time. "Seriously, Scott. A woman needs to be prepared. Do I need bail money? Should I have gotten a Brazilian wax?"

He waggled his brows. "Not today, and you're sexy no matter what."

"Even with a seventies bush?"

"Harlow."

"Fine. But where are we going?"

"It's a surprise," he replied, sighing deep and long, like he was actually annoyed with me. I didn't believe him.

"I don't like surprises."

"Liar," he said with knowing smile, confirming that he wasn't annoyed with me at all. "The fact that you love surprises is the one and only thing that got you out of bed this morning."

"You were using my love of surprises against me?" I nudged his stomach gently with my elbow. "Asshole."

"Not necessarily against you," he answered. "Just using it to my advantage."

"You're such a pain in my ass."

He wrapped his arms around my shoulders and pulled me in for a tight embrace. "You know," he whispered into my ear. "I love your cute and curvy little ass."

I rolled my eyes. "Of course you do. It's a nice ass."

He chuckled into my neck. "It's my ass."

I scoffed. "Pretty sure it's connected to me."

"Yeah, but it's mine. I'm laying claim to it."

"Don't waste your time on the macho alpha male bullshit," I retorted. "It doesn't work on me."

My words didn't deter him one bit, though. His persistent fingers slid down my shoulders to my back until they gripped my ass...*hard.* And in the middle of the crowded subway, Scott tugged my body toward his and kissed me soundly on the mouth.

My first reaction was to pull away, especially considering the crowd surrounding us, but the instant his tongue slipped past my lips, I was a fucking goner. With the warmth of his mouth and the strength of his arms wrapped around me, I couldn't stop myself from melting into his kiss.

Good God, this man can kiss.

He gripped my ass again and whispered, "Mine," into my ear as his mouth moved a trail across my jaw to my neck and then back up to my mouth.

A shiver rolled up my spine, and for some unknown reason, I couldn't find the strength to refute his words.

Because you really like him. Maybe even more than like him...

The subway jolted our bodies a little as it started to slow down, and Scott ended the kiss with a soft peck to my lips. A little whimper of disappointment left my mouth without permission, and he smirked down at me in response.

"We're here," he said, grabbing my hand and linking our fingers together before leading me off the car and toward the stairs of the subway exit.

"Okay. Seriously. What is *here*?" I questioned as we got to the top of the stairs, but Scott was determined and completely unwilling to spill the beans. "Where are we going?" I asked again, and he just laughed.

I sighed in annoyance and petulantly let him lead me toward the unknown.

After a quick stop at Magnolia Bakery for some muffins and two cups of coffee and a quick two-block walk, we stood in front of the doors of St. Luke's Hospital.

Scott turned toward me and smiled. "We're here."

"Huh?" I looked at him and then back at the hospital and then back at him again. "You're taking me to a hospital on our first official date?"

"Yep."

"A hospital?" My brow scrunched in confusion. "Do you understand that a first official date should be something romantic?"

He laughed, but it did nothing to clear my confusion.

"I'm just having a hard time wrapping my brain around how a place of medical emergencies would spell out romance…"

"Today, you get to be Dr. Harlow Paige for the day," he explained with a proud smile. "We're going to spend the next four hours taking care of pediatric patients in my emergency room."

Holy shit.

"Are you serious?"

"As a heart attack."

A barking laugh left my lips, and he grinned.

"There's no pressure," he said and wrapped his arm around my shoulder. "But after you told me about your original goal of becoming a pediatrician, I wanted to give you a chance to really explore it. It sounded like you'd spent most of your life working toward that goal, and plus, you already know I think you'd make one hell of a pediatrician."

God, he remembered all of that?

Not to mention, he'd arranged a whole day for me to experience what it would be like to be a pediatrician on his day off?

A flock of butterflies took up residence in my stomach, fluttering around erratically as I stared at him in awe. These weren't the actions of an asshole. They were the actions of a man who put others' wants and needs before his own.

The exact kind of man I want to spend my life with...

"Wow. This is so sweet, Scott..." I briefly paused as I tried to find the right words—tried not to belittle the gesture with a smartass remark like I normally would. My saliva felt thicker than normal as I murmured the heartfelt truth. "It's probably one of the most thoughtful things anyone has ever done for me."

"It's never too late to accomplish your dreams, Harlow," he answered with tenderness in his voice. "If this is still your dream, then I know you can achieve it."

"You really think that?"

"I'm certain of it," he said and then held out his hand. "Ready to play doctor for the day?"

I smiled. "I'm ready."

My day in the ER had careened by in a blur of adorable tiny humans. Scott and I had managed to see twenty pediatric patients in a matter of three and a half hours, and I'd found myself mesmerized and invigorated by the experience.

Sure and precise and way too much fun, he awed me as a physician. Dr. Shepard was an asset to the city of New York. He had a friendly and playful bedside manner, and even during the most emergent situations, he always found a way to get his patients to relax and laugh, while giving them nothing less than top-notch care.

He was a good doctor, and, I was quickly finding, an even better man.

And I couldn't deny working side by side with him—obviously, with Scott doing most of the actual medical work while I watched— had been the most fun I'd had in a long time. Having already cleared the necessary paperwork with the hospital, he'd handed a permission form to each family we'd worked with and explained that I was simply an intern and not an actual physician. And thankfully, not one family had turned down my participation.

"All right, Dr. Paige," he said with a grin as he handed me the patient's medical chart. "We've got one last patient to see. Go ahead and give me the rundown on what to expect."

I grinned and scanned the chart for the pertinent details. "Josie Morrows. Age five. No significant past medical history. Came in about an hour ago after she fell out of a tree. Only injury appears to be a small gash to forehead."

"Hmm…a head injury? That feels oddly familiar…" he teased, and I nudged him with my elbow.

"Shut up," I muttered, and he chuckled as we headed toward Josie in Bay Six.

Scott winked as he pulled the curtain back to reveal an adorable little girl with a big white bandage taped across her entire forehead. She sat on the exam table with her legs swinging back and forth while her mother stood beside her.

"Hi, Josie," Scott greeted. "I'm Dr. Shepard, and this is Ms. Paige. It looks like someone took a little fall today, huh?"

"Yep." She nodded, and her blond curls bounced with the motion. "Out of a tree in my backyard."

"It's a big tree, but she didn't get very high," her mother chimed in. "One I told her not to climb, by the way," she added with a disappointed glance in her daughter's direction.

Josie frowned. "But Joey did it first!"

Her mother sighed. "Yes, but you're five and he's ten. That's a big difference, sweetheart. You're too little to climb that tree."

"Ugh," she muttered and looked at me. "My brother always gets to do everything. It stinks."

I grinned. "Yeah, but one day you'll be ten too. And then your mom might let you climb trees like your brother."

Josie's blue eyes brightened. "And then maybe I won't get a cut on my head, huh?"

"Exactly," Scott said as he slipped on exam gloves. "Okay, Josie, I need to make sure you didn't injure anything else besides your head, okay?"

She nodded. "Okay."

While he did a quick assessment of the patient, I donned a pair of gloves and got the supplies ready to clean the wound. I was surprised and a bit relieved how quickly everything I'd learned in college was coming back to me. It was like it was yesterday that I was taking pre-med classes and doing short internships at various hospitals in the city.

"Can I remove the bandage so Ms. Paige and I can see the cut, Josie?" Scott asked once he had finished his assessment.

She nodded slowly, but I didn't miss the hesitancy in her response. I couldn't blame her. Head injuries weren't any fun at twenty-nine; I couldn't imagine how scary they were at five. *Fucking Barron the Bore and the Case of the Glass Headboard* taught me that.

"You know," I mused as Scott winked at me and slowly, carefully, removed the bandage. "I once got a cut on my forehead."

Josie's curious eyes met mine. "You did?"

"Yep." I nodded. "Dr. Shepard had to give me stitches."

"Did it hurt?"

"Nope," I answered honestly. "Thanks to the numbing medicine he'd applied, I didn't feel anything at all. Cool, huh?"

Once the bandage was off, both of us took a good look at the gash on her forehead. It was small and, thankfully, most of the bleeding had already stopped.

Scott turned to me. "What do you think, Ms. Paige?"

"I don't think Josie is going to need stitches."

"Me either," he agreed with a smile.

"I'm not?" the little patient questioned excitedly. "I'm not going to need stitches?"

"Nope," Scott said and tugged gently on one of her ringlets. "Looks like you lucked out, little lady. We just need to clean up the cut really, really good so it doesn't get an infection and put a new bandage on it to protect it."

"Oh, thank God," her mother said on a relieved sigh. "I wasn't sure, and I know I probably could have just taken her to her pediatrician, but I panicked when I saw all the blood."

Scott nodded his understanding. "We're glad you brought her in today," he reassured. "Head injuries tend to bleed more than most, and since she's so young, it's always better to err on the side of caution."

"Thank you," she responded and looked at both of us. "You made this trip to the ER a lot easier than I thought it would be. You're both fantastic."

Obviously, I wasn't a doctor, but her words hit me hard.

I really helped…contributed something.

Was it really too late for me to go to med school?

Scott flashed a knowing smile in my direction before whispering for my ears only, "It's never too late, *Dr. Paige.*"

I feigned annoyance with a roll of my eyes, but I couldn't deny that the day had put a bug in my brain. Could I really go my whole life without achieving my dream?

I honestly didn't know the answer to that, but I did know I'd felt more invigorated by today than I had by anything I'd ever done at *Gossip.*

Four hours in the ER with Scott and I felt like I was falling in love with medicine all over again.

Maybe medicine isn't the only thing you're falling in love with.

Oh. Boy.

CHAPTER *twenty-six*

GRABBED MY PHONE OUT OF MY POCKET AS I STEPPED OUT OF THE ELEVATOR ON my way down from the OR.

A man had come in with an esophageal collapse, and we'd rushed him right in nearly the minute I'd started this eight-hour shift. It threw me off a little working a morning shift after working mostly nights—especially after staying up late last night with Harlow—but as soon as that guy had come through the doors in his friends' arms, I'd been wide awake.

On a very important side note: Ever since I'd taken Harlow on a date to my ER about a week ago, late nights—aka lots and lots of sex— together have become our thing.
Neither one of us want to be the first to say "Uncle" to our aching tired bodies or fluttering sleepy eyes. These late night battles with Harlow are my new favorite pastime.

But the surgery had taken nearly five full hours, and after leaving

Harlow sleeping in my bed this morning, I'd wanted to call her before lunch.

I had the screen on recent calls and my thumb hovering over her name when I got interrupted.

"Scott!" Deb yelled, running from the other side of the ER. Assuming her cry was as urgent as it sounded, I immediately dropped my phone back in my pocket, grabbed a pair of gloves from the nearest supply cart, and broke into a jog toward her.

As soon as we were within reaching distance, she swatted the gloves right out of my hand. I watched as they fell to the floor with a soft plop.

Um. Not emergent, then, I guessed.

"Okay, then. What's up, Deb?"

"They just announced this as the most efficient ER in New York City! You're getting an award!"

Me?

"Why am I getting an award?" I asked dumbly, and she rolled her eyes.

"You run this ER!"

Now it was my turn to roll mine. "Not really, Deb. I do some shit, but we all know you're the one who really runs everything around here. This is your award."

"Yeah, well. They don't give this award to nurses. They give it to doctors, and you're the doctor. So just suck it up and accept it. Though, I won't mind if you mention me in your acceptance speech."

"Acceptance speech?"

She slapped at my arm. "Yes. There's a ceremony. Next week. You get a key to the city from the mayor and everything."

Jesus Christmas, that was ridiculous.

"Yeah, I think I'll be busy. Schedule me for a shift then, would you?"

"No. You will go there, you will do this, I will murder you."

"In what order, exactly?" I teased. "It'll be kind of hard for me to show up to the ceremony if I'm dead."

She hit me again just as my phone pinged in my pocket. I held up a finger for her to hold that thought, but she just rolled her eyes and walked away. *I guess she's done with me.*

I swiped the screen to read the new message, noticing at the last second it was from Pam. *Goddammit. Pam.*

Fingers crossed she was just texting about another meeting or the award or something.

Pam: Schedule freeing up? We should get together this weekend.

Or maybe not. Fucking shit sticks.

Me: Still really busy. Sorry.

I mean, fuck. What was I supposed to say? She'd seen me with Harlow, but I'd pretty clearly introduced her as a friend. And although Low wasn't out graffitiing the city with proclamations of our budding relationship, she'd agreed to be open-minded, and more than that, even asked about whether or not we'd be sleeping with other people. Which it was decided that we weren't. Obviously, we were getting there, albeit at the speed of a fucking school zone, but we were definitely getting there.

Which left me to wonder if I should just tell Pam I was seeing someone? Or would she get the hint on her own eventually?

God, this was definitely new territory. Normally, I didn't have to maintain any contact at all, so I just didn't. But with her working in the mayor's office and my whole fucked-up messy involvement in that shitshow, I didn't have the luxury.

Maybe Harlow will know what to do.

Switching over to my messages with her, I started to type out a message when Deb yelled from the other side of the room again.

Fuck. This is why dating and being a doctor never mixed.

Preconditioned to respond to her voice, I looked up immediately.

This time, though, she had her hand on a bleeding chest and a demand that I get the fuck over there immediately in her eyes.

Quick as a flash, I dropped my phone in my pocket and did just that.

"We, the city of New York, pride ourselves on being the best in every category, every profession, every park and skyscraper…"

I rolled my eyes as Brent, the mayor, prattled on about what a goddamn messiah New York City was a week later at the ceremony for my farce of an award.

Harlow was in a meeting. *Thank God.* Otherwise, she'd have been forced to be here covering it for *Gossip*, and I was already distracted enough without seeking her out in the audience every five seconds and wondering if *Brent* was doing the same.

He'd thanked no less than twenty people for their so-called roles in urban greatness, but make no mistake, he'd thanked not one single fucking individual more than he thanked himself.

"…And with me at the helm…"

See?

"And leaders like Dr. Scott Shepard at St. Luke's, I know we can take everything we've achieved and elevate it to the next level."

Christ, this guy was a real crock of shit. *I'm sure my opinion has nothing to do with the fact that Harlow used to bang him.*

But seriously. He sounded like a douche—at least to my ears.

"Today, I'd like to present Scott, and all of St. Luke's Emergency Department, with this commendation of excellence, with specific respect to efficiency and overall treatment experience. Step up here, Scott."

I did as I was told, rising to my feet and trying not to blink too rapidly as the cameras went off in my face. As a public event of the city, the press corner was already bursting with legitimate news outlets, including all of the major networks. But thanks to my current stint on *The Doctor Is In*, it was overfilled, packed to the motherfucking brim by every bloodsucking leech and paparazzi in the city. Though, I guessed the publicity from something like this could really only be good—theoretically, anyway.

Brent reached for my hand with his right and extended a glass statue in the other, all the while smiling in the direction of the cameras instead of making eye contact with me. He was a natural at this whole dog and pony show. Being in the public eye now, I decided to use him as an example of what *not* to do. Not for public opinion—he had that in spades—but for my opinion of myself.

The more I paid attention to all of that fake warmth, all I felt inside was cold.

"On behalf of the city of New York, thank you," he boomed, and I just stopped myself from rolling my eyes all the way when they hit the bottom.

Down in front of me, Pam sat with a smile on her face and applause echoing off of her hands as she looked at me and only me. I looked away as quickly as possible.

Brent squeezed my hand meaningfully.

I cleared my throat. "Uh, thank you," I managed.

His smile deepened, the asshole.

I tried to step away, but he clasped a hand on my shoulder and turned me back.

"Hold on, Scott. Before you run off to save more lives," he said, laying it on thick, "I'd like to take this opportunity to brag a little bit."

Oh, wow. Something new.

"Scott and I have actually already been working together on something that is really close to my heart. I've followed the policy of health and public safety in this city closely for years, and in an effort to make this city even better, stronger, safer, I've appointed Scott as the head of my team for reworking the policies that need work and scrapping the ones that are lacking completely."

Following closely? Appointed me? I approached him!

"I'm looking forward to working together, Scott," he said as the crowd broke out in applause.

Goddamn, he was good. He'd trapped me, and now, thanks to the lives of innocent people being at stake and all, I had no choice but to agree.

"Can't fucking wait."

CHAPTER *twenty-seven*

Harlow

"**K**NOCK. KNOCK!"

Scott's voice echoed off of the walls of my entryway even though the door still separated us. The bastard could definitely boom like no other. I hopped off the couch and headed toward the door to let him in. Just before turning the knob, I caught sight of my nearly blinding smile in the reflection of the large mirror my mother had insisted on placing near the door. I sighed. Boy, I guess I really did like him, huh?

"Hello? Frances?" he teased, impatient as ever, and I rolled my eyes.

Fucking Frances. It would only be thirty-five more years or so before my given name was age-appropriate.

Without humoring him with a response, I took the time to peek at the smartass through my peephole. The longer I spied, the more enjoyment I got. It wasn't until I'd sat motionless for nearly thirty seconds, entranced by the thrumming vein in his corded neck, that I realized what a creeper I was being.

A totally smitten creeper...

Yeah. Even I couldn't deny I was pretty damn smitten over Scott Shepard. The fact that his presence outside my door urged my stupid smile to grow to record-breaking lengths was proof of that.

Damn, he looks good. As handsome as ever, Scott was dressed down in jeans and a white Henley shirt with the perfect amount of scruff covering his strong jaw—the now-growing beard making a much-approved reappearance. And with a pizza from Boca's in one hand and a bottle of wine in the other, he came bearing gifts. Obviously, he wasn't just a pretty face. The man was intelligent to boot. *The full fucking package.*

After one more impatient rap of his knuckles, I put him out of his misery and opened the door.

"Well, *hello*." Scott smirked, not bothering to hide his blatant perusal of my body. I was dressed less than casual in a tank top sans bra—*because fuck bras*—and a pair of little sleep shorts, but I didn't miss the little glint of approval shining from his brown eyes.

His hungry gaze ran the circuit from my legs to my face twice, and when he started round three, an amused smile kissed my lips.

"Do you want to come in or just stand there and gawk at me?" I asked and leaned against the doorframe. Never mind that I'd just spent the better part of three minutes doing the same through a half-inch-diameter hole.

He grinned. "I'm quite enjoying my gawk."

"Okay, then," I said and kicked the door shut a second later. "Just knock again when you want to come inside," I called through the door, and he laughed.

"Let me in, Frances," he demanded, but his voice was more amused than anything else. "I promise I'll behave."

"Stop calling me Frances, and you're a total liar." *I hope.* Scott's version of misbehaving generally ended in orgasms for me. Lots and lots of orgasms, mind you.

"Let me in or else I won't share the pizza."

"Pepperoni?" I asked with skepticism in my voice.

It better be fucking pepperoni. I only ate pizza with pepperoni and extra cheese. Everything else was a waste of time and toppings.

"Yep."

"Extra cheese?"

"Yep."

I opened the door again, and Scott stood on the other side—*looking like the only man in the world for me*—with a giant smile fixed across his mouth. Before he could say anything, I snatched the pizza box from his hands and sashayed my ass down the entryway and into the kitchen.

Luckily, he followed my determined lead, shutting the door behind himself and smiling like a handsome loon once he reached the kitchen.

God, *this* man. I really liked him.

More than like…

The mere idea of that thought should have scared the ever-loving shit out of me, but for some reason, my chest didn't feel tight, and my usual fight-or-flight response seemed to be napping. Which was confusing as hell, but also made sense at the same time.

I liked his mind. And his sexy as fuck body. And the way he could always make me laugh my ass off with effortless, witty sarcasm. And good God, his sexy smiles and sexy smirks—two markedly different things—and his ability to be charming even in the most stressful of times.

I was a sucker for it—all of him. I wanted to lick every inch of him and everything that made him the man I couldn't seem to resist like a motherfucking Charms Blow Pop.

But minus the gum in the middle. Just his perfect penis, preferably inside of me…

Yeah. I liked everything about Scott Shepard.

Do I just like him, though? Or is it something more than that? I thought to myself as I grabbed some plates and wineglasses from the cabinet.

Scott didn't give me any time to delve into that thought process any further. He was always active, fluttering around or twirling my hair or tapping a finger on my leg. It was like he had all of this excess energy when he wasn't on the emergency room floor, but he was an expert in expelling it and being at ease simultaneously. I'd never seen someone manage such a complicated combination so flawlessly before. Tonight was no different.

He spanked my ass playfully, and I turned to find him standing behind me with a flirtatious grin stamped across his mouth.

"What was that for?"

He shrugged. "I blame the shorts."

"Really?" A firm hand went to my hip. "And what exactly did my shorts do?"

"They are driving me fucking crazy," he said and moved toward me in three smooth strides. He wrapped his arms around my waist and lifted me onto the kitchen counter with ease. "I can't stop thinking about what is underneath this skimpy as fuck material." He pushed my thighs apart and eased his body in between them. And with one determined index finger, he ran a smooth line up my calf to my knee until he reached my upper thigh.

I bit back a moan as his finger danced across my skin, just below the material of my shorts.

Holy moly, that feels good…

"What's underneath, Low?" he whispered as he slid his finger underneath my shorts. "Am I going to find a bare cunt?"

Yes. Yes. Yes.

"Maybe," I said on a half moan, half whimper.

His gaze stayed locked with mine as his finger continued the trail beneath my shorts until it reached the apex of my thighs. He brushed through my arousal and let out a little *tsk tsk* from his lips.

"I think someone is a little bit of a liar. This is a bare *and* wet little cunt," he said with a wicked grin as he slid that persistent finger inside of me.

In and out, in and out, he went, and I moaned out loud.

"Guess what we're going to do right now?" he asked and

increased the rhythm of his finger while his thumb joined the pleasure party and rubbed smooth circles against my clit.

Fucking hell. That's good.

"W-what?" I whimpered.

"We're going to eat pizza."

"Huh?"

"Yep," he said and pressed a smacking kiss to my lips. His hand was out of my shorts a second later.

What the fuck?

Had he really just gotten me all riled up so that we could eat pizza?

My eyes popped wide open. "Are you serious?"

He nodded and leaned forward to brush his mouth across my lips and then my jaw until he stopped at my ear. "I'm going to eat pizza for dinner, and then, I'm going to have this delicious little cunt for dessert," he whispered, and his warm breath brushing across my neck pebbled my hypersensitive skin. "Sound good?"

Pizza for dinner and orgasms for dessert? I thought it over for all of two seconds and decided that I could live with that game plan. But no doubt, I'd make sure dinner lasted no longer than ten minutes, tops.

"Sounds good," I agreed and hopped off the counter. I grabbed the pizza and plates and bottle of wine off the counter and marched into the living room as quickly as I possibly could, leaving Scott behind in the kitchen with an amused smirk on his lips.

"In a rush?" he asked as he sat down beside me on the couch.

"You know my favorite part of a meal is always dessert."

"Is that so?"

"Yep," I said and plopped two slices of pizza onto plates. I handed one to Scott and grinned. "Eat up, buddy. You've only got ten minutes."

"You're bossy," he said through a laugh and took the slice of pizza into his hands.

"No," I corrected. *"I'm horny.* And when someone is a fucking tease and makes me horny and then doesn't do anything about it, I get bossy."

He grinned. "A fucking tease?"

"Yep. You're a fucking tease."

"You should talk," he retorted. "No bra. No panties. The shortest fucking pair of shorts I've ever seen. You might as well be walking around here naked."

"Would we have boned on the kitchen counter if I would've been naked?" I asked with far too much hope in my voice. I also made a mental note to answer the door naked the next time Scott came over.

He grinned but didn't offer a response.

"Would we have?" I asked again, but he just laughed it off. "You're not going to tell me?"

"Gentlemen don't kiss and tell."

"Pfft," I scoffed. "That saying doesn't even apply to this situation."

"Eat your dinner, Low," he demanded. "I'm getting hungry for dessert."

He didn't have to tell me twice.

I shoved a bite of pizza into my mouth and got to work.

"Attagirl," he teased, and I rolled my eyes.

"Don't get too cocky," I retorted as I picked up the remote for the television. "I'm only doing it because I'm greedy and selfish when it comes to orgasms."

He smirked. "Good God, I love that greedy little cunt of yours."

"Prove it," I mocked, flipping haphazardly through the channels. Before Scott could offer a retort, his face stared back at us on the television. It was a news station's recap of the press conference Scott had attended earlier in the day to receive an award from the mayor.

"Hey, look! You're on TV!" I stated the obvious, and he groaned around a mouthful of pepperoni and cheese.

"Oh God. Please, turn it off."

"Hell no." I grinned. "It's your big, shining moment! And since I didn't get to cover it live, it's my second-best option. We're watching it, buddy."

"There is nothing big or shining about this moment," he muttered.

And while Scott continued groaning his annoyance, I avidly watched his face on screen. *God, he's handsome. And mine.*

Whoa. Whoa. Whoa. And mine?

God, my thoughts sounded a bit territorial, like I was two seconds away from pissing a circle around him or something.

It's because you l-o-v-e him...

"Fuck, here's the worst part of the whole thing," he announced and subsequently pulled my attention back to the present. I glanced at him in confusion.

"You mean besides the fact that Brent just keeps talking about how amazing he is?"

"Yep," he said with a sigh. "Even worse than that."

I turned my attention back to the television, and that's when the words, "Can't fucking wait," left Scott's lips. Thanks to regulations, they'd bleeped out the fucking part, but yeah, it was more than apparent what he'd said before the edit.

Holy hell, he'd dropped the f-bomb at a press conference with the mayor!

Completely losing it, I snorted and coughed on my own phlegm as I tried to get control of my laughter. "You...cursed...on...stage... with the mayor." Scott rolled his eyes. "At a press conference!" My voice turned nearly shrill. "While you were mic'ed!"

"Yeah, yeah, laugh it up. And here I thought receiving an award couldn't end in bad press. Plus, I'm now an official consultant to *the mayor*. Your fucking ex, of all people. I even have to go to a big municipal event next week."

Any and all waning laughter was renewed tenfold. I wasn't exactly comfortable with all the togetherness he'd be spending with Brent, but holy hell, his own discomfort was amusing.

Suddenly, Scott set his plate on the coffee table and hooked his hands on the line of my jaw. "Go with me."

That made me stop laughing. "What?"

"To the event. Please?"

"Are you nuts?"

"Please?" he asked again. "I want you by my side, Harlow. Nothing feels right without you anymore."

I hated the idea of spending an evening in such proximity to Brent, but Jesus Christ, how could I say no to that?

"Okay."

CHAPTER *twenty-eight*

"SCOTT!"

"Dr. Erotic!"

"Over here, Scott!"

Several paparazzi yelled as I stepped out of the town car I'd hired for the night, buttoned my suit jacket, and turned to hold a hand out for Harlow.

But if I'd thought they were loud or persistent before her fingers—with bright red manicured nails done special for the occasion—settled into the hollow of mine, I was a fucking idiot.

The quiet roar of paparazzi wind turned into a tornado in the span of an instant.

Harlow paused on her exit, but I squeezed her hand affectionately in both support and apology, and she started moving again.

She hadn't told anyone about tonight, not even her boss. I'd wondered to myself if that was a good move for her career, but after the talk we'd had about her life and medical school, it was pretty clear *Gossip* and Harlow Paige weren't a match made in celebrity heaven.

She wanted more out of life, and I wanted it for her. I just had to figure out how to be supportive without pressuring her. Things like emotional support and walking a balanced line for the benefit of someone else weren't exactly my forte.

With her safely to her feet and her long, shimmering silver gown out of the way, I shut the door on the car and took her hand again to step forward. When I linked our hands, interlacing our fingers, and the two of us stepped up onto the curb together, side by side, so obviously a couple in the eyes of the media, everything went white.

At first, I thought maybe I was dying—the moment was surreal—but as Harlow's hand clenched harder and harder in mine, tethering me to reality and her, I knew it was just the cloud of camera flashes assailing us from every angle.

"Scott! Who's your date?"

"Dr. Erotic! Have you finally met your match?"

"What's your name, sweetheart?"

At first, the questions were clear. But after several moments, the shouting started to blend together, and I couldn't have answered even if I'd wanted to.

Hands grabbed at my shoulder, and I tensed in response until I realized some of the mayor's security had noticed the uproar and were coming to assist us.

Up and through the crowd, they guided us without trouble as Harlow did her best to shield her face in an attempt to maintain her eyesight.

"Holy shit," she muttered the moment the doors shut behind us, closing us off to their grubbing questions and never-ending digital assault. "I think I may have underestimated your popularity."

I laughed out loud, feeling all of the anxiety that had built in my chest as a result of the mayhem release. Turning toward her with ease, I put a hand to her jaw and touched her lips to my own. Flashes once again lit up the night behind us.

I rested my forehead against hers. "I guess those are glass doors, huh?"

"Seems like it."

"Sorry," I apologized. I expected her to smart off, to give me some flippant response that I would no doubt love. But she didn't. Instead, she grabbed my hand and gave it a gentle squeeze, her face softening as she did.

"It's okay."

"Hi, Scott," Brent called from the top of the stairs, completely fucking ruining our moment.

As I pulled away from Harlow and looked up to meet his gaze, it was more than obvious he was enjoying it. A smug smile lined not only his mouth but his eyes, and he held on to the lapel of his suit jacket like he was the ruler of the land. Which, I guessed, in a sense, he was.

"Mr. Mayor," I murmured back as Harlow's eyes moved slowly from the floor, up the stairs, and finally landed on the man standing a full floor above us.

"Hey, LoLo."

She sighed, obviously put out by the nickname, and I didn't bother to hide my smile.

"Brent."

A thrill ran up the length of my spine when she literally gave him no more attention than that one fraction of a moment.

Eyes back to mine, she held them tight as she whispered for my ears only, "Ready to get this over with?"

I shook my head, and her face wrinkled. "No?"

"No," I confirmed. "I'm gonna enjoy a night out with the woman I couldn't help but chase."

"Scott," she whispered.

"Come on."

Hand in hand, we climbed the stairs, going a nice slow speed that she could handle in her spindle heels and long knockout of a dress, and by the time we got to the top, the mayor was gone. Back inside, I presumed, to his party and people, but the where didn't really matter. Neither did the why. But the gasp Harlow made when she looked up to make the same discovery made my whole night. Apparently, it wasn't like the overlord to give up so easily.

"I've heard of outrunning people," I teased her. "But being too slow for them is a new one."

"Shut up."

Her lips tasted like sweet surprise when mine landed against them.

One nip turned into two, and by the time I was satisfied, our tongues had danced an entire song's worth of notes. "You look beautiful tonight," I whispered to her, admitting, "You look beautiful always, actually. But tonight, when I look at you, I swear to God, I don't even know my own name."

She smirked and lifted her thumb to rub some lingering lipstick off of my face. "Don't worry, Dr. Erotic. I know it just fine."

"Good Christ, this thing is boring," Harlow whispered as another speaker, some other official for the city of New York, blathered on about whatever these people were pretending to care about at the moment.

"What did you expect? Fireworks?"

"No!" she snapped in a whisper, putting a finger to my lips to shut me up. "But some kind of drama or intrigue wouldn't be amiss. This is politics, for fuck's sake. Where's Kerry Washington with a *Scandal*?"

"Probably working behind the scenes to cover it up."

"You know what I mean. I thought there would be something to make fun of."

"Sorry," I told her, leaning forward to give her a kiss on the cheek. "I'll try to drum up a story when we leave here."

She laughed, albeit quietly since someone was still up there giving a speech, but as her eyes fluttered away from mine and caught on something over my shoulder, it all but dried up.

"Why is the chick at Brent's table looking at me like I'm the Antichrist?"

I took a quick peek over my shoulder to confirm my suspicions, but unfortunately, I already knew who it was.

Pam.

I sighed, and Harlow's eyebrows pulled together.

"Scott?"

"Well, hell. I didn't really want to get into this here, but you asked for drama."

"What drama?" she asked, her voice deepening in a way that suggested she already knew.

I shrugged.

"Oh, Scott. Not that chick. Come on. She's got the eyes."

"The eyes?"

"The crazy eyes. You don't bone and bounce on the ones with crazy eyes. I would have thought a man with your experience would know this."

"I knew," I admitted.

"Then why did you do it?"

"Well…" Something occurred to me suddenly. "Wait…you know this all occurred before you, right?"

She rolled her eyes. "Yes. I may not be prone to relationships, but between your job and the fact that you've basically been stalking me since *Kinky Boots*, you've been too busy to fit in a good-time fuck with crazy eyes over there. Believe me, I can tell that since you've been all about me, you've been *all* about me.

"God, Low—"

"Focus, Scott!" she snapped softly, and I smiled.

I am so fucking hooked.

"Okay… Okay…" I relented. "For the record, my initial plan was not to sleep with her. That just kind of happened."

She quirked a brow. "What was the plan, then?"

"Clearly, it was to win her over with my irresistible charm," I said with a wink, and Harlow giggled. "To make a long story short, even though I knew she had the crazy eyes, I also knew she had access to the mayor. Which I needed in the name of getting our public health policies changed."

"Crazy eyes happened because of Brent?"

I rolled my eyes at her clearly personal knowledge of him. "Obviously, I'd have slept with you to get close to him if I'd known that was an option."

She wrinkled her nose. "Gross."

"Nothing we do together is gross."

She shook her head with a smile, but with one last glance over my shoulder, it was like Pam didn't exist anymore. She could stare at us all night for all I cared.

"Speaking of that…do you think we can leave soon?" Harlow asked, and anticipation jumped in my stomach.

Even better. In two minutes, Pam wouldn't even have us as an option to look at.

"I thought you'd never ask."

CHAPTER *twenty-nine*

Harlow

"**T**HIRSTY?" SCOTT ASKED AS WE WALKED INSIDE OF HIS APARTMENT.

He shrugged off his suit jacket and hung it on one of the barstools by the kitchen island, and, enthralled by the sinewy bulges of his muscles through his dress shirt, I had to shake off the image of ripping it off myself.

We'd left the party on the pretense of sex, but I knew it didn't always have to be only about that. That was the whole point of him telling me to be open-minded about what we were to one another.

I shrugged. "Uh…maybe a little bit."

We'd left the big municipal party before dessert—and probably before Brent's busty assistant could find a way to telepathically light me on fire with her crazy eyes.

It'd come as a little bit of a shock that Scott had slept with her, and yeah, it did sting a little as well. But I understood. Scott wasn't an angel, and he certainly hadn't been celibate before me. His past was his past, just like my past was my past. And Lord knew my past was designed to stay there. Brent had had more than enough stage time at the event tonight; the last thing we needed was to figuratively bring him home with us, too.

What Scott and I were now was still a bit of a mystery to me, though. We'd agreed to be open-minded. And we'd also agreed not to see or sleep with other people.

But did that mean that we were in a relationship?

I had no clue.

Pretty sure the ball's in your court, sister, my subconscious taunted me. *Scott was pulling for a full-blown relationship weeks ago.*

Did I want him to be my boyfriend?

I waited for my body's normal volatile reaction to the word, but nothing came. Not the urge to run or sweaty hands or a violently pounding heartbeat. *Nothing.*

"A glass of wine?" he offered, completely unaware of my mental come to Jesus moment. "Champagne?"

I scrunched my nose at both options. Between the two glasses of champagne I'd had with hors d'oeuvres and the additional glass of wine during dinner, I was done boozing. "How about something less alcoholic?" I asked and leaned a hip against the kitchen counter.

He chuckled and opened his fridge to rummage through its contents. I, of course, took that time to check out his tight and toned ass. *Hot damn, he has a nice ass.* Firm and round with just the right symmetry.

"Stop staring at my ass," he said, his eyes still fixated on the inside of his fridge.

What's he got, eyes in the back of his head?

"I'm not staring at your ass," I denied without bothering to actually stop.

I wanted to grip it with both hands. Maybe even spank it. Hell, taking a big, hearty bite out of it sounded nice.

"Liar," he accused with a grin over his shoulder. I fought the urge to giggle.

"It's not my fault. You're the one who's flaunting the goods."

While he pulled out the drink options and set them on his counter,

230 · max monroe

he shook his ass rhythmically and started singing "Hips Don't Lie" like he was Shakira himself. I couldn't hold back my laughter after that. Flipping imaginary hair from shoulder to shoulder, he swayed and posed and fucking flaunted like he was one of the lead dancers in the music video.

Good Lord, not only was Scott sexy as fuck, he was endearingly charming and had a sense of humor like no one else. It felt like he was the only man I saw anymore.

Because you're in love with him.

At that very moment, my heart attempted its best impression of an Olympic gymnast inside of my chest. Its pounding rhythm felt two seconds away from vaulting directly out of my body and onto the floor.

Holy hell. I was in love with Scott?

The anniversary party cheers. It had to be. *No curse, my asshole.*

"What'll it be?" he asked and gestured toward the counter full of drinks. When his eyes met mine, he tilted his head to the side in concern. "Are you okay?"

No! I'm not fucking okay! I'm not supposed to fall in love, goddammit! Hell, I'm even okay with the boyfriend part! But, love? LOVE? Jesus Christ, what is happening?

"Uh-huh," I said through the dryness in my throat, ironically parched for the first time since he'd offered me a drink. The concern on his face never waned.

"Are you sure?" he asked and moved toward me to put a gentle hand to my cheek. "You don't look okay. Do you feel sick?"

Of course, I'm not okay! You put some kind of voodoo spell on me, and now I'm in fucking love with you!

I cleared my throat with a little ahem and shook my head in response. "I'm just a little tired. Otherwise, I'm perfectly fine."

"Are you still thirsty for something a little less alcoholic?" he questioned with a soft smile.

Drinks! Yes, let's talk about drinks. Drinks are neutral. Drinks are refreshing. Drinks don't give me panic attacks because I'm in love with them.

I nodded. "What are my options?"

"Well," he started and dramatically gestured toward the drink options on the counter like he was selling vacuums and food dehydrators on the Home Shopping Network. "We have a fabulous selection of orange juice, whole milk, water, iced tea, or Coca-Cola."

"Do you have Nesquik?"

"Nesquik?" he asked in confusion. "What's a Nesquik?"

"*What?*" I blinked three times. "You don't know what Nesquik is?" I questioned in disbelief.

"Uh…is that bad?"

"It's like someone admitting they don't know what a Twinkie is."

"I know what a fucking Twinkie is."

Hmm… A Twinkie did sound good right about now…and safe. I can't fall in love with a Twinkie. Well, I guess it depends on the Twinkie…

"Do you have any?"

He quirked a brow in my direction. "Twinkies?"

"No, prune juice. I'm extremely constipated," I teased, and he laughed. "Yes, Twinkies. Do you have any?"

"How did we go from Nesquik to Twinkies?"

"First of all, we haven't left the Nesquik," I clarified with a serious expression. "It's basically the powder form of Hershey's syrup, and it's fucking delicious. If you don't like it, I'll have to revoke any and all of your sex privileges. And secondly, do you have any Twinkies or Nesquik so that I can make chocolate milk, or not?"

He grinned. "You want chocolate milk and Twinkies?"

"Uh… *Yeah.*"

"Let me get this straight," he started with an amused grin. "We just left an event that served the most pretentious five-course meal, along with some of the most expensive alcohol I've ever drunk, and your ideal way to end the evening is with chocolate milk and Twinkies? So much so that you'll refuse to ever sleep with me again if I don't agree with and enable your addiction. Am I hearing this correctly?"

"Yep," I answered without hesitation, and before I could add the sarcastic comment that was on the tip of my tongue, Scott wrapped his arms around my waist and pulled my body against his. He took my mouth in a deep, intense kiss. While his tongue slipped past my lips and danced with mine, his hands skimmed up the material of my evening gown until they reached the bared skin of my back.

I moaned into his mouth, and my body all but melted into his.

This kiss was different. It wasn't just foreplay or the physical act of kissing itself. It was deeper. It was that four-letter word I'd once convinced myself I'd never let myself feel again. And deep down, I knew that little but powerful four-letter word had made a reappearance in my thoughts for a reason—I was in love with Scott.

"God, Low." His teeth nipped at my bottom lip. "I'm fucking crazy about you," he whispered against my mouth before taking the kiss deeper.

With the milk and juice and whatever the fuck else he'd gotten out of the fridge forgotten, our kiss turned urgent. "I need you," I whimpered against his lips. "I need you so bad, Scott."

Funnily enough, despite my pleas for it, this *still* wasn't about sex.

"I need you, too, Low." He leaned back, and his gaze locked with mine. "More than just right now or tomorrow or next week or next month. I *need* you. Always."

God, I felt the same way. I couldn't picture a time in my future when I wouldn't need Scott. Somehow, someway, he'd become a permanent fixture in my life, and I didn't want that to change.

"Me too," I whispered back.

We tumbled into his bedroom in a fit of limbs and lips, and the instant he kicked the door shut, every pretense dropped. The façade I showed the world melted away, and all I wanted was to *feel* him, everywhere and all at once.

Twilight and shadow covered the walls and floor, and Scott stood close enough that I felt enveloped by his musky scent. Without hesitation, and with only the soft inhales and exhales of our breaths peppering the otherwise silent air, he wrapped his arms around my back. In one gentle tug and turn, my covered breasts pressed deliciously against the soft material of his dress shirt.

His right hand dropped to my thigh, and he pulled up my dress enough to reach my already aching skin. I couldn't have moved even if I tried, as if his fingers had short-circuited my mind in the best possible way as they slid up the skin of my thigh and left trembles in their wake.

"God, I'm addicted to you," he whispered, and with two steps back, we toppled onto his bed, his eyes searching mine the entire time.

"Ditto, Doc." I smiled and kissed him again. With my lips, I felt his mouth stretching wider than it should, fighting between grinning and kissing, and I knew mine was most likely doing the same.

We'd done this so many times—kissing, foreplay, *sex*—and somehow, every time, it just kept getting better.

Because this is love.

With our gazes locked, his hand moved down my cheekbones to my lips. "You're so beautiful, Low," he whispered, but he didn't give me time to respond. Between one breath and the next, his mouth was on mine and we were kissing again. Good God, we were kissing—our mouths locked, our lips danced, and our tongues took hungry licks from one another.

Every kiss we shared had this raw intensity—breathing fast, heart rates faster, desperate moans releasing from both of our lungs.

I was addicted to him, too. And I was lost in him. And, even better, found in him.

I was exactly where I should be.

And before I knew how it happened, we were naked and our skin was moving softly against each other, not having sex, but just touching, just *feeling*.

We locked eyes for a moment, only long enough for us to really see each other, and then he was kissing from my toes upward— *slowly, so slowly*—and his hands were on my legs, always just a little higher than his kisses.

Scott's lips and fingers might as well have been electric—every touch, every kiss tingling my skin into a frenzy of static. My back arched in anticipation, knowing where his fingers and lips would soon reach, and my head rocked back against the pillow when he did. I moaned out loud and his fingers slid inside of me from below while he took my mouth in another uninhibited kiss.

"Now, Scott. I need you inside of me," I whimpered against his mouth, and he groaned.

Without breaking our connection, he grabbed a condom from the nightstand and put it on with practiced efficiency. And then he was sliding inside of me, changing my breathing with every thrust, hearing my moans timed to his body.

Fuck, it felt so good. *He* felt so good. God, our bodies fit together as if we were made just for this, to fall into one another, to feel this natural rhythm.

"It's never enough," he panted into my ear. "When it comes to you, I always want more. I'll never stop wanting more."

"Me too," I answered, and my words were followed by a moan as he pushed himself deeper.

His eyes searched mine, and then, he just said it. Out loud and while we were still intimately connected, he said what I'd already been thinking. "I'm in love with you, Harlow."

And I didn't fight it this time. I didn't hold back.

"Me too," I whispered. "I'm in love with you too."

CHAPTER *thirty*

I'D BEEN A WEEK SINCE HARLOW AND I WERE SPLASHED ACROSS THE FRONT PAGE of every gossip column in Manhattan as an item—except for hers—and a week and one day since we'd told each other we were in love. Obviously, it hadn't taken a ton of research for the paparazzi at the municipal event to find out who Harlow was. And to say her boss was unhappy that Harlow hadn't broken an exclusive on her own fucking relationship was an understatement.

And, maybe even more obviously—and simultaneously surprisingly—I was deliriously happy. Me. Happy. In a relationship. Go figure.

Harlow's boss had given her until today to come up with something just as juicy as the story of us—or better—or else.

I'd been trying to gently encourage the "or else" option, making it clear that I'd be a resource at her disposal should she decide to make another go of medical school.

It was easy for the lines to blur, though, being a doctor myself. So I was trying not to push her in any one direction without knowing it was what she truly wanted.

I'd watched her struggle to come up with something good enough to keep her job all week, and she'd texted me late last night from her apartment to tell me she'd finally come up with something.

I didn't know what it was, but knowing how stressed she'd been about it, and how good whatever she'd come up with had to be, I'd set an alert on my phone to go off as soon as her column posted.

Today in the ER had been absolutely fucking crazy with three pedestrian accidents and a stab wound, but that didn't stop me from checking to make sure the volume on my phone was turned on every chance I got.

Still on. Still nothing.

I was just putting the phone back in my pocket when the alert sounded so loudly I jumped and dropped it.

"Shit!" I cursed, picking my phone back up from the harsh hospital tile quickly and flipping it over to inspect the screen for cracks. A small one ran the entire line of the center, but I could still read all the words on the screen, and everything seemed to be in working condition, so I decided to deal with it later.

Quickly, I clicked the link in the alert that took me straight to Harlow's page on *Gossip's* website. A little thrill ran through me at the sight of my name.

Dr. Erotic or Dr. Hypnotic?

I didn't really understand the title, but Harlow had been under a lot of pressure with this one, so I decided not to hold it against her too much when I teased her later.

Scrolling down quickly to the meat of the story, I let myself fall into the article with a twinge of intimate pride coursing through me.

Dr. Scott Shepard isn't new to the *Gossip* scene, and hardly anything about him is new news.

But you should all know by now, I've got the inside scoop on

all of the details.

I smiled in excitement. I hoped she painted me as a sex god. Or, as I considered it, maybe I wanted her to say I was lame.

It might solve some of my overenthusiastic problems with outside interest. *Cough, Pam, Cough.*

They. Are. Horrifying.

He may seem like a charming guy next door, but illusion is a powerful thing.

Entitled and used to getting what he wants, Dr. Erotic is every female's worst nightmare.

The closer you get, the more he reveals, and if your answer isn't yes, that won't stop him.

Look out, ladies. If you don't give Dr. Erotic what he wants when he asks for it, he might just take it.

What the fuck? She basically implied I'm a sex offender.

Frantic, I read on, scrolling painfully through pages and pages of a bitter diatribe about how awful I was in every sense of the word. Not only was I lacking in character and trustworthiness, she spoke candidly and expressly about my propensity not to take no as an answer when it came to women and *my insatiable sexual desires,* as she put it. And, as if that weren't horrifying enough, pointed details accused me of insurance fraud and malpractice, absolutely crucifying everything I'd built as a physician.

Oh shit. Oh Jesus Christ, why would she do this to me? Why would she make this shit up? For what? A fucking byline?

I'd actually been expecting something about us, her little decree of *don't be mad at me for using you shamelessly* last night seeming playful and harmless but telling all the same.

I'd thought maybe she'd finally broken some details about our sex life, the real inside scoop on Dr. Erotic's erotic moves.

But not this. Never this.

This would fucking ruin me.

"Scott?" Deb said hesitantly from the end of the hall as I stood there shaking my head in disbelief.

"Not now, Deb," I said as gently as I could for a guy literally coming apart at the seams. I just assumed she left me to my agony until she called my name again—this time from a lot closer.

"Scott," she murmured in a barely there whisper.

I lifted my eyes to hers, but they didn't stay there long. Two security guards stood behind her. *Good news spreads fast, I see.*

"The board wants to see you," she said sympathetically. I could barely even swallow my saliva without throwing up as I succumbed to my fate.

Just like that, I knew it was over. I was going to lose everything I'd ever had, ever wanted, ever needed, in one fell swoop.

The job and the girl, both a mutilated mess.

I might have been the doctor, but this blood was on Harlow's hands.

CHAPTER *thirty-one*

AFTER A WEEK'S WORTH OF STRESS, MOSTLY BECAUSE OF STELLA RIDING MY ass over the fact that I hadn't been the one to give the personal exclusive on Dr. Erotic's new relationship with yours truly, I'd managed to write a column I was proud of. One that actually made me smile when I read it versus my normal apathetic *meh* reaction I gave most of my columns.

And it wasn't because I thought my writing was shit; it was because I wasn't passionate about any of it. Until now. Until this column. And I owed it all to one very important person—*Scott*.

With him on my mind, I grabbed my phone off my desk and typed a quick message to him.

Me: Did you read it? Tell me you read it and loved it! :)

I watched the message box like a hawk, waiting impatiently for text bubbles to appear from his side of the conversation, but it never came. And before I could call him and demand that he stop saving lives and start reading my latest column, an all too familiar voice of doom grabbed my attention.

"Great work on that article." I glanced up to find Stella standing in the doorway of my office. A proud and even slightly evil smile plastered on her face. "I didn't think you had it in you, but obviously, you did."

"You liked my column?" I questioned with a furrowed brow. This was the absolute last reaction I expected to get from her. If I was being honest, I wasn't sure if I'd still have a job at *Gossip* after she read it. She'd basically given me an ultimatum and made it more than clear that if I hadn't come up with something good, I'd be packing my shit and finding a new job.

And well, this week's column shouldn't have evoked such an enthusiastic response from her.

She nodded. "It was genius. And devious. And I have no idea how you pulled it off, but I definitely loved it. If you keep going above and beyond to bring material like that to me, you'll be promoted and writing only exclusives in no time.

"I guess I should've known there was more to that whole relationship thing with Scott, huh?" she asked with a smile that made a shiver roll up my spine. "You're not the type of woman to settle down with a man, but it appears that you are the type of woman who will do whatever it takes for her career. My favorite kind of woman, by the way," she added with a wink.

The type of woman who will do whatever it takes for her career?

I blinked three times.

What is she talking about?

I didn't even consider this job my career. It was just a fucking job that paid the bills and achieved that without giving me any sense of satisfaction or purpose. I sure as hell wouldn't do whatever it took for *Gossip*.

Something feels real fucking off right now...

The tiny hairs on my arms stood on end. I opened my mouth to ask her what in the fuck was happening, but she chimed in before I could get the words past my suddenly dry and scratchy throat.

"Great work, Harlow. And, for legality purposes, shoot me an email with your various sources for that article. We're already getting phone calls from the media," she said.

And before I could add anything to the conversation, she strode away on her stilettos, her shoes click-clacking down the hallway with every power step while I sat in my desk chair completely confused.

There was no way in hell she was talking about the column I'd written for this week.

Had she run a different column of mine? Maybe one she'd saved up from a previous week or something?

I had no idea, but it only took ten seconds for me to snap out of my trance, and pull up *Gossip's* website to find which columns had run. Dead center, on the very first page sat an unfamiliar article titled: **Dr. Erotic or Dr. Hypnotic?**

But oddly enough, my name sat in the byline. **By: Harlow Paige**

Have they retitled my piece? was my first thought, but then I realized my piece about assisting Scott in the ER for a day taking care of pediatric patients sure as fuck shouldn't have been titled that.

My column had focused around the fact that, although most of the world knew him as Dr. Erotic, his patients knew him as Dr. Shepard—a talented physician who truly cared about the health and well-being of the community. Hell, I'd even gone to great lengths to get Josie and a few of the other pediatric patients we'd seen the day I'd assisted him in the ER to answer questions about Dr. Shepard—who just happened to be unanimously voted as their favorite emergency room doctor in the city, mostly because of his funny jokes and goofy smiles.

Obviously, I'd received nothing less than adorable responses. But none of my words or the patients' answers would've worked with this garbage title.

Quickly, I clicked on the link and started to scan the words, and by the time I got three paragraphs in, I wanted to vomit.

The closer you get, the more he reveals, and if your answer isn't yes, that won't stop him. Look out, ladies. If you don't give Dr. Erotic what he wants when he asks for it, he might just take it.

What in the ever-loving fuck is this?
I didn't write this!

And horribly enough, those words weren't even the worst of it. The article continued for another ten paragraphs and was riddled with accusations including insurance fraud and sexual misconduct.

Basically, it was one giant clusterfuck of horrible and the kind of article that would literally ruin someone's life and career. And to the public, I had been the one to write it.

Oh. My. God.

Had Scott read this?

Well, he definitely isn't answering my text messages…

My stomach fell to the floor, and my chest grew tight with anxiety. I had to do something. I didn't know what, but I knew I couldn't just sit here and let an article like this exist.

With shaky hands and adrenaline coursing through my veins, I grabbed my purse, hopped out of my chair, and sprinted down the hallway like a maniac—completely unconcerned with who I was railroading past.

I had to fix this. Jesus Christ, I *had* to fix this.

Panicked, I picked up my pace to a full-out sprint, and by the time I'd reached Stella's office, I was gasping for air.

"I didn't write that!" I shouted through panting breaths.

She looked up from her desk, and her brow furrowed in puzzlement.

"I didn't write that article about Scott Shepard!"

"What?" she questioned. "What do you mean you didn't write it?"

"I didn't write it, Stella," I tried to explain through the thickness in my throat. "I don't know where that article came from, but I know those are not my words. Yes, my column was about Scott, but it wasn't this fucking mess of horrible accusations." I put my hands on my knees and took big, deep breaths.

With relaxed shoulders and a neutral mouth, Stella continued to sit in her chair—not reacting, not responding—and watched me have a mental breakdown. I wanted to strangle her.

"It was a goddamn personal interest story that showed what an amazing physician he is," I yelled. "Hell, I even had cute interviews in there from his pediatric patients!"

A pregnant pause filled the space in her office, and it felt like an eternity before she finally said, "But that article came directly from your email to my email, Harlow."

"What?" I shouted. "How is that even fucking possible?"

"I'm one hundred percent sure that you're the one who emailed me that article."

"This is completely fucked, Stella! I didn't write this. Take it off the site now!"

She frowned. "That article is the talk of the day at every news source in the city, Harlow. You should be proud of it, not feeling guilty."

"Proud of it?" I exclaimed in frustration. "That article is bullshit, Stella. All of those accusations are untrue. If anything, that article is a lawsuit for *Gossip* waiting to happen."

Her brow popped up in surprise at the word lawsuit.

I guess I'm finally speaking her fucking language.

"Wait…you really didn't write it?"

"I. Didn't. Write. It," I responded. "Those are not my words, Stella. I sent a completely different article to your email that you should've received yesterday around eight in the morning."

"But I received this column two days ago."

"I was still writing my fucking column two days ago!"

She scrutinized my steadfast gaze before muttering, "Fuck," and picking up her phone. Her finger tapped a speed dial button, and she held the receiver to her ear.

"Dave," she greeted. "I need you to look into Harlow Paige's email account. Check all outgoing messages for me over the past seventy-two hours and see if you note anything suspicious."

After a few nerve-racking moments, she glanced up at me with concern creasing the corners of her normally evil eyes.

"Really?" she asked into the receiver. "Two days ago…? Uh-huh… She says the last article about Scott Shepard wasn't from her… It came from a different IP address? Can you do some kind of search to find out…" Her words bled into a hum as my mind reeled.

Hacked. *That's what a different IP address had to mean, right?*

It was literally the only thing that made sense.

Jesus Christ. Who would do this to me? Why couldn't they just send me fictitious emails about being a Nigerian Prince and needing money?

Why ruin my reputation, and more importantly, Scott's life?

He was all I could think about in that moment. I didn't give a fuck about myself or what that article could potentially mean for my career.

I just cared about him. I loved him. I wanted the best for him. And this, well, this fucking article that had been published was the absolute worst.

Had he seen it? Was he okay?

I could only stand in her office for so long before the urge to sprint to Scott's apartment was too strong. Without another word, I turned for the hall and ran toward the elevator.

I had to get to him. I had to make this okay again.

But after sprinting across the city like a madwoman and pounding my arrival against the door to his apartment with my fist, when the door opened, what I was greeted with on the other side made it very clear that everything was the opposite of okay.

It was all completely fucked.

CHAPTER *thirty-two*

AS THE DETECTIVE SWUNG OPEN THE DOOR OF MY APARTMENT, TIME STOOD still and Harlow stood on the other side. Drenched in fresh tears and wild with sweat and anguish, she bounced her eyes off of the detective in horror, only to land on the two uniformed officers standing with me.

Three hours since the article had made its splash in the shark-infested waters of New York City, and my entire life had been dismantled.

I'd met with the board immediately, and while they'd been professionally cautious and respectful, I'd been suspended pending an investigation. They were *keeping it in-house* they'd said, waiting for any allegations from victims to come forward and looking through each and every one of my case files for signs of malpractice before making permanent changes to my position—aka: firing me for fucking forever.

Victims.

Chaos tortured my mind better than any dripping water ever

246 · max monroe

could. If ever there was a time to be clearheaded, I'd have thought this was it. But I couldn't seem to hold on to a single thought long enough to analyze it for fucking anything.

After the meeting with the board, I'd done my best to keep my head high and my mouth closed as I gathered my belongings and left the premises—escorted by security, of course—of a building I'd called home for the last ten years. Sure, I had an actual apartment—I was standing in it—but I'd seen more, done more, fucking grown more in that hospital than anywhere else in my life. Ten years of one-hundred-hour-plus weeks—gone.

I felt like I was trapped underwater, a clog in my ears making everything in the room sound muddled and distorted. I could see the detective's lips moving in front of me, but I couldn't make out a goddamn word.

"Scott," he said again, his voice gentle, if you can believe that. "Let's just go down to the station and talk, okay? You're not arrested at this point. We just can't ignore this public of an allegation without looking into it."

I nodded. Or, at least, I think I did.

But as I stepped forward to gather what I needed, Harlow's raging voice finally broke through the haze.

"No! No, listen to me!"

I looked over the detective's shoulder to see her standing just inside of my apartment, arguing with the two uniformed officers.

"You don't understand, okay? My name is Harlow Paige. I'm his girlfriend, and yes, my name is on the article, but I didn't write that. I'd never write that!"

"Ma'am, you need to calm down, okay?"

"I can't calm down!"

Even though she was responsible for all of this, something inside my heart apparently hadn't gotten the memo yet and sought to comfort her.

"Harlow, it's okay. They're just questioning me. Just calm down so you don't get in trouble too."

A single, beaded tear trailed down her cheek when I finished speaking, her chest rising and falling like she'd run a marathon.

"I didn't write that, Scott," she whispered, almost so quiet I couldn't hear her. "I don't know what happened, but I didn't write that. I would never write that."

I just shook my head, confused and frustrated and so fucking tired, more tired than I'd ever been in my life.

I didn't have it in me to answer her, to address her directly again, and I didn't have the time. Detective Santos had been patient with me up until now, but the strained lines of his face said he was done with this scene.

I could either come peacefully to the station with him now for questioning, or things would get uglier.

Walking calmly to the table at the side of my entryway, I reached for my keys and wallet, settled them into my pockets, and looked back to the detective. "I'm ready."

I wasn't sure what state of mind I'd reached that I was this calm, but everything just felt definite. Harlow, despite her obvious regret, had written something about me that, in the blink of an eye, changed the landscape of my life. I was going to lose my job, despite my innocence, because no matter what, the publicity from this shitstorm would never be wholly positive again.

And now, for the first time in my life, I was headed to the police station to be questioned for serious crimes. Even through rowdy dealings and a partying lifestyle, I'd never been here before. Internally, I laughed sardonically at the thought that settling down was what had actually gotten me into real trouble.

The officers held Harlow out of the way, and I did my best not to look her in the eyes. I was holding it together pretty well, but just one peek into her stormy green irises and I'd be done for.

"No," she muttered, watching as I walked to my door with the detective and stepped through it. "No, no! This is all wrong! You can't take him!"

I clenched my teeth as the throaty scream of her voice turned raw.

"Nooo! He didn't do anything! He's a good person," she cried, and just like that, after all of my effort, I broke. The fabric of my shirt brushed my chin as I turned to look over my shoulder.

The two officers held her by the arms, mostly for her own protection, from what I could see. Her body slumped, and her head hung to the ground in torment.

The sight destroyed me.

Suddenly, almost as if she sensed me, her gaze lifted violently to mine and captured it. Her willing hostage, I watched as she lost control of every ounce of decorum she had left.

"Scott! Scott!" she yelled, the fresh glow of her normally tanned skin turning mottled red with the effort. I tried in vain to look away, but whether I liked it or not, she'd taken me captive—mind, soul, body. It was all apparently hers to command.

"I didn't write that! I didn't, I swear! Scott, you have to believe me! *Scott!*"

She was either the world's best liar or…

My heart shattered. Try as I might, I couldn't come up with another option. My problems were tangible. Her explanation wasn't.

CHAPTER *thirty-three*

Harlow

"**M**ISS, YOU NEED TO LEAVE," THE OFFICER SAID TO ME. "WE HAVE TO LOCK up Mr. Shepard's apartment."

I looked up from my defeated spot on the floor, following the lines of his black shoes to his black pants to his badge until I met his neutral gaze and just stared at him or through him or at nothing at all. I wasn't even sure.

My world focus had tunneled to misery. In the blink of an eye, I felt like my entire life had changed. I'd gone from on top of the world—*in a loving and happy relationship with everything to look forward to*—to the scary, darkened depths of hell.

And that was just me. Not Scott. *No.* He was in a worse place than hell. He'd been accused of some of the most horrendous things inside of an article with my fucking name on it, and subsequently, taken into custody for questioning. To an outsider, it looked like I'd accused my boyfriend of charges that spanned the gamut—some of the worst being sexual misconduct and insurance fraud.

What a fucking mess.

Everything had fallen apart, and the cruelest part of all was that I didn't understand the why or the how. Why would someone do something like this to Scott? And more importantly, *who* would do something like this?

Whomever it was, I hated them. They'd ruined his career, his fucking life—under the guise of my name—and because of that, they'd ruined us. I'd tried to tell him that I hadn't written that column, but the uncertainty in his eyes said more than his words could. He was torn, and from the looks of it, he didn't know what or whom to believe—including me.

Even though it hurt like a motherfucker, I couldn't blame him. I mean, my name was on that column. I'd told him I was writing a column about him. And the column had even come from my goddamn email! It all looked really fucking bad, and everything pointed directly to me.

It looked like I'd ruined his life, and that I'd done it consciously and without any regard for him or his feelings. Like I'd put my joke of a career as a gossip columnist before him.

Fuck.

A quiet sob wracked my body and when visions of Scott being escorted out by the police filled my head, what should have been fresh tears dripping from my eyes came out as nothing. I'd cried more in the past two hours than I'd probably cried my whole life, and it showed. I'd literally run out of tears.

"Miss?" the officer addressed me again. "Is there anyone you can call to come get you?"

There was probably someone I could call, but I didn't want to. I didn't want to see anyone or talk to anyone. I just wanted to go to bed and make this day disappear.

"Miss?" he urged again, and I shook my head.

"No. There's no one," I said and slowly got to my feet. "I'll be fine. I'm leaving."

"Are you sure?" he asked and I nodded.

With my head down and my shoulders sagging forward, I walked toward the elevator. I didn't know where I was going, but I knew I needed to get the fuck out of Scott's apartment or else the police were going to end up escorting me out, too.

Plus, I was probably the last person he wanted to see greeting him at the door when he got home.

If he even gets to come back home…

Fuck. What if they kept him in custody? What if he got charged for those false accusations?

Another sob wracked my body, and it took all of my strength to move on to the elevator and hit the button for the lobby. Once the doors shut, I let my head fall back against the wall with a quiet thud and sighed.

I had to focus on something else besides breaking down. Now was not the time to lose myself to my emotions. I owed at least that much to Scott.

As the elevator doors opened, my eyes were assaulted with the flashes of cameras. Outside of the lobby doors of Scott's apartment stood what felt like a hundred paparazzi snapping pictures and ready to pounce on anyone who left his building.

God, this was bad.

I took a deep breath, and with a hand covering my eyes, I walked outside and faced the media music. Immediately, voices called my name from every direction while the flash and click of cameras filled the air.

"Harlow! It's Harlow Paige!"

"Harlow, over here!"

"Why did you write the article?"

"Did you fake your relationship with Scott?"

I wanted to engage. I wanted to respond. I wanted to tell every single one of these reporters to fuck off. But I knew enough about the media to understand that, although it was tempting as hell, this was not the time or place to issue a statement unless I wanted my words misconstrued and taken out of context.

The only right way to handle this situation was to keep my

mouth shut, my head down, and get the fuck out of there.

But that still didn't stop them from trying to bait me with questions that would strike a nerve.

"Are the accusations true?"

"Is Dr. Shepard a rapist?"

"Did he ever do anything sexually inappropriate with you?"

"Are you going to testify that he raped you?"

Holy fucking shit. Rape? Was this a goddamn joke?

Bile rose in my stomach, and I did my best to navigate through the mess of photographers and news reporters until I was able to hail a cab and slide inside to the safety of the back seat.

"Where to?" the cabbie asked once I shut the door, and I stared at him in the rearview mirror.

"Just… Just get me the hell out of here, please. Drive around until I can think straight."

He nodded, and I sagged into the leather seat.

I didn't know where I was going, but I knew I had to come up with some kind of plan. It was times like these that I wished I had friends in high places.

You do…well, sorta… You have an ex in a high place…

Brent.

Fuck, was I really that desperate to go to him for help?

I scrubbed a hand down my face and hated that my gut response was, *Yes, I am that desperate,* but found myself directing the cabbie toward Brent's office anyway. "City Hall, please," I instructed.

"You got it."

Fucking hell.

Thirty minutes later, I stood outside of Brent's office, at the reception area, where Pam Lockhead—his assistant and the woman who apparently wouldn't give me any other reaction but disdain—stared down at me with narrowed eyes.

I'd already had this argument for five minutes with the receptionist herself, but when I wouldn't give up, she'd made a call to Pam.

"Can I help you?"

"I would like to see the mayor."

She scoffed. "The mayor is a busy man. You have to actually schedule a meeting with him in advance."

Apparently, her assignment was to *handle* me.

"Pam, right?" I asked, and she nodded.

"I used to be a good friend of his, and I just need to speak with him briefly. It's a bit of an emergency."

With her face pinched together like she'd eaten a lemon and her shoulders stiff and rigid, the woman all but bristled in irritation at my words. "Oh, I know you used to be friends, *Harlow*," she retorted. "More than friends, actually."

I furrowed my brow at her words. I honestly had no idea why that was even relevant to the situation. "All right, well…" I started and tried to find a new game plan that didn't require access through this awful woman. "Could you at least let him know that I'm here and I would like to speak with him?"

"I could, but I'm not."

"Uh…"

"Have a nice day," she said and gestured for me to leave through the reception area exit doors, but I shook my head. I hadn't come this far, given in so easily to this impulse, to give up now.

"Yeah. No. This isn't going to work," I denied, and she rolled her eyes.

"I think it's time for you to leave. Or, if you'd like, I can have security escort you out."

Jesus. This fucking woman. She was a witch, who I was pretty sure had breast implants, but that was neither here nor there. I didn't have time to waste arguing with her. I needed to find a way into Brent's office, and I needed to do it now.

Would it be considered assault if I tackled her to the ground before running inside of Brent's office?

Did it really matter at this point?

I mean, my boyfriend had basically been accused of rape in a column that had my name on it. What else did I have to lose?

Nothing.

I stared at her and she stared back at me, and just before I started to rush toward her, Brent's voice was behind me. "Harlow?"

Thank fucking God.

I honestly never thought I'd be happy for his presence, but I'd also never thought someone would write a fake, blasphemous, fucking terrible column about *my* boyfriend under *my* goddamn name and it would get posted.

I turned around and met his eyes. "I need your help," I blurted out.

"I was just getting ready to escort Miss Paige out, Mr. Mayor," Pam chimed in. "I told her that your schedule is too full today for an appointment, but that I would schedule her in for sometime next week."

God, she was a piece of work. And a fucking liar.

"I need your help now," I said, and he nodded.

"Okay." He looked at Pam. "Reschedule my next meeting."

"But…but…" she stuttered over her words.

"Clear it, Pam," he demanded. Her face paled, but with no other choice, she nodded her acceptance and walked toward her desk. `

He gestured me toward his office and shut the door behind us. "Take a seat," he directed, shrugging out of his suit jacket before sitting down in the big leather chair behind his mahogany monstrosity of a desk.

"What can I help you with, LoLo?"

I fought the urge to cringe and focused on the task at hand. "It's Dr. Shepard," I started. "Someone wrote a column under my name, and it was posted this morning. Everything in it is false."

Brent stared back at me without anything but neutral, curious eyes. "If you didn't write it, how'd it get posted under your name?"

"I don't have proof yet," I answered honestly. "But I know someone hacked my email and sent the fake column to my editor."

He quirked one perfectly shaped—*and I strongly suspect, waxed*—brow. "How bad is it?"

"You haven't read it yet?"

He shook his head.

"It's bad," I said through the growing thickness in my throat. Jesus, just thinking about what that goddamn column had done made me feel like sobbing and vomiting simultaneously. "Career-ending kind of bad," I added, and no matter how hard I tried, I couldn't hide the desperation in my voice.

Because, fuck. I *was* desperate. I felt completely helpless, and the most important person in my life had been destroyed by terrible words that were presented as mine.

"That doesn't sound good." He steepled his hands together on his desk. "Is there an IT team investigating it?"

I nodded. "Yes."

"Well, it sounds like you're on the right track then," he responded and stroked his jaw with two perfectly manicured fingers. "I'm not sure what else I can do to help you right now, though. I mean, situations like these need to be investigated, and evidence needs to back up the contrary before any major strides can be achieved. You know how it is, Harlow."

"You're the fucking mayor, Brent," I retorted. "I do know how it is, and I know that you can pull some strings to get this process streamlined and made high priority."

"I don't think that's going to change anything related to Scott, though," he responded in a clear yet infuriatingly calm tone. "But I doubt the police will be able to keep him in custody right now without the right evidence to back up the accusations. They'll just interrogate him for a bit and then release him."

Wait...what? I didn't tell him Scott is with the police...

My brow furrowed on its own accord. "How did you know that he was already in custody?"

"I'm the mayor, LoLo." He chuckled, but there was something off about it and had the hairs on the back of my neck rising. "I know these kinds of things, especially when important members of the community are under investigation."

"But you just acted like you didn't know anything about the situation?"

"I said I hadn't read the article," he corrected. "But I did know that your boyfriend was in custody. Why do you think I cleared my next meeting? I had an idea of the situation. I knew it was urgent. I just wish there was more I could do to help you and Scott. You know that once the police start their investigation, my hands are tied."

I stared at him for a long moment, taking in the relaxed posture of his shoulders, the neutral yet friendly expression etched on his face, and my gut instinct told me that there was more to this story than what he was letting on.

I had no idea what, but there was *something*. I mean, he'd acted like he knew nothing about it when I stepped into his office, but once he'd admitted knowing Scott was in custody, he backtracked, and all of sudden, he *did* know the situation.

The facts weren't adding up. Nor did the kooky behavior his assistant Pam had shown when I requested to see him. She'd been over-zealously defensive, and I hadn't even told her why I was there.

"What's going on, Brent?" I questioned.

"What do you mean?" he asked, and the soft and neutral tone of his voice, and far too relaxed language of his body, urged flashbacks of our past and our relationship to fill my mind.

I'd seen this version of him before. To anyone else, he looked calm and composed. But I'd witnessed him look exactly like this when his then best friend and campaign manager had been investigated, and eventually convicted, for money laundering.

The worst part of the story, Brent had been the mastermind of it, and it was all in the name of greed and power. He hadn't realized I'd overheard his phone conversations when the shit hit the fan, and I'd walked away from our relationship after that with some bullshit excuse of not wanting to be in the public limelight anymore. It had nothing to do with the limelight and everything to do with the fact that I'd realized he was a horrible human being. I got out to save myself.

And even though right now I wanted to say all of the nasty things that rested on the tip of my tongue, I held back. Tempting as it was, I knew taking that route wasn't in my or, especially, Scott's best interest. Brent was a man of power, and he had no moral compass to guide his use of that power in the direction of straight and narrow. If I showed any suspicion that I thought he was involved, I honestly had no idea what lengths he would go to to prove the opposite.

"I—I just don't know how this happened," I muttered and faked a sad sigh. "I don't know how this happened, Brent."

"I wish I could do more, LoLo," he said, and I knew his words were complete bullshit.

I had no idea why he'd be involved in something like this, something that had to do with Scott, but my gut instinct screamed that he was. Sure, a very long time ago, we'd been a couple, but an overt use of his resources for the sole reason of jealously didn't add up.

I also knew I needed to get the fuck out of his office.

"Thanks for listening," I said and stood. "Sorry I screwed up your schedule."

"Oh, come on, LoLo." He grinned his blindingly white politician's smile. "You know you can screw up my schedule anytime. I'll always make time for you."

His words might have sounded genuine, but I knew they were covered in slime.

"Thanks again," I said and headed for the door.

"The offer still stands, you know," he added before I opened it. "I'd love to get together and catch up."

I looked over my shoulder and glanced at the powerful man who sat behind his desk. He might've painted the perfect persona to the outside world, but I knew this was not the kind of man I wanted to keep anywhere but far, far the fuck away. Not only from me, but from the people I loved the most—especially Scott.

"I'll keep in touch," I lied and forced a fake smile to my face and left his office quicker than I'd arrived. Bypassing Pam's desk and the glare I could feel practically burning a hole through my head, I kept my gaze focused on the hallway and walked quickly to the elevator. I didn't want to be around these venomous people for a minute longer than I had to.

Plus, I had bigger fish to fry. I had to find a way to clear Scott's name before he lost everything.

If he hasn't already lost everything...

My heart stuttered painfully at that thought. *Fucking hell.* I had to think. I had to figure out a way to handle this before anything else happened. Once I reached the sidewalk outside of City Hall, I hailed a cab and told the driver to take me to my dad's place in hopes that he'd have the wisdom to help me get Scott out of this situation. And since I knew Nicole was most likely there, I hoped she'd know what to do when it came to getting Scott to believe me that I didn't write that article.

As I stared out the window, mindlessly watching skyscrapers and pedestrians pass by in a blur and worrying a hole in my lip with my teeth, my phone startled me with a text notification. I pulled it out of my purse, and relief bloomed in my stomach once I read the message.

> **Stella: David has definitive proof that your account was hacked. We've pulled the article and posted an apology to the public, and Scott, in its place.**

> **Me: They've taken Scott into custody, Stella. You need to get David to head down to the police station now so that he doesn't get charged with anything.**

> **Stella: He already called. I'm sorry this happened, Harlow.**

I was surprised by her candid apology. Stella wasn't the type of woman to apologize for anything, but it was a relief to see that she had at least an ounce of care inside of her normally dark heart to understand that this situation was not okay. I also hoped like fuck this new information to the police would help Scott immediately.

> *Me: I feel like we need to do more, Stella. Even though my account was hacked, this situation is Gossip's fault. Scott deserves more from us than an apology article. His entire life has been turned upside down because of this.*
>
> *Stella: What else do you have in mind?*
>
> *Me: A press conference. Every media and news source in New York needs to understand that this article is false and these accusations are not true.*
>
> *Stella: I'll get it scheduled for this afternoon.*
>
> *Me: Really?*
>
> *Stella: I might be a hard-ass, but I'm not callous, Harlow. Believe me, I'm sympathetic to this situation, especially to both you and Scott. I'll clear my schedule and get a press conference scheduled for this afternoon.*
>
> *Me: Thank you.*

It might not have been a solution, but it was a start.

Now, I just needed to find a way to get Scott to talk to me, and as I walked up the concrete steps of my dad's place, I prayed that he and Nicole would help me.

CHAPTER *thirty-four*

"I**T'S NOT JUST THE ARTICLE, S**COTT," MY THANKFULLY KIND OFFICER OF THE LAW stated finally, after thirty minutes of mind-numbing circles of question and answer about everything in my life. The hospital, my relationship with the patients—even my relationship with Harlow.

Her article of bullshit had been painfully detailed—I'd noticed that the first time I'd read it—and now I was being forced to relive every false claim over and over again. But while the article itself had been the focus of this interrogation, apparently now there was something more.

"What? What else?"

Detective Santos sighed. "We got an anonymous call as soon as it broke. She claimed to be scared to come forward personally, but strongly suggested the allegations against you were factual in nature."

My face felt clammy in my hands. The urge to bury myself in them had been pressing all day, but at this bewildering and shittacular news, I couldn't fight it anymore.

"Oh God."

"Scott."

"It just doesn't make any sense," I muttered, head still firmly in my hands. "Never. I would never do anything with a woman without consent. Hell, enthusiastic consent. If I'm touching a woman, you better believe she's told me she wants me to. Period."

"Look, we're going to look into this."

"Can you…I don't know…trace the call from today? Find out who this woman is?"

He looked at me with wrinkled eyes and a slightly downturned mouth.

"Sorry. You're the detective here."

He smiled then.

"I know this is not how you planned on spending your day today."

I laughed, completely devoid of humor. To say the fucking least. The last week with Harlow had been perfect. Literally everything I'd never known I wanted. Everything I'd distinctly thought I *didn't* want.

But Christ, it was good.

Finally, some of what she'd been so vehement about this morning broke through. "She says she didn't write it," I whispered, mostly to myself.

Detective Santos didn't think anything I said in an interrogation room was to myself. And he was right.

"Yep. I heard that too, and it's worth looking into. You've been an upstanding member of the community long enough that I'm willing to give you the benefit of the doubt until something proves to me I shouldn't. You stitched up my daughter's chin when she tripped and fell into the coffee table, for shit's sake, Scott."

He sighed.

"I don't want to see you here any more than you want to be here."

I nodded, bit my lip, and turned to the side.

"So, here's the plan," he declared, sinking a hip onto the shiny metal table in front of me and leaning into his thigh. "You're going to be released. You're not going to leave the city, and you're not going to go out to the clubs or the bars or whatever."

I snorted, and he narrowed his eyes.

I straightened up immediately. "Sorry. Just...yeah...you don't have to worry about that. Pretty sure I'm going to lock myself in my apartment and sleep until this nightmare is over."

He smiled. "Good plan. We'll look into everything, and if no one comes forward with serious evidence, something we could take to court on this, we'll release a statement that you've been questioned and cleared."

I shook my head and then nodded. I knew it was a confusing mess of opposites, but I couldn't help it. That was what I was feeling. Because everything he said was great. I knew I hadn't actually committed crimes against women. In a perfect world, I'd be cleared, they'd make a statement, and that would be that.

But in the real world, I had someone falsely accusing me, my girlfriend was at the center of this shit, my job security was questionable at best—even if they cleared me—and no statement to the media would ever completely clear my name.

Innocent in the eyes of the law and innocent in the eyes of the public were two different things, and it was a pretty short trip from Dr. Erotic to Sex Offender in the world of reality TV.

"Come on, Scott," Detective Santos said, pulling me from my seriously depressing thoughts. "I'll walk you out."

I nodded and stood, following him out of the room and through the bullpen as he led the way to the front doors. There was a set of stairs that led down to the entrance, but the doors were glass. I could see pretty well that it was a goddamn media circus out there just as it had been outside of my apartment when we came here.

I groaned. "Great."

Detective Santos followed my gaze. "Ah, shit. All right. You can go out the back entrance. Come on."

"Thank you, Jesus," I said aloud, happy to be free of at least one current burden.

Detective Santos smirked. "It's pronounced Hey-Zeus."

Safely back in my apartment building—Detective Santos had been nice enough to have a cruiser give me a lift to a block up from the building—I stepped onto the elevator, waited for the doors to close, and then sank into the back wall.

All of my energy was gone.

The last ten hours felt like two hundred, and I hadn't been lying when I told Detective Santos I would just sleep until it was over. Honestly, that felt like the only way to survive this shit.

The ding of the elevator pulled me from my thoughts, so I opened my eyes and stepped off as soon as the doors opened.

Digging the keys from my pocket, I inserted them in the lock and gave them a turn when the knob pulled right out of my hand.

"Harlow?" I asked, scrubbing at my face as she held the door open and gestured for me to come inside.

This is my apartment, right? What the hell is going on here?

"What are you doing here?" I asked. "How did you get in?"

Guiltily, she glanced behind her and then looked back to me. "With the help of my dad and your mom."

"Christ."

I looked past her to the couch. Bill and my mom sat there, hand in hand.

The last thing I wanted was to have to face my mom right now.

"Jesus Christ, Harlow!" I scrubbed a hand down my face and sighed in exasperation. I was fucking done. Part of me believed everything she was saying, but another part, the part that had literally been through the emotional ringer, didn't have its usual ability to align important things like *fault* and *consequences*. "Don't you think you've done enough?"

She jerked like I'd struck her, and my mom jumped to her feet. "Enough, Scott. Come sit down and hear her out. We did, and that's why we're here. We all know you didn't do this." She moved closer, around the couch to right in front of me and took my hand. "*All of us,"* she stressed.

I pulled her into my arms and buried my face in her neck, a few tears pooling in my eyes. Sometimes, even at thirty-five years old, you just needed your mom.

She let me hold her for several minutes before she spoke again. "Come on, now. Let's sit down."

I nodded and moved with her, around the couch and the coffee table, and took a seat on a chair. I didn't have it in me to sit next to someone right now.

"Harlow, honey," my mom prompted. "Why don't you tell Scott what you told us?"

Harlow nodded and took a seat on the couch. She looked like it killed her to do it, but she knew I was trying to put space between us, and by some miracle, chose to respect that.

"Okay. Well, you know I'd been struggling to come up with an article for this week."

I nodded.

"And you know I told you last night that I'd finally come up with something."

I nodded again.

"And you know that I asked you not to be mad?"

"Yes, Low. I know all of these things. What I didn't know was that you were accusing me of being a rapist!"

"Scott, calm down, son," Bill advised, taking a stand and putting a hand to my shoulder.

Harlow's face lost all of its careful calm though. She charged, grabbing me by the jaws and ignoring all of the carefully constructed space I'd erected.

"I. Didn't. Write. That."

I stared back at her, a goddamn mess, fighting to let her words sink in.

"Scott, I fucking promise you. I didn't. Those were not my words," she whispered, and tears started to drip from her lids and down her cheeks.

God, she looked desperate.

And Harlow Paige never looked desperate, not for anyone or anything.

There were sad lines around her normally bright eyes, and her small shoulders, sagging forward noticeably, appeared to be carrying the weight of the world. But mostly, it was her determination and the way she refused to break eye contact with me that made my heart start talking some sense into my stubborn head. The anger, the honesty, the affection in her eyes. It finally all sank in. I nodded and took a shaky breath.

"Scott, I didn't write that," she whispered again, more tears rolling down her cheeks.

I nodded again, and she repeated herself. "I didn't. I wrote an article about what an amazing doctor you are. I even did interviews with a few of the pediatric patients we'd taken care of in the emergency room. It was sweet and adorable, and it definitely wasn't what they published," she explained on a shaky breath. "That awful fucking article they published wasn't mine. I'd never do something like that. Not to anyone and especially not to you. I love you, Scott."

Realization turned into conviction. She *didn't* write that article. Harlow might've been a gossip columnist, but she had morals and strong convictions and she'd never write something to intentionally destroy someone's life. She might have held her heart pretty fucking close to the vest, but that heart of hers was huge.

I tried to focus on what she had to be going through, feeling like she was responsible for so much turmoil in my life when she actually wasn't, but I had a whole litany of my own problems, despite her innocence.

I nodded, her lips sinking closer to mine, more tears spilling from her eyes. "I'm so, so sorry."

The salt of her tears stung on my tortured lips. I'd been chewing on them for hours.

"I believe you."

Her breath was audible and shaky as she touched her lips to

mine, once, twice, three times, and climbed into my lap.

"Thank God," she mumbled as she buried her face in my neck and let a few tortured sobs bubble all the way out. I gave her a moment to compose herself before ripping off the comfort of her Band-Aid.

"But what are we going to do about all of this? I'm so fucking glad it wasn't you, but it was someone. How am I supposed to handle that?"

"With your head high," my mom interjected, reminding me she was there.

My face pinched in disbelief. "You want me to shrug this off? Act like it's no big deal?" Steadily and with each word, my volume increased until I was nearly at a yell.

Harlow sensed how close I was to the edge and put her hands to either side of my jaw to turn my face back to her.

With soft green eyes—the softest she'd ever bestowed upon me—Harlow did her best to heal the hurt inside of me with nothing more than a look.

I wrapped her up as tight as I could manage.

I still didn't know what the fuck was going on, but if she didn't write it, when all was said and done, I knew I had at least one thing left to hold on to—her.

"You don't shrug off anything. *Gossip* already did a press conference, admitting that because of a computer security issue, they're uncertain of the source of the article or the validity of the statements within it. I know that doesn't help much—"

"They already did a press conference?" I asked, mystified. "When?"

"This afternoon while you were still in police custody," my mom offered helpfully.

Christ. Police custody. How was this my life?

At the thought of what my visit to the precinct had entailed, I shook my head. "Well, that's good I guess. But that doesn't clear me completely. According to the detective, they got an anonymous call from a woman claiming I'd assaulted her."

"What?" Harlow shouted as my mom gasped.

I nodded, pulling back from Harlow enough to scrub a hand down my face. "I know. It's not good."

"Who the hell would do that?" my mom asked, distraught. I'd never seen Nicole Shepard distraught in my life, and I decided in that moment I never wanted to see it again.

Harlow just looked angry. The line of her eyes changed from a curve to a point, and her mouth set in a firm line. "I've got a fucking idea."

CHAPTER *thirty-five*

Harlow

A few weeks later...

"THANKS FOR COMING DOWN," DETECTIVE SANTOS GREETED US AS WE walked into his office.

"Not going to lie, this is always the very last place I want to be," Scott muttered, but it was in a teasing tone.

Detective Santos chuckled softly and gestured for us to sit down in the chairs across from his desk. "I promise, it's all good news from here on out," he said, and Scott sighed.

"Even if it is good news, anything related to *this* always feels like bad news."

He had a point. This entire situation had been one giant cluster-fuck of awful since it began. And even though it had been made clear that the article was faked, there were still people in the public who believed the lies it had bled.

But no matter what, we still had each other. I put my hand on top of his thigh and squeezed gently in reassurance, and he offered a soft smile in return.

"You were right, Harlow," Detective Santos stated simply. Unsure to what he was referring, I sat there dumbly while Scott nodded without understanding. I could tell by the creases at the corners of his eyes that he didn't have any more clue what the detective was talking about than I did.

"About?" I finally asked. It felt like if I didn't pipe up, Scott would just keep nodding forever.

"Well," Detective Santos started, "after a lot of searching, we traced the initial tip-off call to the station and verified that it came from Pam Lockhead."

"Are you fucking serious?" I blurted out. "It *was* her?"

I'd had a hunch, sure, but fuck if I thought I was going to be right. I didn't have a degree in Criminal Justice.

He nodded. "Apparently, she made the call from a burner phone that had been bought with cash and had no name associated with the account. It wasn't an easy trace, but thankfully, the computer system in the cell phone store along with their security cameras helped verify that it was her. We also have suspicions that she might be involved with the hack to *Gossip's* email database. She was brought into custody this morning and is now being investigated."

"So, what happens now?" Scott asked.

"Well, your name, as well as Harlow's, has been officially cleared from this. We'll be issuing a statement to the public this afternoon, along with an explanation of the evidence that we've found so far in this investigation."

"Thank God," I muttered. "I guess maybe there is a light at the end of the tunnel."

Scott rested his hand on top of mine and squeezed, practically begging me not to jinx this shit. "Is that all you need from us?"

"The only other thing we need to know is, once all of the facts are found, do you want to press charges against the people responsible?"

"Of course, he fucking does!" I shouted, and Detective Santos chuckled.

"Should I take her word for it?"

"Yes." Scott grinned. Fucking grinned. For something that was almost unavoidable in the past, he'd done very little of it in the last few weeks. I was fucking thrilled to have it back. "I definitely want to press charges."

Scott's happiness only egged my craziness on. I didn't want it to go away.

"We want to press charges and nail these fuckers into the ground! We'll accept nothing less than a life sentence," I added enthusiastically, and Scott laughed.

He fucking *laughed*.

My mind raced as I tried to come up with my next off-the-wall remark, but Scott was pretty well done with the whole scene, overtly amusing girlfriend or not.

"Yeah, if that's all you need from us, I think we'll be leaving now."

Detective Santos smirked. "Have a good one."

"You too," Scott said and grabbed my hand to pull me to my feet. "Come on, Low. Let's go get some lunch before you try to join the police force."

"Oh! I'd be an awesome cop!" I said, basking in the glow of his willingness to joke. *It's so good to have him back.* He all but dragged me out of the detective's office.

"No," he refuted as we wove our way through the bullpen. "You're going to be an awesome pediatrician. You don't have time to learn how to shoot a gun and put bad guys in handcuffs while you're going through med school."

"Oh my God! I'd get handcuffs, too," I whined. "Maybe I need to think this whole cop thing over a little more before I make any career changes."

"You're crazy," he muttered, pulling his sunglasses from his shirt, putting them on, and yanking the folded up baseball hat out of his back pocket to put it on. "I fucking love you, but you're crazy."

Before I could offer a sarcastic response, the familiar and always blinding flashes of cameras went off like fireworks in front of my face.

Ever since the article had been published, the media had been following us around like fucking vultures. And it didn't matter how discreet we were, they always managed to find us.

Jesus, when would this end?

Scott wrapped his arm around my shoulder protectively and tucked me into his side. "Just keep your nose to the ground and stay close to me, okay? I'll handle the rest," he whispered.

"Okay," I agreed, letting him lead us through the throng of vipers trying to get our attention.

"Scott! Harlow! Over here!"

"Did you really believe she didn't write the article, Scott?"

"How can you trust him now, Harlow?"

"Are you getting married?"

"Is Harlow pregnant?"

God, it never ended, and it didn't matter that the police had cleared Scott's name and that *Gossip* had done the press conference as well as printed a statement that the article was fake. The media still wanted to keep the spotlight on the two of us. And they didn't want happy endings; they wanted fucking blood. *If it bleeds, it leads* sort of thing.

There was no doubt that pictures of the two of us leaving the police station were worth their weight in gold. And with the enthusiastic—*and extremely overwhelming*—way their cameras were snapping photos, it was a safe bet that they'd be hot on our trail all goddamn day.

"I guess we're not going to lunch, huh?" I whispered to Scott as we walked across the sidewalk and he hailed a cab.

"Nope," he muttered. "Let's just get home and order takeout, okay?"

"Good idea."

Even though things were looking up and the truth was coming out, that fucking article had stolen our freedom. Eating out, walking the streets, riding the subway, they were each a thing of the past. We couldn't do any of it without being assaulted by the press's questions and cameras.

And the terrifying part of it all was that we didn't know when it would finally blow over or get better, and neither one of us was certain we could live our lives like this for much longer.

One cab ride and thirty minutes later, we stepped inside of Scott's apartment. Both of us sighed in relief once the door shut behind us. I slipped off my flip-flops and plopped my tired ass down onto the sofa while Scott grabbed us sodas from the kitchen. The remote was in my hand, and I was scrolling through the Netflix options moments later.

I needed to decompress, and generally speaking, binge-watching Netflix shows was the answer. Hell, I think most people used it as an actual coping mechanism now.

Writer's block? Watch Netflix.

Just got dumped by your boyfriend? Watch Netflix.

Too many items on your To-Do List? Watch Netflix.

Too stressed out to adult? Watch Netflix.

See? Obviously, it was a multifaceted kind of coping mechanism that could be utilized in almost any situation. Now, I wouldn't say it actually solved anything, but that was neither here nor there. If I needed something to help me forget that I was procrastinating on my responsibilities or avoiding my problems, Netflix was my number one homeboy.

But as I started watching an episode of *Parks and Recreation*, I quickly realized I had too much on my mind to experience the full escape my homeboy generally provided.

It shouldn't have come as a surprise, though. Life had been a bit of a fucking roller coaster for Scott and me, and it felt like our cart had managed to get stuck on the very tip-top of the first big hill that makes your stomach fall into your shoes.

"I know all of this bullshit will eventually die down, but fucking hell, it's kind of awful," I muttered, probably more to myself than Scott. "I mean, when will it end?"

He sat down beside me, set the glasses of water on the table, wrapped his arm around my shoulder, and tucked me close to his side. "This is just a temporary kind of hell, Low. It won't last forever."

I sighed and rested my head onto his shoulder. "Yeah, but the fact that you just called it a temporary hell says everything."

"Yeah, but I'd go through all of that bullshit again if I knew it would lead me right back here. With you," he said, and I lifted my head to meet his eyes. "You're it for me, Harlow. And I don't care if three years from now we're still in New York being chased around by paparazzi or if we've moved to a new city and are starting over. The only thing that's important to me is *you*." He kissed my lips softly. "You're my home now. Everything else is just minor details."

He was right.

If there was one thing I learned from this experience—*besides the fact that Pam Lockhead is a total cunt*—it was that I loved Scott. And I not only wanted to be with him, but I *needed* to be with him. Nothing felt right without him.

"I love you," I whispered, and he kissed my nose.

"I love you, too, Frances," he said, and I rolled my eyes.

"Ugh. Don't ruin the moment with my awful name," I scolded, but secretly, I loved it. I wanted Scott's teasing and smiles to last a lifetime.

"We're having a moment right now?" he questioned playfully.

"Well, we *were*," I muttered. "We're definitely not anymore."

Scott laughed and flipped me onto my back before I could stop him. His large body hovered over mine as he grinned down at me. "You know what I think?" he asked and peppered my jaw with kisses.

"What do you think?"

"I think you need to follow your dream."

"Become a stripper?" I asked in jest, and he chuckled.

"No." He shook his head with a grin. "Your original dream. Although, please feel free to practice your stripping skills anytime. I volunteer as your lap."

"And my pole?" I asked with a waggle of my eyebrows, and he licked his lips.

"Yes, motherfucking please."

"Fantastic. It's settled. I'll become a stripper."

He groaned. "Christ, the thought of you as a stripper is making it hard to concentrate, but you know what I'm really talking about."

I did know. Scott wanted me to follow my original dream of becoming a pediatrician. And ever since we'd been in the middle of this media shitstorm, and I'd had to take a leave of absence from *Gossip* in the name of sanity, he'd been occasionally bringing it up. Not pressuring me, but just encouraging me and reassuring me with kind words.

I stared up at the handsome man above me and sighed. It was a dreamy fucking sigh, and I earned one hell of a Scott smile in return. Not only did he encourage me to follow my dreams, but he was also sexy and fucked like a god.

Damn, I really was the luckiest woman on the planet…

"You really want me to go to med school?"

He nodded, and his lips pressed soft kisses against my skin and his nose brushed my cheek as he did. "It's your passion."

"That's a big commitment, Scott. I mean, before I could even apply to med schools, I'd have to study my ass off and pass the MCAT. And even if I managed to achieve that, who knows if and where I'd get accepted."

"I'll help you study," he declared, and I giggled.

"Let me guess, naked study time?"

"Whatever it takes, baby." He smiled against my skin. "I mean that. Whenever, wherever—"

"We're meant to be together?"

He laughed and lifted his head to meet my gaze. "Well, yes. And I really appreciate your knowledge of Shakira. But I mean we follow your dream wherever it takes us."

"That could be anywhere." I searched his face for any hint of uncertainty, but he didn't falter under my scrutiny. His mocha eyes stayed locked with mine. "What if I end up going to med school on the West Coast?"

He shrugged. "Then, I guess I'll be working in an emergency room on the West Coast." He smirked. "And reaping the benefits of you in bikini weather."

"*Really?* You'd do that?" I asked, because holy hell. That was a big commitment. That was Scott letting my future career path guide us. That was...*everything.*

"I'll follow you anywhere, Harlow," he said. "And if your dream keeps us here, then we'll find a way to deal with the media until it dies down. All that matters is that we're together."

I wrapped my arms and legs around his strong body and pulled him closer to me. This man had me. He so fucking had me. "I love you," I whispered into his ear. "You make me so fucking happy."

Because he did. My life wasn't the same without him in it. And, even though we were in the middle of a *temporary hell,* as he put it, with the whole media shitstorm following us around, it didn't matter. That was just minor details in comparison to what we had together. And nothing could affect that kind of happiness.

He winked, picking up both glasses of water and handing one to me. "To love," he said with a smirk, taking me back to the very beginning with the toast at his dad's anniversary party. I clinked my glass to his, and he smiled. "Cheers, *Doc.*"

CHAPTER *thirty-six*

Seven months later...

"SCOTT!" HARLOW YELLED, HER VOICE CARRYING UP THE STAIRS AND INTO THE loft.

"Yeah?" I yelled back as I pulled the protective wrapping off of my diploma from NYU and set it to the side to reveal another frame. The quilted padding of the moving blanket and tape concealed its contents completely, but I knew what was inside.

Years of studying, years of training, and years of service to the citizens of New York City, all symbolized in one framed, white coat. It was a source for a million memories, and despite knowing this move was going to be everything I'd ever had in New York and more, I wasn't sure if I was ready to open it yet. Sometimes memories—especially those that carried a tinge of melancholy—had the ability to feel more potent than the present. But happiness feeds the soul, and it wouldn't be long before Harlow's smiles and flirty fun were the only thing I could feel.

"Scott!" Harlow called again, now impatient.

Fuck. "Sorry! I zoned out!" I shouted, keeping my sentimental moment close to the vest. I didn't want her to think I had any resentment about leaving New York and starting over with her—because I didn't. The life we were leaving behind had really started to feel like no life at all. Although we were blissfully happy together, the media was a constant circus, and everything we did played out under a microscope of public scrutiny. But I guessed that was what happened when you were at the center of a scandal with the mayor of New York City.

After a fairly lengthy investigation, both Brent and Pam had been indicted on a litany of charges. Not only had Pam falsified statements to the police, but she'd been the one to organize the actual hacking of Harlow's email account. The fine law enforcement of New York had taken the cybercrime pretty seriously. While jealousy and scorn over our non-relationship had been the weak board underneath her, it was her naïveté and willingness to consort with Brent that had turned her life upside down. Apparently, I wasn't the only one who'd slept with the wrong person in an effort to get to the top.

Brent, though less directly in contact with the actual dirty work, had bigger fish to fry—likely the ones at the bottom of the bay. As in, he swam with them.

Okay, so he wasn't dead, but for a driven egomaniac like him, the demise of his political career and the distinct possibility of prison had to feel like it. His trial date was scheduled for the end of the year.

"What's up?" I called over the railing.

"Have you seen my masheew?" Harlow asked loudly.

"Your masheew? What's a masheew?"

"No!" she yelled through a laugh. "My nuschmoo!"

"Why are you garbling this word so much?" I shouted with a smile. I moved directly to the stairs, knowing she was just stubborn enough to keep yelling until the end of time despite our gap in communication and the simple solution of a short trip up one flight of stairs. "I understand everything else you say completely, and then, as soon as you get to the important word, all ability to speak is lost."

I wasn't even fully on the landing when the weight of her body hit mine. I went back and down, putting a hand out behind me to brace myself on the steps as she fell on top of me.

She giggled the whole way, shrieking a little when we hit bottom and the force of her body on my stomach made me grunt.

"What are you doing?" I asked with a chuckle as I shifted my now bruised back off of the wooden riser and settled my ass onto a stair instead. She straddled my lap, adjusting easily to the new position and wrapping her arms loosely around my shoulders. "Are you trying to send us both to the hospital?"

"Just think how fun of an introduction that would be to your new coworkers," she teased.

I narrowed my eyes. "Not fun at all."

While the shitshow with the media had been one driving force for our move to San Francisco, my job was another. Just as I'd suspected, being cleared of any and all charges didn't mean being cleared of the consequences. While the hospital couldn't legally fire me, the whole dynamic of my working environment had shifted to something I didn't enjoy. Constantly watched and criticized, my teasing good-natured fun wasn't allowed, and all of the joy had left along with it.

We were hoping starting over at San Fran General would bring some sense of normalcy and enjoyment back to the career I truly loved. I didn't even know how to be a good doctor without being a smartass. Just like with my musical warm-ups, that shit went hand in hand.

And it didn't hurt that little Harlow had been accepted to the University of California, San Francisco School of Medicine and would be starting her first semester tomorrow.

"Really?" she questioned, grabbing me by the hair at the back of my head and playfully shaking it back and forth. "I think it'd be great. Injuries bring people together. Look at what it did for us."

"That's true," I mused. "If only I'd known about the power of a head laceration earlier."

"What? You would have used it sooner on another woman?"

I shook my head and touched my lips to hers. "What other women? Do other women exist?"

She smacked me on the chest and rolled her eyes at my theatrics, and only then did I remember what had brought me down the stairs in the first place.

"Now, what is it you're looking for? A schmoodle? Or a hot s'more? I've got no fucking clue what you were saying."

"Oh." She laughed. "Yeah, I was just making up words. I knew you'd come down if I kept it up long enough."

"Oh yeah? Did you miss me or something?"

"Mmm-hmm." She nodded and rubbed the tip of her nose against the tip of mine.

"What part of me did you miss most?" I asked softly, the succulent skin of her lips tickling the nerves in mine as they skimmed together.

Her eyes widened, almost comically because of our proximity, and I laughed at the words she didn't have to say.

"Yeah, I thought that might be your favorite."

"I was thinking about your brain," she lied.

I nipped at her lips and then skated my own down the silky skin of her neck. "Sure you were."

"I was! I'm starting medical school tomorrow, and I could really use your knowledge. Can you take all of my tests for me?"

I laughed and squeezed her hips, scrunching my nose. "I don't think that'll help you actually treat patients. And since you want to treat kids—"

"And kids are your weakness," she finished for me with a roll of her eyes. "Yeah, I get it. You don't want my incompetence to kill them. It's really selfish of you, but I guess I understand."

My phone buzzed on my ass and made me jump.

It took some work to shift Harlow enough to get to my back pocket to retrieve it, but somehow, I managed—not that Harlow helped at all.

She laughed when she got a look at my exasperated face. "What? I'm more important than your phone."

She had no idea how right she was. Lips to hers, I parted the seam with my tongue and showed her.

Our breathing was noticeably heavier when we broke apart—at least at the mouth. Our bodies were still a tangle of limbs.

"You're the most important. This phone call could be the President of the United States for all I care."

Of course, it was more likely that the call was actually from my mother. A week we'd been gone, and she already thought living on opposite coasts was the worst thing ever to happen to her and called me at least once a day to remind me.

Harlow's face softened into a thoughtful frown. "Are you going to miss New York?"

I lifted my hand to her jaw, stroking the apple of her cheek with my thumb, and shrugged. "I don't know, doll. But I'm fine as long as I don't have to miss you."

She sighed. "I love you, Scott."

"Frances," I started, causing a playful frown. I wiped it away with my thumb. "You have no idea."

epilogue

Scott

One year later…

"I PROMISE TO LOVE AND HONOR YOU IN ALL THE WAYS THAT COUNT," SHE RECITED from the small, worn piece of paper in her hands.

Her vows. I'd watched her rub them nervously all morning, so much so that the paper felt soft to the touch. I could tell by the way she rubbed at it to steady all of her shaking nerves.

It was a big day.

Maybe the biggest. And I'd been expecting it since that first night at *Kinky Boots.*

Flowers dotted every flat surface of St. Matthew's Cathedral, and the colorful light filtering through the stained-glass windows made the whole room feel like magic.

"I'll do my best to give you the space you need when you need it, and fill that very void the rest of the time.

"I know I'm crazy and impetuous—"

I bit my lip to contain my laugh at her truth in reporting and got a stern look from the green-eyed goddess across the aisle. Apparently, this wasn't the time to goof off.

"But you know just how to handle it. Thank you for loving me for who I am at the same time as making me want to be a better person. Most people don't have it in themselves to watch calmly from the sidelines as I do ridiculous things."

No longer able to contain my laughter, I drew the attention of everyone in the church, including one particularly unhappy bride.

My mother.

"Scott!"

"Sorry, Mom," I apologized quietly. "Continue." Harlow's smirk warmed me from her spot across the aisle as "best man" to her father.

We'd flown in three days ago for the start of the wedding festivities for Bill and Nicole soon-to-be Paige, and there hadn't even been one solid hour that passed without someone making a joke about Harlow and my new relation—stepsiblings, as it were.

Harlow's dark red lips moved silently. "You're naughty," I could have sworn she mouthed.

I winked, mouthing the word "Later" back at her.

Bill cleared his throat and pulled his own vows out of his breast pocket. Apparently, we'd moved along while I was busy checking out my woman.

"Nicole."

He took a deep breath and cleared his throat again, reaching up to swipe underneath his eye.

He was crying. *Another perfect match.* Tanner and Linda, Harlow and me, and now, Nicole and Bill.

"This far into the total expectancy of my life, I'd thought I was done. Done with the major milestones and the greatest joys. Done learning new things and meeting new and unexpected people. Done making major changes to my very routine life.

"I was happy. I had friendship and the love of a great daughter, and I didn't feel unfulfilled."

Choked up again, he had to pause and lick his lips while he

composed himself.

I was feeling a little emotional myself. And, when I glanced up and across the space to the love of *my* life, it was pretty clear I wasn't alone.

Fresh tears marred her wedding makeup and her bottom lip quivered, but Harlow looked content. I didn't see even an ounce of the unsettled energy that used to consume her—the energy of a woman who'd decided to settle on a life she didn't want in an attempt to avoid heartache.

My transformation wasn't any less significant. The Scott of old at this wedding would have had one distinct thought. *Danger, ladies! Take a look at the kind of man Scott Shepard will never be!*

As it turns out, I could be wrong occasionally. I never would have thought.

"I had no idea," Bill Paige continued. "No idea what life could be if I just opened myself up to it. With you, I know I'll be forever grateful that I did. Thanks for waking me up, baby. I promise, when it comes to us, I'll never sleep again."

Harlow's eyes glowed majestic as they held mine. I was spellbound, now and forever.

Right on, Bill.

Who needed dreaming when this was what it felt like to be awake?

Harlow

"Another beer, Frances?" Amanda half slurred and flashed a lazy grin in my direction. Her blond hair glided across her shoulders as loud laughter left her lips.

I grinned. Life was good. I was on spring break from my fourth year in med school, currently living it up in the city that would always hold a special place in my heart with the only man ever to have my heart. Life couldn't get any better. Not to mention, Amanda was drunk *and* visiting home with her Spanish lover. Well, now husband.

Yes. She'd not only fallen in love with her client, but she'd up and married the man and changed her nationality in the process. Officially a citizen of Spain for the past two years, my best friend had never looked happier.

I missed her like crazy, but God, I was happy for her. Happy for both of us, actually. And although our lives had taken completely different paths, we were still as close as ever. FaceTime and Skype and twice yearly visits to see one another helped with that.

As the four of us sat inside of Radio Star, a popular karaoke bar in Midtown, drinking beer and watching the crowd showcase their drunkest vocals, I knew with certainty that life couldn't get any better than this.

"Are you gonna be a little pussy, Lances?" Amanda all out slurred this time, and I flipped her the bird from across the table.

"Shut up, drunky."

"I'm dot srunk! You're drunk!" she shouted back, and I couldn't fight the smile that consumed my face.

"Exactly."

Mateo wrapped his arm around his wife and chuckled. "I think you've hit your quota, *mi amor.*"

She raised her glass directly in front of his face and frowned. "But I'm all out."

Instead of responding, he merely set her glass back down on the table and kissed his wife until she basically forgot her fucking name. It was more than apparent that the man knew when to pick his battles. I liked him on principle alone.

Scott wrapped his arm around my shoulder and tucked me close to his side. "What's the over under?" he asked on a whisper, and I tilted my head to the side in confusion. "How many minutes will they last until they have to leave to go do the sex?"

"Hmmm…" I tapped my chin with my index finger and glanced

back at Amanda and Mateo. Considering they were still engaged in a battle of the lips and tongues, something had to give soon. "I give them another ten minutes tops."

Scott grinned. "I'm going with five minutes."

I quirked a surprised brow. "Five minutes? Really?"

"Yes, really," he answered and kissed the corner of my mouth. "What are we wagering?"

I shrugged. "What do you want to wager?"

"If I win, you have to promise to actually consider the idea of marriage."

I rolled my eyes. "And if I win?"

"No proposals for the next ninety days."

"Ninety days?" I blurted out before I could stop myself.

He raised his brow. "Do you have a problem with that?"

"Of course I don't," I answered quickly. Probably too fucking quickly with the way Scott was grinning at me like the Cheshire cat. "It's a deal, buddy," I said and held out my hand.

He shook it without blinking an eye, and I didn't like it.

The bastard was pretty damn confident. Too fucking confident, in my opinion.

And unfortunately for me, not even two minutes later, Amanda and Mateo were able to break their lips' suction and stand up from their seats.

"We're leaving!" she shouted so loudly that her voice carried over the woman on stage singing "Like a Virgin" at the top of her lungs. "I want to have sex!" she added, and Mateo just smiled his million-dollar smile.

Seriously. His smile was literally worth one million dollars. Not only had he obtained quite the success in his music career, he'd also become the apple of a lot of women's eyes.

"No, don't go! Stay a little longer," I exclaimed and hopped to my feet. I glanced down at my watch and noted that I literally needed another six minutes to pass to even come close to winning the bet. "Just six more minutes, please!"

Amanda shook her head. "Nope. I want the sex. With my husband."

"But you can always have sex with your husband," I whined, and Scott chuckled softly beside me.

"Sorry, Low," Amanda said and hugged me tightly. "Call me in the morning so we can meet for breakfast, 'kay?"

"But…but…" I started, but Amanda and Mateo were on a fucking mission. They tossed out their goodbyes and were out the door before I could come up with any other excuse.

I sat back down in my seat on a sigh.

Fucking hell.

"Tough loss, huh?" he whispered into my ear.

I shook my head. "I'm ignoring you."

Obviously, I was a sore loser. But, seriously? I'd only lost by mere minutes.

Goddammit, Amanda. Why did my best friend have to be such a dirty slut for her husband's penis? What happened to the marriages that made people want sex less? If anything, since she'd married Mateo, she only talked about how she wanted sex more.

Maybe I needed a new best friend?

While Scott tried to coax me into a conversation, I turned my head back toward the stage and watched as the fortysomething woman continued to sing her off-tune rendition of Madonna into the microphone. "Like a virgin! Ohhh! Ohhh! Ohhh! I'm a horny virgin!"

"Horny virgin?" Scott whispered to me. "I don't remember those lyrics."

I couldn't stop myself from laughing at the absurdity and met his gaze with a grin. "I think she's freestyling."

He quirked an amused brow. "Freestyling? In karaoke?"

God, my man was handsome. After being together for over four years, I couldn't believe how one simple look into his gorgeous brown eyes still had the power to take my breath away.

"You should know," I retorted. "You're the karaoke expert."

He winked. "All I know is that I can't wait for your performance."

I scrunched up my nose. "I might have agreed to come to this karaoke bar, but I'm not fucking getting up on stage," I declared, and he just grinned.

As the last beats of "Like a Virgin" left the speakers, the MC for the night hopped on stage and took the microphone from the woman's hands before she could start an encore.

"All right," he announced to the crowd. "Next up, we have Frances!"

I looked around the room for the next victim, but when no one stood and he shouted Frances into the microphone again, I looked at Scott with a scowl.

"No fucking way," I muttered. "Tell me you didn't sign me up for this shitshow."

He nodded and smirked. "What are you waiting for, Frances? Get up there and show 'em what you got!"

"Come on, Frances," the MC said again. "Don't be shy, sweetheart!"

I looked at Scott and then back at the MC. I had two options: I could either lose both battles for the night, or I could at least walk away with one victory.

Obviously, I needed a victory, and I knew exactly how I could get it.

After a quick smile flashed into Scott's oblivious direction, I stood up from my chair and hopped on the stage and took the microphone from the MC.

"My boyfriend is a little shy," I told the crowd. "I think Frances just needs a little bit of reassurance," I said and pointed straight at Scott.

His jaw dropped as I continued to point at him and chant, "Frances! Frances! Frances!"

Once everyone else in the bar joined me, a giant smile consumed Scott's face.

"Come on, Frances! I know you can do it!" I cheered. "Everyone wants to hear your beautiful voice."

Scott got to his feet and jumped on stage beside me. After one quick spank to my ass, he took the mic from my hands and whispered into my ear, "You're so getting it later."

I sure fucking hoped so.

But I didn't waste any time dallying on stage, I quickly got back to my seat and left Scott to deal with the now overly enthusiastic crowd wanting to hear Frances sing.

For once in my life, that goddamn name actually worked to my benefit.

"Just bear with me for a second," Scott told the crowd and leaned over to the DJ to tell him something.

Once they appeared on the same page, he looked toward the crowd and grinned.

"This one is for my beautiful girlfriend, Harlow."

"Awww!" one woman in the audience sighed.

"God, he's hot," another one chimed in. "I wish he was my boyfriend!"

I flashed a glare in the last one's direction. *Slow your roll, lady. He's mine.*

Once the initial beats of a song I'd figured was Shakira's "Hips Don't Lie" began, I settled into my seat to enjoy my handsome and very sexy boyfriend's performance.

But "Hips Don't Lie" didn't come.

I didn't recognize it right off the bat, but it was definitely something else. The beat was a bit slower but still upbeat and pop nonetheless.

Once the lyrics started to leave his lips, I couldn't believe my fucking ears.

Scott was belting out "Marry Me" by Train.

What the what?

Surely, it was just for fun. I mean, I knew I'd lost that bet, but he wouldn't ask me to marry him right now, in a fucking karaoke bar, *right?*

I shook off the crazy thoughts and just focused on how goddamn sexy he looked up on stage. But my focus went to shit when not even halfway through the song, he stopped singing and the DJ cut the music.

Scott got down on one knee.

And pulled a small black box out of his pocket.

Oh. My. God.

My heart stopped beating for what felt like a minute before it stuttered back into a pounding rhythm.

"Harlow Paige," he said into the microphone with his gaze locked with mine. "I love you. You are my heart. My home. My life. I want to spend the rest of my life making you smile and laugh. I want forever with you, Low."

"Are you really doing this right now?" I called toward him and he grinned.

"I really am," he answered. "And, if I do recall, you just promised that you'd consider the idea."

Holy shit. My hand went to my mouth on its own accord.

"Frances Harlow Paige. My lover. My best friend. My sister," he added with a teasing grin. "Will you marry me?"

"Oh my God, stepsister! Don't make people think we're inbreds," I corrected, and he just chuckled in response.

"Get your ass up here and tell me yes, Low."

This wasn't his first proposal. Over the past six months, Scott had made a game of playfully asking me to marry him. He'd proposed in the grocery store. At the gas station. Even while we were waiting in line at a fast food drive-thru. And every single time, I'd answered no. But, this time was different. He didn't have to tell me twice.

In six quick strides, I was out of my seat and up on the stage. And with Scott still on his knee, I stared down at the one and only man who could ever really have my heart.

"Yes," I said and wrapped my arms around his neck. "I love you."

After he slid the ring on my finger, and with me still hanging off of him like a monkey, he stood and took my mouth in a mind-blowing kiss.

"I love you," he whispered against my lips.

"I love you too."

"Not gonna lie, that yes came a lot easier than I expected," he admitted, and I grinned. "I think that's proposal number fifteen if I'm keeping count correctly."

I giggled. "Yeah, I might have finally said yes, but you still have to convince me to actually plan the wedding."

He grinned down at me. "Is this going to be like the months of chasing it took to get you to agree to be in a relationship with me?"

"You mean the months of stalking?" I teased with a smile, and he laughed.

"Is this how it's always going to be with us?"

I shrugged. "Probably."

"Thank fuck for that," he said and lifted me into his arms. "You're my favorite challenge," he whispered against my lips. "I'll spend the rest of my life chasing after your feisty ass."

Can I let you in on a little secret?
I'm going to find a way to convince Scott to fly to Vegas tonight and make it official.
The only reason I've been waiting is because I wanted to be done with med school.
And since I only have one month left, it's motherfucking time to make this man officially mine.
God, I really am one lucky bitch, huh?

Kisses forever,
Harlow Shepard

Love Scott, Harlow, and the St. Luke's crew?
Preorder the next in the series, Dr. NEURO,
coming August, 29th 2017!

BUT FIRST!
Get ready for something new from us!
Still hot, still sexy, STILL funny, but this time, a little twisted.
#AlexinWonderland #July25th #DarkRomanticComedy
Why does being bad have to feel so good?

Stay up to date with them and us by signing up for our newsletter:
www.authormaxmonroe.com/#!contact/c1kcz
You may live to regret much, but we promise it won't be this.
Seriously. We'll make it fun.
If you're already signed up, consider sending us a message to tell us
how much you love us. We really like that. ;)
You don't want to miss Dr. Nick Raines, do you?
#DrNeuro #DrNEUROtic #HeadvsHeart

Follow us online:
Facebook: www.facebook.com/authormaxmonroe

Reader Group:
www.facebook.com/groups/1561640154166388

Twitter: www.twitter.com/authormaxmonroe

Instagram: www.instagram.com/authormaxmonroe

Goodreads: https://goo.gl/8VUIz2

acknowledgments

First of all, THANK YOU for reading. That goes for anyone who's bought a copy, read an ARC, helped us beta, edited, or found time in their busy schedule just to make sure we didn't completely drop the ball by being late. Yeah, that's us—sliding in fifteen minutes behind schedule. Actually, that's 95% of our characters too. We guess art imitates life.

Thank you for supporting us, for talking about our books, and for just being so unbelievably loving and supportive of our characters. You've made this our MOST favorite adventure thus far.

THANK YOU to each other. Max is thanking Monroe. Monroe is thanking pizza. Wait…what? Just kidding. Monroe is thanking Max, too. And we're both thanking pizza. P.S. We're going to keep doing this forever.

THANK YOU, Lisa, for always saving our asses. Even when you're in Berlin. Will you be our editor forever?

THANK YOU, Amy, for understanding that when we say we're going to send you our next manuscript soon we actually mean we're going to send it 2 weeks from now and you'll only have 24 hours to read it. You're the best agent in the whole wide world.

THANK YOU, JoAnna & Sandra, for being superior Counselor Feathers. We love you. You are the reason Camp Love Yourself is the coolest place to be (cough, it sure as hell isn't us. #multitaskingfail)

THANK YOU, Sommer, for always creating the hottest covers. And for giving us options even though we both know we'll always end up choosing your choice anyway.

THANK YOU, Stacy, for always putting up with us. Without you (and your patience), our books would be a poorly formatted hot garbage mess.

THANK YOU, Bex Harper Designs, for making awesome graphics for us. And for being so freaking adorable that we want to put you in our pockets.

THANK YOU to every blogger who has read, reviewed, posted, shared, and supported us. Your enthusiasm, support, and hard work do not go unnoticed. We'd offer to get you an appointment with Scott as thanks, but we've tried that a couple of times and Harlow isn't fucking having it.

THANK YOU, to the people who love us. They support us, motivate us, and most importantly, tolerate us. Sometimes we're not the easiest people to live with, especially when there is a deadline looming. And since we always have a deadline looming, it's safe to say we're stressed out asshole 50% of the time. Good thing we're so funny and charming, huh? We love you.

P.S. We know you love us, too.

THANK YOU, to our Camp members! You guys are the best! Meet us in Bora Bora (okay, Denver) someday soon (July 2018 for Book Bonanza)? We'll bring the wine. ;) No, seriously, meet us in Denver. We're coming out, betches!

As always, all our love.
XOXO,
Max Monroe

10/17

DATE DUE

Montgomery County Public Library
215 W. Main
Troy, NC 27371

Made in the USA
Columbia, SC
14 October 2017